CARRIER
OF THE
MARK

CARRIER OF THE MARK

LEIGH FALLON

HARPER TEEN
An Imprint of HarperCollins*Publishers*

HarperTeen is an imprint of HarperCollins Publishers.

Carrier of the Mark

www.epicreads.com

Library of Congress Cataloging-in-Publication Data
Fallon, Leigh
Carrier of the Mark / Leigh Fallon. — 1st ed.
p. cm.
Summary: Instantly drawn to a mysterious, alluring boy in her class,
teenaged Megan, an American living in Ireland, discovers that they are
linked by a supernatural destiny that gives them powers Megan never
knew she possessed.
ISBN 978-0-06-202787-0
[1. Supernatural—Fiction. 2. Magic—Fiction. 3. Love—Fiction.
4. Ireland—Fiction.] I. Title.
PZ7.F19596Car 2011   2010050516
[Fic]—dc22   CIP
                                                                     AC

Typography by Ray Shappell
11 12 13 14 15   CG/BV   10 9 8 7 6 5 4 3 2 1
❖
First Edition

FOR MICHAEL, MY WINGMAN

CARRIER
OF THE
MARK

PROLOGUE

Flames engulfed the boat, and my lungs ached as dark, noxious smoke filled the air. I struggled off the dirty makeshift bed and shuffled across the floor, the cable ties binding my hands and feet making my progress slow.

Suddenly a wall of water smashed through the cabin, dulling the flames.

Seizing my opportunity, I threw myself toward the wooden stairs, where the remains of the fire licked their way upward to freedom. I gritted my teeth and reached over to hook the cable binding my wrists on a jagged piece of scorched metal that I could see through the flames. Turning my face away from the searing heat, I tugged down sharply and felt the tie snap. I screamed as the flames burned my skin, but I didn't have time to worry about the pain. I needed to get out, to warn the others. I had to make sure they were okay.

With my hands free, I released my ankles and scrambled up the still-burning stairs to the deck. Through the haze I could see a group of people on the shore. They stood motionless, staring at the ground. My eyes followed their horrified gazes to the body lying facedown on the water's edge.

One

FIRST DAY BLUES

Four months earlier . . .

My first day at a new school . . . again. I pulled on the school uniform and eyed myself critically in the mirror. A uniform! I couldn't believe it. Back in Boston, only the fancy private schools had uniforms. But after some extensive Googling I learned that in Ireland, everyone wore them. Mine was a royal blue V-neck sweater (the letter from the school called it a jumper—I guessed I was going to have to get used to Irish phrases), a gray skirt, and a blue-and-yellow-striped tie. Hideous, of course, but it could be worse; at least I'd blend in.

I scowled at my reflection and tugged at the elastic

holding up my wavy brown hair. I seriously needed a little makeup—at the very least, some mascara and lip gloss—but the school had a strict no-makeup policy—a throwback to its convent roots.

Finally semisatisfied with my appearance, I went downstairs, where I found my dad in the kitchen playing on his laptop and mumbling about cables.

"Morning, Dad. Did you get that thing working?"

"Hey, Meg," he answered, looking confused. "Yeah, it was working fine and then it just died on me."

"It helps to plug the charger into the wall. That's what actually charges the battery." I walked over to the socket, plugged it in, and pressed the power button on the computer.

"It's back!" he cried.

"The wonder of science," I said over my shoulder as I popped two pieces of bread into the toaster. "So how do you like your new job?"

"It's great. Why don't you come down to the club after school? I'll show you around. I have a feeling about this place, Megan. This could be the one."

I hoped that was true. It would be nice to stay in one school for an entire year, even if it meant living in Kinsale.

"Sure, Dad," I replied. "I'll stop by after school." My toast popped up and I buttered it quickly. "I should get going. I have to figure out where all my classes are."

"Good luck," he said, glancing up from his computer with a reassuring smile. "You'll be fine. I'm sure you'll fit right in."

The school itself wasn't far from my house, and on my walk over (all downhill, thankfully) I saw lots of kids making their way in that direction. Nobody really paid any attention to me; in fact, people didn't even seem to notice I was there. Score one for my unexceptional appearance. At five-foot-five, with pale skin and a sprinkling of freckles, I blended nicely into the sea of faces. I guess I could even pass for Irish, with dark green, almond-shaped eyes, courtesy of my dad, and my mom's small oval face.

Turning the corner, I caught sight of the school gates, and my stomach fluttered a little. The school, a long, low building all on one level, had a parking lot in the front, and was bordered by basketball courts and grassy soccer fields in the back. I took a deep breath and made for the main entrance, when a pair of eyes caught my attention. Just inside the gate, a tall boy, leaning against a lamppost, was staring at me. A chill ran through my spine and my hands tingled. I balled them into fists and glanced down. *What the hell?* I was so distracted that I took a step forward and walked straight into another girl.

"I'm so sorry," I yelped, as we stumbled and caught

each other. I quickly glanced back at the lamppost, but the boy was gone.

"No problem," a friendly voice chirped back. "Looking for someone?" She followed my gaze with a curious expression.

"Oh, no. Well, yes, actually. I need to find the principal's office."

"New?"

"Am I that obvious?" I asked, laughing.

"I'm Caitlin," she introduced herself. "Are you in fifth year?"

Another term I was going to have to get used to. I was a junior back home. "Yep. I'm—"

"Megan," she finished for me, and smiled apologetically at my shocked face. "It's a small town. We were wondering when you were going to show up." She pointed toward the school. "The principal's office is through the double doors and to the right. Sister Basil." She pronounced the name with an ominous tone.

I could feel my face paling. *Great. A scary nun.*

"She's not that bad really," Caitlin reassured me. "She's strict, but fair. Keep eye contact with her and agree with everything she says and you should be sorted."

"Thanks," I said, turning to leave. I massaged my hands, trying to ease out the pins-and-needles feeling that still prickled through them.

"Good luck! I'm sure to be seeing you later. We're

bound to share some classes." She waved and walked off.

Thanks to Caitlin's advice, I got through my meeting with Sister Basil easily. She dispensed with the formalities quickly, gave me my schedule and the school map, then ushered me out of her office.

Classes in Ireland were divided into higher and lower curricula depending on ability. Luckily, I'd made the grade for higher English and I had that class first. I walked down the hall, following the map Sister Basil had given me. When I got to the room it was only half-full of students, most of them talking among themselves. I sat down at the first available desk, opened my copy of *Hamlet*, and tried my best to look engrossed while furtively listening to the chatter around me.

I still couldn't believe how fast people here spoke, and I was having some trouble getting used to the musical accent. Dropping my pen (accidentally on purpose), I leaned down to retrieve it and took a quick look around. I was surprised by how nervous I felt. I had always taken pride in my ability to adapt—a talent that years of new schools and new friends had helped me perfect—but something about this day felt off. I scratched my neck. It always got itchy when I was nervous. And that prickling feeling I'd had in my hands earlier was back, leaving them cold and stiff. I stuck my fingers under my legs, hoping the heat and the pressure would get the circulation working properly again.

Just then, Caitlin came in. Smiling broadly, she walked toward me.

"See, I told you we'd share some classes," she said, dumping her books on the desk beside me. She glanced over my head, then did a double take before sitting down and leaning in. "Do you know Adam?"

I shook my head. "Who?"

"Adam DeRís, the guy down the back. Don't look now, but he's staring at you."

I felt red heat climb slowly up my neck, stinging as it passed over my scar. I ached to turn and look.

"I don't know anybody here."

"Well, he appears to know you. He's still staring. It's weird; he's normally only aware of his own self-importance. Oh, crap," she said, flicking her head back to me. "He just caught me looking. Like he doesn't have a big enough head as it is."

I strained my eyes to the side, twisting my neck slightly to try to get a look at him, but just then the teacher walked in and promptly got into some heavy Shakespeare.

At the end of the period, Caitlin packed up her books and notes. I stalled, wanting to give this Adam guy a chance to leave so I could catch a glimpse of him as he left the room.

Caitlin slyly glanced back and stood up. "He's still looking," she mumbled through barely moving lips as she turned to talk to the girl sitting behind me. "I'll tell you when he's coming."

Just then I heard the screech of a chair on the tiles and Caitlin nudged me, raising her eyebrows. I knew I was being stupid. I was seventeen, not twelve. But I felt compelled to see who this guy was. I glanced up furtively as I heard him come near. It was the guy who had been watching me at the school gates. My heart began thudding loudly and my hands went rigid and tingly. The heat rose up my face.

"Ohhhhhhh, new girl has the hots for Adam," scoffed the blond girl behind me. "Don't waste your time, honey," she said, putting on an American accent.

"Jennifer! Play nice." Caitlin gave her a playful shove as Jennifer pushed past us to leave.

Adam glanced back at me and collided with the door frame. He winced and, rubbing his shoulder, made a hasty exit. Jennifer turned to us with her mouth hanging open, and then walked out after him, laughing.

Caitlin grabbed my arm and we made our way to the crowded hallway. "Don't mind Jennifer. She's just ticked off because he's never even looked at her. He's a bit of a funny fish, him."

I nodded, barely listening. I was so embarrassed by my bizarre reaction to Adam.

Caitlin saw the look on my face and quickly changed the subject. "Let me see your course list," she said, peering at the piece of paper on top of my folder. "Oh, great, you're in the same French as me. Wait until you meet Mr. Flood, our teacher."

Relaxing, I smiled at her. "Why?"

"You should see his face! Only a mother could love it, and that's not the worst of it."

I looked at her questioningly. "What's the worst of it?"

She scrunched up her nose in disgust. "You'll see."

We moved quickly to our next class, and I soon found out why Caitlin very wisely steered us toward seats at the back of the room. Mr. Flood liked to put lots of emphasis into his pronunciation, something he very obviously took great pride in. The first row was a testament to that. There was a lot of scowling and wiping of faces. One of these faces belonged to Jennifer, who'd arrived late. She wiped her face with the sleeve of her sweater, and I giggled. Justice was served.

As much as I tried to focus on the class, my mind kept drifting to Adam. There was an air about him, something different. He oozed arrogance, from his perfectly straight nose to his carefully disheveled dark hair. Not my type at all. Not that I really had a type. We'd never stayed in any town long enough for me to develop anything more than friendships.

Suddenly, I noticed Mr. Flood standing over me. *"Excusez-moi, mademoiselle, mais peux j'ayez s'il vous plaît votre attention,"* he said into my face with a liberal spraying of saliva.

"Oui, monsieur, je suis désolée," I said, snapping out of my reverie. It was a good thing Adam wasn't in this class because I really needed to focus.

Mr. Flood walked back to his desk and I quickly mopped my face while he wasn't looking. "He lives up to his name, doesn't he?" I whispered to Caitlin.

The first half of the day passed quickly, one class running into another, and soon it was time for lunch. Caitlin and I sat on the grass in front of the building eating our soggy sandwiches. There were others scattered in groups around the grounds, enjoying the sunshine. It was still warm for September, and I was just rolling up my sleeves when Jennifer joined us.

As she passed me she fluffed my hair. "Sorry about earlier; I was only playing. No hard feelings?" She sat down and smiled at me.

"Sure," I said, a little taken aback by the turnaround.

Sitting side by side, Jennifer and Caitlin were like night and day. Jennifer's hair was highlighted and straightened and her skin was a smooth, perfect tan—which I assumed was fake. She was pretty, but she clearly worked at it; I could tell she had plenty of makeup on. So the strict no-makeup policy was not quite so strict. I could definitely get away with some.

Caitlin, on the other hand, was completely natural. Her light brown hair hung in long layers, framing a friendly, pretty face. She had a huge smile that touched her warm brown eyes, and she wasn't wearing any makeup so far as I could tell.

Jennifer stood up and waved at two boys by the school doors, trying to get their attention. One had curly blond hair and bounded over with a big smile on his face. I noticed Caitlin blushing faintly as they approached. She glanced up at the blond shyly. The other guy had dark hair that was coaxed upward into messy peaks.

"Hi, Jennifer," the dark-haired guy said.

"Darren, this is the new American girl I was telling you about, Megan," Jennifer announced.

"Ah, so you're the reason DeRís has been tripping over himself all morning. Can't say I'm not enjoying seeing him stumble around like that. Nice work, Megan. Welcome to the metropolis of Kinsale."

"D'Reese?" I asked, looking at Caitlin.

"Adam DeRís, the guy from this morning," she explained.

"Don't get too close," Darren said with a smirk. "Or he'll turn you into a toad or some—" A soccer ball came sailing through the air and smacked off the side of Darren's head. "That hurt, you plonkers!" he shouted to a group of guys standing around the goal nets.

"Come on, Killian, they're starting without us," Darren said, kicking the blond boy, who was looking down at Caitlin. "Jennifer, I'll meet you at the front gates after school?"

"Sure," Jennifer replied, fluttering her eyelids. Then she turned back to us. "I have to agree with him. It's great to see Mr. Über-cool and Collected make a twat of himself." She looked me up and down appreciatively. "I have a feeling you are going to be a very useful addition to our circle. Now . . . isn't someone going to ask me what happened over the weekend with Darren?" She smiled expectantly at Caitlin.

"Oh, go on. Like you need to be asked," Caitlin said, rolling her eyes.

Jennifer launched into an all-out explanation of how she and Darren hooked up over the weekend, making sure to include every incidental happening. The more excited she got, the faster she spoke, until I couldn't understand her anymore. It didn't even sound like English. My mind drifted to Darren. What had he said about toads? Jennifer's voice faded into the background as a familiar profile caught my attention.

Over by the school gate, Adam appeared to be arguing with someone. I could see that his eyebrows were furrowed together and his body was rigid. The other guy's dark hair was wavy and long enough to spill out over the collar of his leather jacket. He pointed toward the school, his face screwed up in irritation, and then turned and walked away. Adam watched him leave as he rubbed his forehead with his hand.

I wonder what that was all about. Suddenly, Adam turned and looked at me, right into my eyes. Burdened by the weight of his stare, I dropped my gaze before he did and rubbed my tingling neck. When I looked up, he was gone.

Jennifer's voice came back into focus; she'd come to the end of her story. She sighed and looked a little dreamy.

"That's so cool, isn't it, Meg?" Caitlin said, turning to me.

"Um, yeah. Great," I replied quickly.

"So, Caitlin, when's the big move on Killian going to happen?" Jennifer asked.

Caitlin flushed.

Jennifer rolled her eyes. "Oh, come on. You've been hankering after that boy for two years now. It's getting old! It's so obvious that you're mad into him."

"Oh, shut up, Jennifer," Caitlin said, but not in a mean way. "Come on; it's time to get back to class." She jumped up and hauled me to my feet.

"Holy crap, your hands are cold," she said, letting go of me to retrieve her grass-covered sweater from the ground.

"I know; they've been like that all day." I shook my head in frustration, and pulled my sleeves down over them as I followed her inside.

Caitlin caught up to me as I was walking to the gate at the end of the day and took out her cell phone. "What's your number? I'll definitely need it for some late-night bitching."

I held up my still-tingling hands. "Sorry, I haven't got an Irish one yet, but I'll get right on it."

She made a face of mock horror. "No phone! How have you existed here this long?"

I cracked up. "I promise I'll have one by the end of the week. I'm meeting my dad now; I'll put on the pressure."

But my laughter quickly died in my throat. A little down the road, Adam was leaning against the chipped paint of an old Volkswagen Golf. He was talking to the guy he'd been fighting with earlier. Adam's mouth curled into a smile as the other guy gave Adam a mock punch before climbing onto a motorcycle.

Caitlin followed my stare and sighed. "Trust me, you don't want to go there," she said, stepping into my line of sight.

"What do you mean?"

She lowered her voice. "He's a snotty, stuck-up git. He'll mess with your head. Just do yourself a favor and keep walking. I have to leg it now or my mum will kill me." She slowly turned and walked away.

My freezing hands shook. I shoved them in my pockets, but stayed rooted to the spot. Adam was relaxed, still laughing at something the other guy said. I gazed at his eyes, bright green, set wide apart, whites perfectly clear, framed with thick, dark lashes. I took in the curve of his lips, the high angle of his cheekbones, and his long jaw that gently rounded to his chin. I caught my breath when I saw there was a girl sitting in the car's passenger seat.

"Figures," I muttered.

Adam glanced in my direction and said something to the girl. She looked at me warily and I felt a flush of embarrassment creep up my neck. Was I that obvious?

Get a grip. Squaring my shoulders, I turned to walk into town. I didn't see the old man approaching me until I was right in front of him.

"Oh, I'm so sorry." I smiled, expecting him to apologize too, or perhaps step aside to let me by. But he just stood there, his watery gray eyes focused on mine.

"Well . . . excuse me," I said, stepping off the sidewalk and quickening my pace. I looked back at the old man. He was wearing a brown cloak with a rope around his waist like some bizarre monk. His long gray hair hung loose down his back, and his beard was tied with a leather clip. His expressionless face turned to me.

I whipped my head around and didn't glance behind me again. Odd; I felt like his face jogged a memory, but I couldn't quite place it.

I focused on navigating the ten-minute walk to the marina where my dad worked. The club, though small, was world-renowned, and this manager position was

Manhattan-Elwood

Public Library District

Date: 4/27/2018

Time: 12:45:35 PM

Name: BUSLER, HOLLY A

Fines/Fees Owed: $0.00

Total Checked Out: 0

Not Checked Out

Note: Some information may not be available for all items listed.

Title: The Carrier of the Mark / Leigh Fallon.
Barcode: 38001001011950
Reason: This item cannot be renewed. Please see a staff member for assistance.

the opportunity of a lifetime for my dad. Pulling on the shiny brass door handle, I walked inside and went straight to the receptionist's desk.

"Hi, I'm Megan Rosenberg; I'm here to see my dad, Caleb."

"Ah, Mr. Rosenberg's daughter—I wondered when I'd see you. Did you enjoy your first day at school, pet? It's a nice school we have here. My own daughter was a student there until last year. She's in college now in Limerick."

Not knowing what else to do, I nodded.

She cocked her head to the side and gave me a big motherly smile. "I'll just call him and let him know you're here, dear."

A few minutes later, my dad came wandering in. "Megan!" he exclaimed. "How was your first day?"

I pulled my dad away from the reception desk. "It was mostly good, I think."

"Make any friends?" Dad said, following his usual first-day script.

"I made a few friends. One girl, Caitlin, is really nice."

"Caitlin Brennan?" the receptionist piped up.

"Er, yeah," I replied slowly. Wow, this really was a small town.

"Her mother owns the Misty Moorings bed-and-breakfast." She smiled.

My dad discreetly rolled his eyes and directed me out

the front door. "Sybil," he said, as if that explained it all. "Tell me, what was your first day really like?"

"Honestly, it was one of the better ones. Something feels different this time."

"I know what you mean, Meg. I think your mom's looking after us," he said wistfully, glancing up to the sky.

"Maybe."

"Or it could be that Irish blood in you; it's back on home turf."

"I have Irish blood?"

"It's pretty diluted, but it's definitely in there. Your mom's grandfather came from somewhere near here, I think. Somewhere in County Cork."

"I guess that explains the freckles," I said, inspecting my arms. "So, are you going to show me around your vast empire?" I put my arm in the air and waved it around extravagantly. "It looks very fancy. Is your office nice?"

My dad was happy to give me the grand tour: the boats, the marina, and the club. I tried to look interested, but water and boats were never my thing. Truthfully, water had always sort of freaked me out. It held an allure for me, but one that felt dangerous, so I generally gave it a wide berth.

"I'm so proud of you, Dad," I said, after he had shown me everything there was to see. "You're definitely onto a winner here. How did you manage to swing this job?"

"I'm still not sure," he replied. "Someone recommended me, but I don't know who. I just wish I could thank whoever it was. I'll never get an opportunity like this again."

"Well, you deserve it." I paused. "One thing, though."

He looked at me nervously.

"I'm seriously going to need a cell phone."

He looked relieved. "We'll get right on that! Come on. I'm finishing up early, and I'm going to treat you to a big bag of fish and chips. When in Ireland, do as the Irish do!"

"Sounds good," I said, hooking my arm into his. "Lead the way."

Dad pulled the door open for me and I found myself face-to-face with a shocked Adam DeRís.

"Mr. Rosenberg," Adam said, avoiding my eyes.

"Hello, Adam. This is my daughter, Megan," Dad introduced me. "Adam is one of our instructors."

I didn't know where to look.

"Nice to meet you, Megan," he muttered, and started backing away, tripping over himself. "I'm sorry, Mr. Rosenberg, but I'm in a hurry."

"Of course, of course." My dad's forehead was crinkled in confusion as he leaned closer to me. "That was weird. He's normally so friendly. Never mind, let's get those chips."

With my stomach twisting uncomfortably, the last thing I felt like was fries. I glanced over my shoulder at the fast-departing Adam.

"Don't worry about him, Dad," I said, faking a smile. "I'm not bothered."

But I was lying. Adam's reaction did bother me. It bothered me so much it hurt.

Two

DAY TWO

I got up the next morning with one intention: to prove to myself that Adam DeRís was nothing more than the usual seventeen-year-old guy. I was sure that seeing him again would break whatever spell he'd put on me. There was no way he could be as breathtaking as my memory painted him; my mind was playing tricks on me. As soon as I had that clear in my head, I would be able to start fresh. Perhaps I could even claw back a little bit of my dignity in the process.

And that was why I found myself standing at the school gates forty-five minutes before classes started.

Half an hour went by, and while other students had

started to pour in, there was no sign of Adam. I looked anxiously up and down the road.

A hand tapped me on the shoulder, and I jumped.

"You came back." It was Caitlin, beaming at me. "We didn't scare you off then?"

I laughed. "Not quite; I thought I might risk one more day before I run screaming to the U.S."

"Come on, we'd better get inside. If we're late to biology, Psycho Phil will go ballistic."

My heart sank a little. I'd forgotten the class schedule here changed every day. I wondered if Adam would be in my biology class. I was just going to ask Caitlin who Psycho Phil was when I realized my hands were tingling again. A black Volkswagen came into view and swung into a parking space across the road. Adam opened the car door, stepped out, and threw his bag over his shoulder in one fluid movement. Then he leaned over the roof of the car, talking to the girl who was getting out of the passenger side. It was the same girl I had seen him with yesterday. She was tall and slim, and her smooth, black hair was cut in a blunt bob.

They started walking toward the entrance, where I was standing with Caitlin. Adam was grinning, and her face looked up into his with a sly little smile, her eyes gleaming with a witchy edge to them. Adam walked by without a glance. She looked at me sheepishly, then quickly walked on.

"Bitch," I muttered. I hated to admit it, but I was

totally jealous. She was stunning. I could never compete with that. To top it all off, they were probably laughing at me and my completely transparent infatuation with Adam.

"Earth to Megan; come in, Megan," Caitlin said as she snapped her fingers in front of my face. "Megan, are you with me?" she said a little louder. "Or are you with a certain tall, dark, and outrageously handsome Mr. DeRís?" She followed my gaze.

"I wish." I stared after them. There was no point in trying to hide my glaringly obvious emotions. "They look good together," I said, somewhat begrudgingly.

"They would," she said. "They're twins. And did you not listen to a word I said? Honestly, don't bother. Now come on." She grabbed my arm and started dragging me up the hill. "We're definitely going to be late!"

We ran down the hallway to our class.

"Twins," I said at the door, as we paused to catch our breath.

"Yes, twins. Her name is Áine." She shook her head in irritation. "Really, Megan, no offense or anything, but let it drop. You're wasting your time. He's a total plank, and has the personality to match. Now, shush," she whispered, putting her finger over her lips before pushing the door to the biology lab open. I followed, wondering what a "plank" was.

"Ah, ladies, nice of you to finally join us," said a

sarcastic voice as we filed into the room. "I'm assuming this is our new class member, Miss Rosenberg." A man with beady eyes and more hair on his face than his head glared at me. "Well, Miss Rosenberg, let's hope this is not how you intend to continue your education in this school, and if it is, perhaps you could be so kind as to not drag Miss Brennan down with you."

"No, sir," I muttered, and fled to the nearest available desk. I was starting to understand the "Psycho Phil" nickname.

As soon as I realized we were talking about the lymphatic system—something I had studied last year—I tuned Psycho Phil out and my thoughts drifted back to Adam. The image of him smiling and leaning on his car crept into my mind: his head thrown back in laughter, his green eyes glittering with mischief. I pushed the picture from my mind and reminded myself that I was trying to purge him from my system, not reinforce my feelings. I rubbed the scar on my neck; it was itchy again. I couldn't believe how much it had been irritating me. It never really bothered me before, but then again, I'd never gotten all flustered over a guy like this before either. I idly traced its circular shape and lost myself to memories of my mom. The scar would always be a painful reminder of the last day we spent together.

I was six. Mom and I had gone to see my grandmother, who was living in a retirement village. We had a great time playing games, Gran telling me stories of when my mom was my age. After dinner Mom and I set off in the car for the three-hour drive back home.

Rain began to fall, and soon the wipers had to work overtime to keep the windshield clear. My mom turned up the radio and we sang along tunelessly, laughing at each other as we made up our own words to the songs. Then there was a sheet of metal coming straight at us and a screeching noise that hurt my ears. I screamed.

The next thing I knew I was in a hospital bed with tubes sticking out of me and beeping machines by my side. My dad was holding my hand.

"You came back to me," he said, tears spilling down his face. Later he told me my mom had died instantly in the crash. I'd been unconscious for days. By the time I woke up, Mom had already been buried. I would never see her again.

My memories of the crash were still vivid all these years later, but now I felt detached from the event. All that was left was the scar, my dad's sadness, and the guilt I felt when I tried to remember my mom. I kept a photo of her with me, so I wouldn't forget what she looked like.

The bell broke my reverie. Caitlin turned to me.

"So did you choose home ec or art?"

"Art," I answered, as I gathered my books.

"Well, you're on your own for this one. I'm off to bake a cake. I'll see you in maths. The art rooms are back up the corridor; turn right and they're on your left."

"Caitlin, what's the deal with Adam and Enya? Why don't people like them?"

Caitlin laughed. "Her name is *Áine*. You know, like *Awn-ya*. You're going to have to get used to these Irish names. Anyway, it's just . . . well, they're stuck-up and a bit weird." She leaned in closer. "There are rumors about their family. I don't think I believe them, *really*, but you know what they say—there's no smoke without fire."

"What kind of rumors?"

"There's been talk of 'odd' goings-on. And Adam and Áine don't do much to persuade people otherwise."

"So when you say 'odd,' you mean . . . ?"

"Really odd. You know . . . things-that-go-bump-in-the-night odd."

"You're joking, right?"

She raised her shoulders and half smiled. "I don't know. But you've been warned." She wagged her finger and left the class.

I wasn't much good at art, but I did enjoy it. I was happy that the art teacher ignored formalities and got right down to business. She handed me a sketch pad and pointed me toward a desk with a drawing board on it. I glanced at the still life of white daisies in the center of the room and picked up my pencil, but a shiny black bob on the opposite side of the room caught my eye.

Áine DeRís. She didn't look at me, just kept sketching. What was it with the DeRís twins? I couldn't get away from them. I looked up at her again and this time her eyes met mine. She quickly looked away, and I rubbed my neck in annoyance. Now that I knew Adam and Áine were twins, the similarities were obvious: the dark, rich hair; the green eyes; and the strong facial features. They both oozed the same quiet self-confidence, the type of arrogance that came from a life of privilege. Odd, though. Adam's old car seemed to suggest they weren't rich.

I sketched away as I thought about them, flicking glances through the limp-looking flowers when Áine wasn't looking. By the end of the class I was pleasantly surprised with what I had produced. I finished off the sketch and went to get the fixing spray. I was just returning to my desk when Áine passed me. She brushed the display table in her haste to get by and nearly knocked over the vase. Saying nothing, she righted the vase, picked up a daisy that had fallen to the floor, and gently placed it on my desk. Giving me a cautious smile, she walked out.

Caitlin was right. Weird. I grabbed my bag and glanced at the flower she'd left on my desk, doing a double take. I could have sworn it had been a tired-looking white daisy when she picked it up, but it was most definitely a healthy-looking *pink* daisy now. I chucked it into my bag with my things and went to my next class.

After math (I couldn't imagine ever feeling comfortable calling it "maths"), Caitlin and I went outside for lunch. Jennifer, Killian, and Darren were already there, stretched out in the sun. Everyone was chatting happily, and I munched on my sandwich and listened intently, catching up on the gossip. At one point, Darren turned to me, then looked back in the other direction, and then at me again. I watched him, bemused.

"Darren, what are you doing?" Jennifer asked.

"I was just wondering who Rían DeRís was glaring at, and it would appear to be you, Megan. Bloody hell, what did you do to deserve *that* look?"

"Ree-in?" I glanced up and found the face in question. It was the guy who'd been fighting with Adam yesterday, the guy with the motorcycle. He was Adam's brother! His eyes boiled with such intensity that I had to look away. "Why would he be looking at me? I've never met him," I said uncertainly.

"He shouldn't even be here. He finished school last year. I'd watch out if I were you, Megan. Rían will put the evil eye on you. People around here think the DeRíses are witches, ya know," Darren replied, standing up and waving his hands around like a magician.

"Darren, that's rubbish. You listen to too many old wives' tales." Jennifer gave Darren a look and tugged on his shirt to make him sit down. "And anyway, the rumors are of their being druids, not witches."

Darren leaned closer to me. "My granddad reckons they're related to the old Killeen coven that hexed the town back in the eighteen hundreds."

"What! You've got to be messing with me. Is that what you meant by 'odd,' Caitlin?" I asked.

"Darren, shut up. You're going to scare her," Caitlin said with a slight edge to her voice.

They all looked at me with serious faces. Then they burst out laughing.

"Don't mind us," Caitlin said, gently rubbing my arm. "Yes, there are rumors, and there have been 'incidents,' but none of us actually believe the stories. Do we, guys?"

"What stories?" I pressed.

"Tell her the one about the cat!" Jennifer exclaimed, elbowing Darren excitedly.

"Ooh, that's a good one," Darren declared, leaning into me. "A long time ago, there was a woman who lived here. Her name was Elizabeth Killeen. Rumor has it she's, like, the DeRíses' great-great-grandmother or something. Anyway, she was a bit of a babe, and all the menfolk of the town had a *thing* for her. Of course, all the women blamed Elizabeth for the wandering eyes, and one unfortunate lady actually went to confront Elizabeth. When she did, Elizabeth morphed into a ferocious cat and lashed out at her, plucking an eyeball right from her head. The cat reportedly ate the eyeball, and then morphed back into Elizabeth. At least, that's how One-eyed Lily tells the story."

"One-eyed Lily?" I asked.

"Yeah, she's the great-granddaughter of the woman who had her eye swiped out. One-eyed Lily says her family is now cursed, and since that day, all the female children have been born with one eye."

Caitlin threw the crust of her sandwich at Darren. "What rubbish. One-eyed Lily is a crazy alcoholic who fell asleep drunk on the pier and lost her eye because a fisherman accidentally lodged a hook in it. Don't listen to him, Meg. He's only winding you up."

I glanced around at their faces. Darren smirked at me, and Jennifer had gone back to inspecting her hair for split ends.

"So who's signing up for the school's sailing classes?" Killian asked, changing the subject.

Caitlin looked excited, while I cringed and pretended not to hear. I personally couldn't think of anything worse.

Caitlin eyed me. "Would you be up for it, Meg?"

"No way," I replied, laughing nervously. "Water and I are not friends!"

"Oh, you should," Killian begged. "It's going to be fun." He looked pointedly at Jennifer and Darren.

"It's a tad remedial for me." Jennifer sighed, sticking

her nose in the air.

Darren snorted. "Come on, Jen. Sitting on the deck of your dad's day cruiser in a bikini does *not* equal a qualification in sailing!"

She pouted at him as Killian looked back to Caitlin, his eyes pleading. "Come on, Caitlin; will you?"

Caitlin melted under his gaze. "I'd love to, but I'll have to run it by my mum."

"Excellent." Killian smiled at her.

"Who's running the course?" Darren asked.

"The yacht club and the outdoor education center; I'm sure the alleged druid himself, Adam DeRís, will be doing some instructing," Killian replied.

I felt a flicker of interest register on my face. I fought to hide it, but Caitlin didn't miss a beat. She immediately went to work on my weakness.

"Oh, come on, Meg; it could be fun, and we'd get to miss Friday-afternoon PE for five weeks."

I groaned inwardly. I was totally witless around water, and here I was being coerced into a sailing course! *You know you want to,* a voice in my head chirped. *One-on-one time with Adam DeRís.*

"I'll think about it," I said.

"I guess you can count me in too," Jennifer added, not to be left out.

Caitlin was bouncing up and down. "Come on; let's get inside." She looked like she was going to explode.

33

"We still have ten minutes before class starts," I said as I ran after her.

"Will you really do the sailing course?" She turned to me.

"I hate water," I replied, cringing, "but if you *need* me to . . ."

"Oh, I do need you. I do," she said in a gush. "Killian will be there, and he seemed to want me to be there, didn't he? Maybe it's time to up the ante on Operation Snag Killian."

"Operation Snag Killian?" I repeated, laughing.

"Oh, shut up. I nearly have to mop up the drool that pours from your mouth every time Adam comes within ten feet of you."

"You'd better be nicer to me if you want me to do this sailing course," I warned.

"Okay. I promise, I won't mention Adam again!"

"Fine. You're on."

"Yay! And to show my appreciation, this weekend I'm going to introduce you to the many delights of the Kinsale Equestrian Center. You're going to love it," she declared.

"Your bringing me to the equestrian center wouldn't have anything to do with the fact that Killian's parents own it, would it?"

She raised her eyebrows questioningly. "How did you know that?"

"It's a small town," I replied, mimicking her voice.

"And Jennifer mentioned it earlier."

She smiled sheepishly. "Well, there're some fine animals there . . . and some great horses too," she added with a smirk.

"You're impossible! Come on; let's get to class and get your head out of rippling muscles and firm hindquarters. And the horses, for that matter."

She exploded with laughter, and we made our way to class.

That night I ran the sailing course by my dad. He was startled, to say the least, since he knew how much I hated the water. But of course he was delighted.

"This place is good for you," he said. "I can't quite put my finger on it, but you're glowing." He paused. "Hey, are there boys involved in this sailing course?"

"Dad, it's not like I go to an all-girls school. Yes, there are boys involved."

My dad looked a little uncomfortable. "Has anyone caught your eye?"

"I've been at school for two days; give me a chance to get settled."

"I didn't mean it like that; you've just been acting different. I thought there might be an outside influence."

"No, Dad. No boys."

He looked back to the TV, where the news was playing softly. "That course is being run through my club, isn't it?" he asked, without turning to me.

"Yeah. Why?"

"Just wondering. I think one of our guys is helping run it. Adam DeRís. He's the one we ran into yesterday, remember?"

"Yeah, he's in a few of my classes."

"You should have heard the stories that Sybil was spinning about his family—all nonsense, of course, but wow, can that woman tell a tale."

"What did she say?"

Dad leaned forward. "She said that the DeRís land is bewitched. People won't even walk there. There have been reports of flocks of savage birds that attack if you get too close. And the farmers claim that the crops won't grow where their land meets the DeRíses'."

"Did you hear the one about the cat?"

Dad nodded his head and laughed. "Oh, yeah, that was a doozy. Anyway, Adam's an excellent instructor. You'll be in safe hands."

If only I were in those very safe hands right now, I thought, smiling. Oh, God, I was absolutely pathetic.

Later that night I remembered the daisy that Áine had given to me. I threw myself onto my bed, dipped my hand into my bag, and pulled it out. It was as perfect as when Áine gave it to me. I twirled it around in my fingers, inspecting the delicate petals, allowing my mind to wander to the DeRís family. A scratching noise at the window drew my attention, and I saw a big black crow looking in at me. He had a ring of silver feathers around his right eye that made him look like he was winking.

"Shoo," I said, waving my hand at him. He flew away.

Without giving it any more thought, I placed the daisy on my nightstand and curled up in bed, pulling the quilt tightly around me.

Three

THE EQUESTRIAN CENTER

My first week was over, and I couldn't believe how settled I felt after such a short time. In all the towns I'd lived in and schools I'd attended, I'd never clicked with anyone like I did with Caitlin. I had a feeling she was going to be a keeper. And Jennifer, Darren, and Killian seemed like people I would count as true friends.

I also felt myself softening toward the quirky, slow-paced way of life. It was strange to say, but I was even looking forward to school next week. Of course, it helped that I had nothing to really miss from my old life. We'd moved almost every year since my mom died.

As soon as the anniversary of her death rolled around, I would notice my dad getting restless. Before I knew it, the bags were packed, the car was loaded, and we were off again to "start over." Our last "home" was Gloucester, Massachusetts. We'd lasted there longer than most places, but before I dared to hope for a second year in one school, Dad got the Kinsale offer.

My friends in Gloucester were nice, but I had never had a best friend. It was my own fault, I guessed. One thing I learned early was not to form attachments—they only ended in tears. But now that I had a taste of how things could be, I didn't want to go back to our odd sort of half life. I no longer wanted to feel displaced.

The only blip in my new life was Adam DeRís. I couldn't get him out of my mind. From my first day at school, he'd occupied my thoughts. His staring and awkwardness combined with my constantly tingling hands made me hyperaware of his presence in school. I ached just to get a glimpse of him.

Saturday was torture. No school, no Adam. I spent most of the day at my desk, trying to catch up on schoolwork. It was three weeks into the school year here. I had missed the first two weeks and I had some serious studying to do. Senior cycle in Irish schools consisted of fifth year and sixth year, and at the end of sixth year students took a big exam that sounded like the SATs. It was called the Leaving Certificate, and what you got on the exam determined what you could study in college. True, I wasn't set on going to college in Ireland, but I didn't want to bomb any major tests either. I was ahead in some subjects, but way behind in others. Caitlin said she would help me out if I needed it, but Saturdays were busy for her, as she helped her mom out in their B and B.

My torture was somewhat alleviated on Saturday night, when my dad arrived home and handed me a brand-new cell phone. Caitlin and I texted each other all night, plotting our visit to the Kinsale Equestrian Center the next day. Finally, Sunday arrived.

Before we headed over, Caitlin swung by to pick me up. I was eager to show her around my new house, which I loved. It was set high up above the multicolored houses that crept along the sides of the roads in town. The harbor below us was banked on all sides by houses, shops, and restaurants, all stepped up on the surrounding slopes.

From our porch, you could see the water from the harbor snaking its way out to sea and blending with the horizon. Our house was up a very narrow, steep road, through iron gates set into piers that were made of a red and sandy-colored stone. The driveway curved around in a big circle with a green in the middle of it. Dotted along the curving road were eight large, slightly elevated houses. They were all painted different colors. Ours was apple green.

Caitlin had a quick look around the house and my

room, but she seemed anxious to get moving. The call of the equestrian center was obviously too strong to ignore.

"Come on, Megan, you're going to love this," she urged.

I smirked. She would love it, but I imagined my role would be more of a supporting one. I didn't mind, though. Caitlin had informed me that Killian was teaching the lessons in the afternoon, and this was too good an opportunity to miss. We would get to gawk at him for a couple of hours. Lucky us.

It was another lovely day. The weather had been really nice since we arrived. Apparently it wasn't normally like this; any day now the clouds would come and it would probably rain for six months solid. I planned to enjoy the sun while it lasted.

We walked down past the school in the direction of the Bandon estuary, which swept its way into the harbor. When we came to the water's edge, we turned right.

The water was still, just a few small boats bobbing gently at their moorings. The reflected sun sent out sparkles in all directions. They were hypnotic. It took me a moment to tune back in to what Caitlin was saying.

"I was thinking of getting a fringe; what do you think?" she asked, holding her hair across her forehead.

"A fringe?"

"Oh, yeah, what do you call them again? Bangs." She rolled her eyes. "Never mind. Did you see Jennifer in geography on Friday? I love that girl, but *what* was she thinking? That skirt could not go any higher! Mr. Murphy nearly had a hernia; he couldn't take his eyes off her legs for the whole class."

"Poor Mr. Murphy, it wasn't really his fault. How could you not look?" I replied, sticking up for the unfortunate geography teacher. "Anyhow, Sister Basil sorted her out. I don't think we'll be seeing that skirt return to such dizzying heights anytime soon."

I laughed, but realized I had lost my audience. Caitlin had stopped and was staring into the field at the side of the road. She leaned against the fence, and I followed her gaze. There was a large horse being put through his paces in the paddock. He was a beautiful chestnut color; his coat gleamed and his well-toned muscles rippled as he cantered by. The rider put the horse over a series of cross poles, jumping each one perfectly.

"Gorgeous, isn't he?" Caitlin said, letting out a sigh.

"Yes, he is. He has great form."

"The rider, Meg, not the horse."

I peered closer, taking in the face under the riding helmet. It was Killian Clarke, of course. He wore black jodhpurs, knee-high black leather boots, and a purple-and-white-striped polo shirt. His blond curls were darkened with perspiration. I had to admit, he really did look amazing up there. I definitely understood what Caitlin saw in him.

Just then he looked up and a huge smile spread across his face when he spotted us. He steered the horse in our direction. "Caitlin, Megan, what are you doing here?"

Caitlin looked at me and flushed. "Megan was thinking of taking some lessons. I thought maybe you could give her the tour."

"Excellent," he said. "You'll be looking for a commission soon, Caitlin; you're great at generating business for us."

Her cheeks grew a darker red.

"I'm nearly finished here, and I'll meet you in the yard for the grand tour in a few minutes." He winked down at us and cantered away.

I elbowed Caitlin in the ribs as we started walking. "How many times have you been down here gawking at him? Caitlin, you seriously have to make a move; this isn't healthy."

"I know, I know. But I'm not good at, you know, making moves. I'm hoping *he'll* make his move during the sailing course. If he doesn't we'll need to strategize."

It wasn't long before we heard Killian coming up the concrete path into the large barn. He pulled the horse up and swung his leg over its back, slid down the leather saddle, and landed solidly on the ground. One of the young stable hands, eager to help, ran over, fluttered her eyelashes at Killian, and took the reins from him.

"So, Megan, you want to learn how to ride?"

"Well, sort of," I replied. "I've actually been riding off and on for the past ten years, but I'm a little rusty at the moment."

"Great! We have some excellent classes and hacks for the more experienced rider," Killian said, leading us through a barn lined with stalls full of sleepy-looking ponies.

He then directed us to a huge indoor arena and a spectator area. We sat down and listened as Killian gave us the lowdown on some member of the center who'd been caught red-handed with the wife of the local farrier in one of the stalls. Caitlin was hanging on his every word. I gave up trying to follow along and watched a girl on the other end of the arena instead.

She was on a huge white horse that must have been at least seventeen hands high. The horse's neck curved in with her head tucked neatly toward her powerful chest. She moved so gracefully.

The rider was wearing white jodhpurs and long black leather riding boots. She was completely in control, barely touching the reins. I squinted, trying to see who she was.

"She's really beautiful, isn't she?" Killian said, interrupting my thoughts.

Caitlin gave the rider a murderous glare.

"She's an Andalusian purebred mare. There aren't many of them in this country." At this, Caitlin's face relaxed. "She's a complete bugger to work with, though, and extremely difficult to ride."

I found that hard to believe, watching the horse and rider move with such grace.

"She's vicious in the stables too, damn near killed my old Labrador the other day," he continued. "I think we'd have sold her if it weren't for Áine. She has a way with the mare. It's almost as if they can speak to each other. That, and Áine works for free in return for ring time and use of the horses."

"Áine," I repeated, startled. "Isn't that Adam's sister?"

"The very one. She's like a horse whisperer or something. Our vet bills have plummeted since she's been working here. My parents will do just about anything to keep Áine happy."

At that, Killian got up and told us he had to give another lesson, so Caitlin and I got ourselves a couple of Cokes from the vending machine and settled in for a marathon session of gawking at Killian. Well, Caitlin gawked. I couldn't stop myself from focusing on Áine. The way she moved on the horse was breathtaking. I couldn't help but wonder: Did Adam have the same gift as his sister?

The afternoon crept by and finally Caitlin looked at her watch. "We'd better go," she muttered, sneaking another glance at Killian. "My mum will have dinner ready, and if we stay here any longer we could be accused of loitering, or stalking, or both, for that matter."

We got up and made our way out of the barn to the driveway.

"Oh, crap, I forgot my jacket," Caitlin announced.

"Yeah, right. You just want to get one last glimpse," I teased.

Caitlin blushed. "I'll be back in just a sec. Wait for me!"

Dusk had cast a gloom over the parking lot. I was just approaching the gate when I noticed Áine standing under a canopy of trees. She was dimly lit by the orange light of a street lamp that had just flickered to life, and she was laughing quietly to herself while gently waving her arms around. I slowed, stepping back into the shadows, and watched her delighted face as a cloud of white moths began to gather above her head. Where had they all come from? She swayed her arms to one side and the fluttering white cloud of moths danced to her command. It was a strangely beautiful sight. Then she held out her arms to each side and the hovering mass of insects descended on her, smothering every inch of her silhouette in the delicate beatings of white wings.

Stunned into stillness, I stayed where I was. The crack of a branch above my head made Áine flick her eyes in my direction. As quickly as the moths had arrived, they disappeared like a wisp into the darkness. Áine looked right at me, then above my head.

Caw! A crow swooped out of the tree and flew to the lamppost beside Áine. They both stared at me. Then the bird winked. No, he wasn't winking. It was the crow with the ringed eye. He cawed again and took flight, disappearing into the distance.

"Sorry I took so long, Meg. I couldn't find it anywhere," Caitlin called breathlessly as she jogged toward me. She pulled up short when she saw my face.

"What's wrong?"

I didn't know what to say. The beauty of the moths had sent a chill through my entire body and left my skin tingling. It was the oddest sensation, sort of like what had been happening with my hands, but somehow gentler.

Áine stepped out from under the canopy and walked toward me.

"It's Megan, isn't it? I'm Áine. We have art together, but we haven't been introduced yet," she announced, looking at me warily. She stopped short, keeping her distance from me.

"Yeah, hi," I said, taking a step closer and attempting to shake her hand.

Ignoring it, she scratched her neck and cocked her head to one side, focusing on something behind me. Her eyes slowly slid back to mine and she looked at me thoughtfully for a few moments. Her eyes were so like her brother's that it was unsettling.

Then a battered-looking Land Rover Discovery pulled in behind her. I peered into the car, but couldn't see through the tinted windows in the half-light. The driver's window opened just a little bit and a gruff voice called to Áine to get into the car.

"Must dash." She looked at me guiltily and jumped into the front seat. Before they pulled away she rolled down her window and stuck her open palm out of the car. On it was a big white moth that must have strayed inside. She smiled at me and gently blew the moth off her hand, then raised her finger to her lips. Seconds later, the car took off, leaving dust and spinning stones in its wake.

"That was weird," Caitlin said.

"Totally," I agreed. "Come on, let's get home."

The last of the sun was setting over the Bandon estuary as we walked along the river. It had turned the still water a molten orange and red.

Caitlin looked at me. "What's with all the silence? Are you okay?"

"I'm fine. It's just . . . I saw Áine doing something really weird with all these white moths. It's hard to describe. She sort of had them dancing."

"She was dancing with the moths?"

"No, she *made* the moths dance."

"I don't get it." Caitlin snorted, giving me a sidelong glance.

"I'm not explaining it well. I just . . . Do you think there's any truth in the rumors about their being . . . you know?"

"Stop it! You're giving me the creeps."

We made our way up the hill past the school and then turned toward town. Just ahead of us I saw someone who looked like the old man from the other day. I started to slow down, not wanting to have to deal with him again. He turned his expressionless face to us before slowly crossing the road and disappearing into an alley.

Caitlin glanced back at me. "Are you sure you're okay?"

"What is it with the creepy monk guys around here?"

"Oh, they're just the brothers from the friary. They're all really nice."

"What about that one, the one with the long gray hair and beard clip?"

"Can't say I've ever seen a monk with a beard clip," Caitlin said, laughing. "I think you have an overactive imagination. I'm going to have a word with the lads. No more scary stories for you."

"He was just walking in front of us." I pointed to where he'd crossed the road.

"Sorry, I must have missed him. My mind was more *agreeably* engaged." She winked at me. "Thanks for today; I know it wasn't exactly your bag of chips."

Still really freaked out, but not wanting to make

her worry, I smiled. "Today was great. Your idea was inspired. Riding in the evenings could be just what I need." I hugged her. "See you tomorrow."

"Yes," she replied, "but I'll talk to you first." She waved her phone at me.

"Definitely," I said, waving mine back at her.

I started huffing and puffing my way up the hill. When I was halfway home, I leaned against a tree to catch my breath. There was a squawk from the branch above my head. I jumped and looked up into the silver-ringed eye of a familiar crow.

"And what are you looking at?" I said to him. I took another deep breath and battled the last of the steep hill to my house.

"Hi, Dad! Wait until I tell you what I saw," I shouted as I let myself in. "Dad?" There was nothing.

I went into the kitchen and flicked on the lights just as my phone beeped with a new text.

Having dinner at work. Order pizza. See you later.

"Oh, Dad." I sighed. "Of all the nights for you not to be here."

My stomach was still in knots, so I decided to skip the pizza. I picked up the remote and turned on the TV for some much-needed background noise.

The sound of a cracking branch drew my attention to

the window. There, in the tree just outside, was the same weird crow. His beady eyes glared at me in the half-light of dusk.

"Yah!" I shouted at the window, but the bird simply jumped to another branch. With the hairs standing up on the back of my neck, I hastily pulled the curtains.

Four

SAILING LESSONS

$\mathcal{I}$ couldn't believe a month had passed since we moved to Kinsale. Time had flown by, and I had settled into a comfortable routine: Monday to Friday I did the whole school thing, and then on the weekends I hung out with Caitlin and Jennifer, either at one of our houses or in one of the coffee shops in town.

I hadn't ventured into Cork City yet, though there was a trip planned for a week from Saturday. Caitlin had even been given a pass on her usual cleaning duties in the B and B. I was really looking forward to it. As much as I liked Kinsale, it was hardly Rodeo Drive, and I was desperate for new clothes. My pursuit of Adam might be futile, but I needed to look good anyway. Making myself a tad more visible couldn't hurt either.

It was funny: When I first arrived here Adam seemed to be everywhere. True, besides the odd looks and furtive glances, he generally ignored me, but he was a regular presence. Lately, though, Adam had been keeping a lower profile. He was in school, but I was seeing him less and less.

I had even asked my dad about him. He said Adam was still working at the yacht club, and sailing and instructing more than ever. Strangely, Rían, who'd graduated last year, still skulked around the place. It was creepy. What on earth was he doing lurking around the school anyway? Shouldn't he have been in college or something?

And while Adam had been pulling a disappearing act, Áine had become more approachable since our meeting at the equestrian center. But though she was always nice and friendly, she never got too close. One day in art, I plucked up the courage to ask her about the moths.

"Áine . . ." I chickened out at the last minute. "Could you pass me a red oil pastel?"

"Sure," she replied, handing it to me. I noticed she avoided touching my hand, though. *Weird*.

I swallowed hard and tried again. "Do you mind if I ask you something?"

She looked at me, half-wary, half-surprised. "Sure."

"What happened with the moths that night at the equestrian center?"

"I don't understand what you mean," she said quietly, and turned back to her drawing.

"They were all around you, dancing. I saw them covering you."

She laughed, not making eye contact. "That's a good one."

"But I saw—"

"I don't know what you saw, Megan, but whatever it was, it had nothing to do with me."

"Oh, I'm sorry. I just . . ." I felt my face redden. *She must think I'm deranged.*

She looked at me with pity. "Don't beat yourself up over it. The light can play tricks at dusk." She tapped her hand on mine in a reassuring way.

We both jumped. The zing that passed through us was short, but strong. It was like a static shock, and the tingling that had been flickering through my arm before was gone. I looked at her now pale face.

"Was that static?" I asked, looking from her hand to mine.

"Yeah, ouch. I gotta go. . . . I'm not feeling too well." She turned to the teacher. "Miss, I feel sick. Can I be excused?"

"Of course, Áine," she replied, and Áine fled the room.

She hadn't sat next to me in art since then, but Caitlin

told me not to worry about it, that Áine was, after all, a DeRís, and oddness was to be expected.

My Adam drought came to an abrupt end the first day of our sailing course. While most students were excited that they would be getting out of gym for five weeks, I was dreading it. Boats, water—ugh! The only thing keeping me from dropping out of the whole charade was the thought of seeing Adam, being close to him.

When school broke for lunch, people who were signed up for the sailing course were allowed to go home to get their gear. Once home, I changed, grabbed the bag containing my new wet suit (yeah, attractive! But a must with the freezing Irish waters), and set off to the marina. Now that I was so close to seeing Adam, my body was fizzing with excitement. I took a deep breath and tried to calm my nerves, but it didn't really work.

Caitlin and Jennifer were waiting for me at the club.

"Hurry, Meg. Dump your bag," Caitlin said, pointing at the clubhouse.

Jennifer looked at her nails, oozing a lack of interest. "Yeah, Meg, come on; let's get this over with." She flicked her blond hair over her shoulder. The appeal of the hair flick was lost with the very unflattering gray-and-pink wet suit. I suppressed a smile.

"I'll be right there," I called, running up the steps. I glanced back at them and ran slap into Adam's hard chest at the door. Winded by the collision and teetering on the edge of the step, I grasped in vain at the handrail. He put out his arms behind me and caught me before I fell, pressing me against his solid body. He looked down at me with an inquisitive glance, and I tilted my head toward his face, then jumped back from him, realizing I had paused a second too long, giving away far too much. *Get out of here quick*, I thought to myself, and ran for the locker room. I poured myself into the wet suit, then dashed back down to Caitlin and Jennifer. They were chatting in excited voices with Darren and Killian. Nausea washed over me. I wasn't sure whether it was the impending sailing or my run-in with Adam, but I could feel the bile stir in my stomach.

Caitlin and I paired up and we were assigned a tiny two-person boat. We were instructed to drag the boats, which were on little wheels, down the slipway and into the water.

I can't believe I signed up for this. What was I thinking? We started walking down the concrete slipway. The water lapped up at us halfway down. Green slime and seaweed swirled around my feet. My stomach churned uneasily. I needed to get out of here. I was looking around for a private place to puke when Killian came up to me and put his hand under my elbow.

"Jeez, Megan, you okay? You look like you're about to hurl."

Caitlin turned from the front of the boat at the sound of Killian's voice. "You do look awful. Do you need to sit this out?"

Killian put his arm around me. "Come on; I'll help you back up to the club."

At that moment Adam walked down among us all and stopped at the end of the slipway. I shook my head back and forth; I had to snap out of it.

"No, Killian, thanks. I'll be fine." I felt myself cool almost instantly. Then the prickling started working its way through my body. The sensation no longer startled me. In fact, I found it soothing today. I could feel my stomach settling and my color returning to normal.

"Only if you're sure," Killian said in a worried tone.

"Honestly, I'm fine. *Caitlin*, tell him I'm fine."

"Thanks, Killian, but it looks like your knight-in-shining-armor skills won't be needed," Caitlin said, glancing at Adam.

"Well, if I can be of any help, just give me a call." He smirked and winked at her.

Adam had made his way to his boat in the front and was running though some notes. He looked so vital, so full of life. The rest of us looked hideous in our wet suits and life vests, but he still looked gorgeous. How did he do that?

He flicked his eyes around at us and started giving a lecture on water safety and dos and don'ts while operating leisure craft, his green eyes holding everyone's attention. I idly rubbed my tingling neck and tried to listen to his instructions, but it was useless. I felt my body melting toward him, my breath catching. I dropped my eyes and tried to refocus. I quickly risked a look back up to him under my eyelashes, but his eyes caught mine at the same time and he immediately looked away, dropping his clipboard in the process. Caitlin elbowed me in the ribs.

"Focus, Meg," she whispered under her breath.

We cast off into the water somewhat successfully; it was actually quite fun, as long as I didn't look into the deep, dark liquid swirling around us. It was reassuring to see that Adam treated everyone else with the same level of reserve as he did me. He called us in two boats at a time to do some work on knots and lines. He was giving a complicated demonstration on the importance of tying up pulleys or something; I wasn't really listening. I assumed Caitlin was—well, at least I hoped she was. But when I looked over at her, she was gazing at Killian, who was concentrating hard on his ropes and mimicking Adam. Panic hit me. *Oh, crap!* I tried frantically to catch up with what Adam was saying and doing, but it was too late.

"Go out twenty yards and keep plenty of room from each other, and, working as a team, tie in your lines and secure your sails," Adam shouted as he moved on to the next pair of boats.

I glanced at Caitlin. She was still looking dreamily over toward Killian's dinghy.

I kicked her. "Cait, did you get any of that?"

"Huh?" she said, with a vacant expression.

I flushed with embarrassment. God, could we be any more pathetic?

"Don't worry, Meg. It looks pretty simple. I'm sure I can figure this out," Caitlin said, as she started pulling at ropes and levers.

I looked back at Adam, who was giving a helping hand to one of the other pairs. He was so gorgeous; his lightly tanned skin rippled over his toned body. His dazzling eyes were hidden for the moment behind a pair of dark sunglasses. His defined cheekbones were flushed red from the sea air. His full, curling lips were slightly parted; I wondered what they would feel like, taste like. . . .

Bam! I was interrupted by a hard thump on my head.

The shock of the cold water was temporary. It was replaced by fear as I gasped for air. Whatever hit me had snapped all of the oxygen from my lungs before dunking me in the sea. I sucked in a vast breath and choked on the salt water that swirled its way into my body. I couldn't figure out which way was up. I knew I was wearing a life jacket, but I couldn't find the surface; there was no air. Then I got warmer, my breathing became easier, and the strangest sensation of calm came over me. I was underwater, but no longer felt the panic of water filling my lungs. My head was spinning and pounding with pain, but I was breathing. The sound was muffled, like I was cocooned.

A firm arm supported my back.

"Megan." I heard my name being called in the distance. "Christ, Megan, answer me! Megan, come on; can you hear me?"

I wanted to open my eyes, but even the slightest movement hurt my head.

"Oh, Megan, Megan, I'm so sorry," I heard Caitlin crying in the background.

"Caitlin, please stay back," the voice instructed. "Come on, Megan, open your eyes." It was Adam's voice, calling me back to consciousness.

I obeyed him and opened my eyes, trying to focus on his. I was lying in Adam's arms on the slipway. His face was so close to mine I could hear his ragged breath and taste the warmth of it.

"There you are." He smiled in relief.

The sun was shining behind him and I couldn't see his face clearly. I tried to sit up and coughed, attempting to clear the burning stinging in my throat. I became acutely aware of a throbbing sensation in my head; it spun and little stars twinkled around Adam's face.

I gasped at the pain and put my hand to the back of my head. It felt warm and sticky. When I looked at my hand, it was all bloody. I tried to get to my feet, but fell forward. Adam's strong, warm arms caught me.

"Whoa, take it slowly."

He put my arm around his shoulders and his arm around my back to support me. I gasped at the warmth and closeness of his body; it was like a static shock. Misinterpreting my gasp as pain, he swung me up into his arms.

An orange lifeboat pulled alongside the slipway. "Hi, Adam, you need help? We were just coming in from a call and noticed all the commotion," a crew member shouted up.

"We're all good here now, thanks, Dave. Actually, can you do me a favor and see that the class gets the dinghies back into the yard, while I look after this one?"

"Sure thing," Dave replied.

As Caitlin walked past me up the slipway she gave me a tearful smile. "Are you sure you're going to be okay? I'm so sorry; I let go of the rope that controls the boom and it just shot out."

"Don't worry; I'm good."

"Go on, Caitlin; join the rest of the class," Adam said.

It was quiet and calm for a moment, and then I remembered I was in Adam's arms. I was sure I weighed a ton, but I felt faint and my head pounded. I let it fall against his chest. I could hear his heart thudding away. I was so comfortable there; I felt so safe. My eyes were fluttering again, and the last thing I saw before losing the battle with them was the gray monk, standing at the gates to the yacht club. His watery, expressionless eyes met mine; then a hint of a smile touched his lips.

My head was throbbing. I opened my eyes and reached for the back of my head, only to encounter a hand and an ice pack. Startled, I sat up.

"Dad!"

My dad's worried face softened into a smile. "God, Meg, you gave me a fright! How do you feel?"

"Sore. Where am I?"

"The Kinsale clinic. I wanted to take you to the hospital." I stiffened. I hadn't set foot in a hospital since the crash and I intended to keep it that way. My dad reacted immediately. "It's okay, I won't make you go. Let's see what Dr. Forrest has to say, okay? Look, here he is now."

"So, Megan, how are you feeling?" Dr. Forrest asked, shining a light into my eyes.

"Okay, I guess. My head hurts."

"Luckily the wound is superficial, but even so, I'd like to have you under observation for twenty-four hours." He looked sternly from me to my dad.

My dad squeezed me tighter. "I'll keep a close watch on her at home."

Dr. Forrest smiled. "Good. Well, here's a prescription

for the pain. If there's any swelling or nausea, call me immediately."

My dad helped me up from the bench and opened the door of the exam room. "We better let Adam know you're all right."

"What! He's still here?" I gasped, stepping into the waiting room. Sure enough, there he was, sitting in a low, comfy chair, a small smile playing on his face.

Oh, cringe. I just wanted to get out of the room. And what was he smiling about, anyway? For God's sake, it was hardly a big smiley moment.

I couldn't talk to him with my dad in such close proximity, but Adam's eyes met mine, this time holding them. What was that in his gaze? Humor? No, but there was something, an intensity. Something had changed. I yearned to know what. His eyes were laden with meaning and questions; I was desperate to know them, to answer them.

"Come on, Meg; I think your sailing career is over. Let's get you home." Dad turned to Adam. "Thanks again, Adam; I can't tell you how grateful I am. She's all I have and so, so precious." He said it with such emotion. I felt a mix of intense embarrassment and love for my poor dad.

"No problem, Mr. Rosenberg. I completely understand." Adam strode across the room and firmly shook Dad's hand.

I struggled to say something, anything. But the words wouldn't come. I just stood there, looking at him awkwardly, then shuffled out of the room.

I caught a last look at his exquisite face. He had one hand in his hair and the other held the back of his neck. His eyes, clouded by confusion, followed mine until the door closed silently on his gaze.

Five

AFTERMATH

School on Monday was all drama, drama, drama. Everyone wanted to hear what had happened and how the heroic Adam had come to my rescue. I didn't really want to relive the experience—it was embarrassing the first time around and it became more so with each retelling.

After first period, Caitlin grabbed my sleeve and pulled me into one of the girls' bathrooms.

"So, what happened after Adam carried you off?" she asked.

"I passed out, I think. I just remember waking up in the clinic."

"Did he say anything? Did he mention the accident?"

"No. Why?"

She leaned back against a sink and chewed on her bottom lip for a second. "I swear to God, I saw the freakiest thing."

"What do you mean? What happened?"

"Well, after you fell in, I couldn't see you for a few seconds. I was shouting and grabbing at the water, but there was no sign of you. Within seconds Adam had dived in and swum to you. Like, I mean, *seconds*. I've never seen anything like it. Then, before he got to you, there was a glow in the water. It's hard to describe. It looked like a golden light just below the water's surface. Then suddenly, there you were. I could see you perfectly, but here's the weird thing. You weren't in the water. You were under it, but not in it. Your hair was hanging down normally and . . . and . . . well, you looked content. I swear to God . . . I'm so freaked out right now. Nobody else saw it. I'm beginning to think I imagined it all. I was hoping you might remember." She ran her hands through her hair, shaking her head.

"Caitlin, don't stress yourself out. Maybe it was the sun playing tricks on the surface of the water."

"Maybe you're right. It all happened so fast," she muttered, looking confused.

The door to the bathroom swung open and Jennifer flounced in. "What are you two doing skulking in here?" She went into a stall and slammed the door shut, but kept talking. "Did you guys hear about Killian's dog? He followed Killian to school today and one of the school buses ran over him."

"Oh, no! Is he all right?" Caitlin gasped.

"The bus was doing the poor dog a favor, if you ask me. He's so decrepit! He should have been put down years ago," Jennifer replied.

"No, you numpty. I meant Killian," Caitlin said in exasperation.

"Let me finish! Anyhow . . . Áine arrives just as it happens and runs over to help the poor mutt. She just put her hands on his head and hey, presto, the dog stood up and headed off home."

Caitlin and I exchanged startled glances as Jennifer flushed the toilet, opened the door, and walked over to a sink. "How freaky is that? I mean, I could have sworn the wheel rolled over the dog. Then the thing just gets up and trots off. There is something strange about that girl. She's working some kinda voodoo, if you ask me." She looked at us with her face all scrunched up. "You don't find that odd? Am I the only one who thinks it highly unlikely the bus missed *all* of the dog's vital organs?"

"It's a possibility," I piped up.

"Well, I think it's weird. But then, when have the DeRíses ever been normal?" Jennifer said, leaning into the mirror and reapplying some lip gloss.

It was pouring at lunchtime, so the boys decided to play indoor soccer. Jennifer went along to support Darren, and Caitlin and I found an unused classroom and sat in two desks at the back. The rain had been falling all day and now it ran in torrents down the windowpane. The glass was all fogged up on the inside, distorting the greenery beyond.

"Caitlin," I started.

"Yeah," she replied, not looking up from her soggy sandwich, which she was opening up and peering into in disgust.

"I . . ."

"Come on; spit it out." She paused. "Do you know what that is?" She opened her sandwich wide and put it up to my face. I wrinkled up my nose and took a little sniff.

"I'm not sure. Um . . . cheese, maybe?"

"Well, I'm not risking it." She threw the sandwich back into the aluminum foil, picked up her apple instead, and took a big bite. "You were saying?"

"Adam." I paused, thinking where to go from here. "What's the deal with him?"

"Even after everything we've told you, you're still besotted with him," she said with a faint smile.

"I'm not *besotted*."

"Oh, come on, Meg, be honest with yourself. You are and have been since your first day here. It can't have escaped your attention that he is fairly taken by you as well," she continued.

"If he really liked me, he'd ask me out. Anyway, that's not what I want to talk about. I've been thinking—"

"I hope you didn't strain yourself." She laughed.

"Seriously, Cait, listen to me. Ever since you told me about seeing that light in the water I've been racking my brain trying to remember what happened. I don't remember a light, but I vaguely remember a warm, floaty feeling."

"You think there's something to what I saw?" she asked, leaning toward me.

"There might be. Remember the dancing moths down at the equestrian center? I couldn't explain that either. Then today there was the incident with the dog and the bus. I think there are too many coincidences with the DeRíses. What's their story? I mean, they're not exactly your straightforward, run-of-the-mill family, are they?"

"Far from it. I don't know all the details, but apparently their parents died in some tragic car accident years ago. They were orphaned and had no other relatives, so an old family friend took them in. They moved around with him for a couple of years and then settled here in Kinsale at the Killeen estate, which has been in their family for generations. That estate has been shrouded in mystery since . . . well, forever. You've heard the stories.

And there was the hex that everyone talks about."

"I haven't heard that one."

"Really? Well, the Killeens used to be the big land-owners in the area. At some point, the locals began to resent the land charges they were forced to pay, and then in the summer of 1842 something happened over at the big house and darkness descended on their lands. Literally. Clouds rolled in off the sea and settled over the entire estate. The land turned brown and every-thing started to die. It was like a plague. The crops failed and the 'sickness' radiated out farther and farther until the whole of coastal West Cork had been affected. The townspeople believed the Killeens had hexed their land and town as punishment for their insubordination. But who knows how much of that is true. . . . It was around the time of the Great Famine, and they may have just been looking for someone to blame."

"Wow. Imagine trying to shake that kind of association."

"Yeah, that's got to suck. But honestly, they do noth-ing to endear themselves to the locals. When they first moved here three years ago, we were all a little bit in love with them. Rían was, like, sizzling hot, and Adam was swoon-worthy, but they were absolutely obnoxious and shunned anyone who tried to make friends with them. Áine was more approachable, but she always lurked in the shadows of her brothers, so we eventually stopped trying. The DeRíses seemed to like the distance, and then all the old stories started popping up again."

"So who's the guy in the Land Rover?" I asked, totally engrossed.

"Oh, that's Fionn."

"Fee-un?"

"Yeah, the guy who took them in, Fionn Christenson. He is *so* hot . . . well, for an oldie, that is. Wait until you see him!" She nibbled the last bits of her apple and then threw the core in the trash. "He's some sort of consultant, and he travels a lot. When he's not traveling, he works from home. He has this sexy English accent, so Darren's convinced he's working for Her Majesty's Secret Service . . . you know . . . MI5." She laughed. "Darren and his conspiracy theories!"

"Are you serious?"

She nodded and rolled her eyes.

"What about Rían? Do you have any idea why he's still hanging around the school?"

"I don't know what his problem is. He finished school last year, and from what I'd heard, he was due to start at Trinity College this year. I'll tell you one thing for sure: He's not too keen on his brother having the blatantly obvious hots for you!"

I flushed. "Áine seems pretty nice, in a strange way," I said, moving swiftly on from Rían.

"Oh, yeah, she's fine. Actually she's been much better

since you've been here. Before you came she was as bad as the other two. She would always have one of them by her side. They're a bit overprotective, don't you think?"

"I guess so. Maybe being orphaned at such a young age made them that way."

"Maybe." She looked at me thoughtfully. "Do you really think the DeRíses have magical power?"

"I don't know what I think. But there *is* something really odd about them."

She laughed. "Haven't I been telling you that all along?"

Six

DINNER

I decided to quit the sailing classes. I hated being a quitter, but the truth was, I was not meant for water. I was better off accepting my fate now; otherwise fate would come looking for me . . . again. So on Friday, the gang went to the marina and I changed my clothes for dreaded PE. What a way to finish the week. Yuck. After a riveting class of running laps around the hockey field while Miss O'Toole flirted with the groundskeeper, I packed my stuff and headed home. I was red faced and sweaty by the time I got to my house, thanks to the laps and the uphill struggle with my ever-increasing-in-weight backpack. I opened the door and dumped the monstrosity inside.

I tried to shake off my bad mood. I knew I was only cranky because all my friends were currently under the tutelage of the gorgeous Mr. DeRís and I was not. I was just about to head upstairs to take a shower when a text came in on my phone.

Don't forget. Dinner tonight 7 p.m. I'll be home to pick you up at 6:30. Dad.

Oh, crap. I had forgotten all about it. Dad wanted to introduce me to the who's who of Kinsale, most of whom I already knew through idle gossip and their kids who attended the school. He also seemed pretty eager for me to try out a fish restaurant in town, the Crab Cage or the Lobster Pot or something like that.

I got a glass of water and went to my room—my favorite place in the house. White walls, oak floors—and two dormer windows flooded the room with light by day, making it cheerful and homey. It also contained my prize possession, my bed, which I had brought with me from the U.S. It had been my mother's bed before mine, and it made me feel close to her. Its white wrought-iron headboard was an intricate mesh of flowers and leaves that twisted and spiraled from one side to the other. I threw myself down on the pillows, kicked off my shoes, and tried in vain to piece together all the little bits of oddness that made up Adam DeRís. My eyes wandered to my bookshelves. I glanced at some photos and mementos of my life before Kinsale, a life that I rarely thought of. These things had meant a lot to me a few short months ago, but now their significance had faded.

I closed my eyes, willing myself to sleep, but it just wasn't happening. *I may as well start getting ready for tonight.* I'd just grabbed a towel when something behind me started tapping and scratching. I tiptoed to the window and pulled back the curtain. I wasn't at all surprised to see my feathered friend sitting on my windowsill. This time I stared back at him. The crow angled his head and glared back at me with his winking eye. I stuck my tongue out at him and went in for a shower.

Feeling refreshed, I got dressed in my soft, comfy jeans and a long-sleeved T-shirt. Then I slicked on a little black mascara and pink lip gloss and threw myself back onto my bed to do my math homework while I waited for Dad to get home.

At six forty-five I heard the key in the front door.

"Megan, are you ready?" Dad called into my room as he passed. "I'm just going to change my shirt and we'll go, all right?"

"Yeah, Dad, I'm ready." I grabbed my purse and went downstairs to wait for him.

He was down in double-time, smelling nice and his face flushed.

"Ohhh, you're putting in an extra effort tonight, Dad," I teased him.

"No more than usual," he said, carefully inspecting his reflection in the hall mirror.

"Yeah, sure." I gave him a sidelong look.

There was obviously something very appealing about this restaurant, and I had a feeling it wasn't the crab cakes. As we pulled away from our house, I looked back. The crow was perched on the highest point of our roof, watching me leave. Was that bird really following me? No. That was insane; birds didn't stalk people. I pushed the thought out of my head.

The restaurant was lovely, quaint, and totally jam-packed. The food was amazing. Too bad the people surrounding us were so dull. They were bigwigs in town: the superintendent from the Kinsale Gardaí (the Irish police), who, at seven feet tall, towered over us all; as well as the owners of the various town shops and businesses. Killian's mom and dad were there (Caitlin would be seething that she missed this one). Then there was the owner of the restaurant, Petra Van Meulder. Judging by all my dad's excessive laughing and beaming, she was the object of his extra efforts.

To be fair, she was lovely and really pretty. Petra told me she was from Holland and that she had come to Ireland to forget a bad divorce and never went home. I appreciated that she was making an extra effort to include me in their conversation, but I couldn't help feeling like a third wheel. It was great to see Dad actually getting a life, and

I wanted to leave them to it. We were just finishing up the meal and thinking of ordering dessert when I saw an opportunity to escape.

I nudged my dad. "Do you mind if I go for a walk?"

"Meg, it's late. I don't think so."

"Caleb, let her go for a walk. It's very safe around here, and she's well able to look after herself," Petra said, giving me an understanding smile.

My dad caved. "Okay, but stay close and don't be too long, okay?"

"I won't. I'm just going to wander down to the marina."

I stepped out into the night air and filled my lungs with a deep, fresh breath. I exhaled slowly, looking up at the stars, and then started walking along the waterline. The yachts swayed gently where they were moored, creating a musical tinkling sound. I punched in the code to the jetty at the marina and opened the gate. Finally I found a secluded spot and sat down between two big yachts. I let my feet dangle over the edge, toward the water. Funny, it didn't look scary at night. In fact, it had an almost magical quality in the dark.

I was so caught up in my thoughts that I almost didn't notice the person gliding quietly up the gangway in my direction. The flat, calm water shimmered and pulsated, then rose slightly up, as if there was something just below the surface. I watched in amazement as the water took on a life of its own and followed the person as he walked along the wooden jetty and then moved out of sight behind a boat. I shrank back into the shadows of the yachts as he walked past.

"Adam," I breathed quietly, enjoying the tingling sensation that ran through me.

He was wearing heavy sailing pants, boots, and a padded sleeveless jacket. He climbed nimbly into the yacht beside me and disappeared inside. My heart was pounding. Then I heard the flapping sound and a cawing. I looked up. That freaky crow was sitting on the railing of the yacht, his head cocked to the side, watching me.

"Go away," I whispered, but he cawed down to me again and disappeared in between the boats. Just then two big boots hit the deck above my head and Adam peered down over the railing, squinting into the darkness.

"Who's there?" He turned on a flashlight and shone it down in my direction.

I played with the idea of pulling myself farther into the shadows and hiding, but quickly realized that it was virtually impossible.

I leaned out into the beam of light and waved up at him. "Hey, Adam."

He looked around worriedly. "How long have you been down there?"

"Don't worry; I won't say anything."

"What do you mean?"

"About the water. I saw it, but I won't say anything."

"I don't know what you're talking about. Really, Megan, you shouldn't be hanging around the marina at night. It's dangerous. You should go home."

"But . . . the water . . . it was glowing." I stopped, doubting myself for a second.

"Megan, honestly, you've lost me. I'm guessing you've been listening to all the stupid stories about my family. Do yourself a favor—go home." He sighed and started to turn away.

My temper flared. What made him so goddamn superior? "Hey," I called up at him, "that's not fair." I stumbled in my haste to get up off the gangway and teetered on the edge. He jumped down and steadied me.

"You were saying?"

"Oh, nothing." I was furious at myself for still aching to touch him.

"Wait," he said, rubbing his jaw. "I'm sorry."

"You should be."

He laughed and turned off the flashlight. It took a few moments for my eyes to adjust to the darkness again. "I mean it," he said softly, very close to my face.

I could hardly breathe. "Forget it," I managed, and turned to flee.

But he was quicker; he caught my hand and spun me back to him. "Honestly, I'm sorry." He lowered his eyes to mine. "But the marina is not the place to be hanging around after dark."

I lifted my chin defiantly. "You're here, aren't you?" I looked him straight in the eye.

He held my glare for a moment or two; then his eyes softened. All traces of my irritation melted away as he moved closer.

I felt like we were being pulled together by some unknown force. With his face now only inches from mine, I could feel his hot breath on my lips; it tickled the end of my nose. Every nerve in my body was screaming for me to throw my arms around his neck, but his eyes held me still. My lips parted, eager to taste his breath on the tip of my tongue.

His eyes shifted and flickered up toward the pier. He took a step back, the spell broken.

"Yeah, but I work here," he said softly. "See you at school on Monday."

He walked back down the gangway into the shadows and disappeared into the blackness.

"Megan," my dad called from the pier. "Are you down there?"

"Yeah, Dad," I shouted back, still looking in the direction where Adam had disappeared.

"Come on. It's getting late."

"I'm coming." I ran up the gangway to the gate and into my dad's view.

My crow swooped up the gangway above my head

and landed on the gate by my dad.

"What is it with these Irish birds?" my dad said. "They're persistent, aren't they?"

"You've noticed too!" I blurted out. "I thought it was just me. That crow is a menace. I swear he's been following me."

"Have you been reading Stephen King again?" he asked, laughing. He threw his arm over my shoulders and changed the subject. "I didn't get a chance to talk to you much at dinner. How's school been?"

"It's fine. I wish people would stop talking about my stupid drowning incident, though."

He chuckled. He knew I despised being the center of attention.

"Caitlin was talking about going into Cork City tomorrow. Can I go with her?"

"Sure. You haven't been outside of Kinsale since we got here, and you need to learn how to get around."

"Great! I'll let Caitlin know I can go. Thanks, Dad."

"Come on. Let's get back to the car; it's getting cold," he said, pulling me closer. "Did you see how tall that guy from the guards was?"

"I did. He was pretty hard to miss. And it's pronounced *Guard-ee*, Dad. The 'i' with the fada on it is pronounced *ee*."

"Since when do you know so much about the Irish language?"

"Since I discovered half the population of the school has unpronounceable names," I said, laughing.

Seven

CORK CITY

He walked toward me, holding me in his gaze, his eyes wide with intensity. His pupils were dilated black and deep, ringed by a circle of yellow that fanned into the green that made up his irises. The green was enclosed by a thin black ring, encasing all that intensity, holding it there. They shimmered. I tried to take a step forward and realized I was underwater. He held out his hand to me. I couldn't grasp it.

"Don't leave me," I screamed over and over. My head was swirling. "Come back."

"I'm here, Meg, don't worry," my dad said, sitting at my bedside. Confused, I glanced around the room. It was a hospital room.

"You came back to me. . . . I thought I lost you," he said, smiling at me with sad eyes.

My eyes flickered behind him. The gray monk stood there with a hand on my dad's shoulder. His eyes gazed at me softly and he smiled gently before dissipating into a shimmering mist.

I threw myself forward and nearly tumbled out of bed. My breath was ragged, my head disoriented. Glancing around, I saw that I was back in my bedroom at home. A dream. It was only a dream.

Breathing a sigh of relief, I allowed my head to drop back onto my feather pillow. My damp hair clung to my cheeks and I rubbed it off in irritation and threw back the duvet. Needing air, I crawled out of the bed and opened the window. It blew fresh and salty onto my clammy face, and I breathed deep as the memories of my encounter with Adam last night washed over me.

"Good morning," I croaked at the crow who was sitting on my windowsill, as I'd known he would be. He cocked his head and bowed it a little, then flew away. "See you later, Winky." I watched him soar down toward the harbor, until he was just a dot in the distance.

My cell phone vibrated on my bedside table with a message from Caitlin.

On my way! Will be at your place in ten. Be ready.

Crap! I'd better hurry. I chucked on what I was wearing last night, giving it a quick sniff to make sure it didn't smell like fish; then I pulled on my Converse and ran down the stairs. I gasped in horror as I caught sight of myself in the mirror. *Whoa, hair. Calm yourself.* I quickly pulled it into a ponytail and slicked on some lip gloss and mascara. Just as I was finishing up, there was a knock at the door.

"Hi," Caitlin sang, sticking her head into the hall. "Bring your raincoat; it's starting to drizzle."

On the way out, I noticed a white envelope with my name on it. Inside there was a wad of euros and a little note.

Have some fun on me!

Dad, you're the best, I thought as I pocketed the cash.

"Let's go," I said, and pulled the door firmly behind me.

"The bus will be here in ten minutes, so we'd better leg it. Jennifer's meeting us in Cork. She went in with her dad earlier." We set off quickly down the hill and made it just in time.

"So . . . how was dinner last night?" Caitlin asked as soon as we sat down on the bus.

"Okay. Nothing too riveting."

"Weren't Killian's parents there?"

"Yep. How did you know?"

"I have my sources. Next time, try to get me an invite. It wouldn't hurt to get some insider info, you know." She smirked and raised her eyebrows.

I smacked her arm, laughing. "You have it so bad! We have to sort that out soon before you injure yourself. So . . . I bumped into Adam last night."

"No! Tell me all the sordid details."

"Nothing sordid, unfortunately, but I think you might be right about him liking me! I'm pretty sure we came close to a kiss."

"Agh!"

"I know. It was all very intense."

"Details, please."

I gave her a rundown of the previous night's events, and then paused.

"Are you keeping juicy bits from me?"

"Not juicy bits, but, well . . . there was all this weird stuff happening with the water when Adam was around. It started to shimmer and bulge up."

"Agh! Just like when you fell in. Holy crap, now you've seen it too. I'm telling you—there's something up with them!"

"But that's crazy!"

"I've been doing a little digging. I only came up with the usual tales of witchcraft blah, blah, blah, but do you know what's really strange? These are old stories. There's been nothing new in ages. All this strange stuff has only been happening since you've been here."

We went quiet, lost in thought as the bus pulled into the city station and we jumped off and started walking toward the main shopping area around Patrick Street.

"Do you think it's you? You know, with Adam fancying the pants off you?" Caitlin asked after a few minutes.

"Don't be ridiculous. How could it be me? This was all going on long before I arrived. I think Adam just got caught out when I fell into the water."

"Then how do you explain Áine?"

"Oh, I don't know. Honestly, Cait, is it possible we are adding one and one and getting three? I sort of mentioned it to Adam and I felt *really* stupid afterward. He told me I was imagining things."

"Well, he would say that, wouldn't he?"

"I guess."

"Wouldn't it be cool if they were, like . . . magic? Hey! You should ask him to the Halloween party." Caitlin looked at me with excited eyes.

"What Halloween party?"

"Oh, yeah . . . breaking news; the social event of the year is happening next Saturday night. Jennifer has all the details. Look, there she is," Caitlin said, waving across the road.

Jennifer was standing in the doorway of a department store, talking into her cell phone.

"Hey, Jennifer! What's the story? Any news on the party?" Caitlin asked as Jennifer ended her call.

"Yep. We are 'G' for go. My dad is throwing a huge Halloween bash at the yacht club, so while all of our parents are getting their groove on at *that* party, we will have free rein to have some serious fun at *our* party. It looks like there's going to be a full student-body turn-out, so, girls, we'd better get shopping." She grabbed our arms and marched us in through the brass doors of the store. Jennifer led us right to the very expensive floors full of designer clothes, far beyond anything I could afford. Jennifer, however, made several purchases.

"This place is great for getting ideas before we hit the more affordable shops," Caitlin explained as we stepped onto the escalator. She winked. "Now, here's the main reason for hitting this store first."

We were greeted by the smell of perfume.

"The makeup department." I sighed.

We proceeded to work the entire floor. By the time we reached the doors at the other side, we were creamed, preened, and perfumed within an inch of our lives. We looked and smelled fantastic. The doorman in his top hat and tails opened the door with a flourish and we walked out of there feeling like royalty.

We crossed the vast street, completely ignoring the crosswalks, just like everyone else. This whole place was a lesson in jaywalking. I followed Caitlin and Jennifer onto a small lane that led to a maze of narrow cobbled alleys. Caitlin told me it was called the Huguenot Quarter. It was a really old part of the city and a treasure trove of boutique shops and restaurants. We browsed through them, picking up bits and pieces for ourselves in the process.

We were just looking for somewhere to have lunch when we heard loud knocking on the window beside us. We peered in through the fogged-up glass and beyond our reflections. Inside, smiling and waving at us, were Killian and Darren.

"What is Darren doing here?" Jennifer said, putting her hands on her hips and tapping her foot. "I told him we were having a girls' day."

Caitlin bolted for the door. "Come on," she murmured. "Maybe I won't have to wait for the party. Let's put some of that plotting into practice."

Killian moved over on his bench, pointedly making room for the suddenly very shy Caitlin, while Jennifer immediately launched into a deep discussion with Darren about his invasion of her girls' day.

"What are you all doing in town?" Darren inquired, breaking away from Jennifer. "If we had known you were going in too, we could have come in together on the same bus." This earned him a look of pure poison from Jennifer.

"I was getting an introduction to the delights of Cork," I replied.

Jennifer scowled at Darren's back and raised a very pointed middle finger in his direction.

Suppressing a smile, I kept babbling to keep Darren's

attention on me, as Jennifer continued the sign-language attack behind his back. "I really like it here."

Seeing Killian laugh, Darren turned to look back at Jennifer. She quickly flicked her gaze over to me and looked suitably aggrieved. "I can't imagine why! I can't wait to start university, so I can get out of this dump!"

"Hey, that's a little harsh," Darren said.

"Whatever," she bit back.

"Ouch! What's up with you?" Killian asked, looking at her.

"Nothing." She stood up and pouted at Caitlin and me. "Girls, want to ditch the boys and do some shopping?"

"Ah, Jen, we just got here, and I'm starving," Caitlin said.

"Suit yourselves. I'm outta here," she announced, turning to leave. "Text me when you're finished."

"And that, unfortunately, is my cue." Darren frowned. "Man, is she high-maintenance," he whispered to us before he ran to catch up with Jennifer.

We ordered lunch and Caitlin and Killian chatted easily about school and the impending midterm break. Talk moved on to the big Halloween party, and I think Caitlin noticed I was starting to feel like a third wheel, because she suddenly turned to me and asked if I thought I would be able to go.

"Probably; I'll have to run it by my dad."

"You'll be there, Caitlin, won't you?" Killian asked eagerly.

"I sure will." She smiled.

"You know, I might meet up with Jennifer after all," I said, getting out of my seat. "I still have to buy something for the party. Do you mind?"

Caitlin looked at me, not quite sure what to say. I quickly intervened. "Killian, you can take good care of my friend here for an hour or so, can't you?"

"I'm sure I could manage that. It will be a burden, but I'll cope." He laughed.

"Great, so I'll see you guys later then!" I raised my eyebrows at Caitlin to let her know that she should use the time with Killian wisely, and set off down Patrick Street in the direction of Grand Parade. I texted Jennifer to see if she was up for more shopping.

Within seconds my phone beeped:

Definitely. Let me just ditch Darren. Meet you in five at the fountain on Grand Parade.

Darren was kissing her good-bye when we met up. Then he waved to us and set off.

Jennifer sighed once he was out of sight. "I guess I shouldn't be so hard on Darren. It turns out it was Killian who coerced him into 'accidentally' meeting us. Killian is *finally* going to ask Caitlin out."

"That's awesome! I'm glad I left them alone so it could actually happen!"

"Yeah, well, it's about time. Now with her sorted it's just you we have to worry about. Are you still hankering after Adam?"

"I don't think I was ever *hankering* after him."

She gave me one of her withering looks.

"Okay, so I did some hankering," I admitted. "I don't know; I guess I still am, but as you've all pointed out, he's a no-go."

"Listen, if Adam DeRís showed even the slightest bit of interest in me I'd snap him up. When a guy's *that* gorgeous, he could sprout wings and sport a tutu and I'd still have a bit of him."

"I'm just not big on making the first move . . . and he doesn't seem too hot on it either."

"Oh, dear Lord. It's like the Caitlin/Killian fiasco all over again. Just grow a big pair of cojones and ask him out. The Halloween party is the perfect opportunity. Now, come on. We need to do something about that wardrobe of yours."

I pressed the button at the crosswalk and waited for the little red man to turn green. Then I heard a caw.

I glanced up in disbelief. "You've got to be kidding me."

"What did you say?" Jennifer said.

"Oh, nothing. Just talking to myself." That crow

really was following me! Now that I had noticed him, I saw how he shadowed our movements from shop to shop. *This is crazy.*

Later, Caitlin texted for us to meet her. She and Killian were standing outside the café waiting for us, and her face relaxed when she saw us walking toward her.

"Finally!" she exclaimed.

I noticed Caitlin and Killian had their fingers linked casually. I made no comment, but winked at Caitlin when I knew Killian wasn't looking.

"Are you ready to go?" she asked.

I nodded and she turned to Killian. "So, I'll see you Monday?"

"It's a date," he replied. "I'd better check in with Darren."

"I'll go with you," Jennifer said, linking her arm through his. "See you guys later."

Once they were out of earshot, I spun around to Caitlin.

"Tell me everything! What happened?"

"Oh, Meg," she said breathlessly. "Wait until I tell you! He is mad about me, has been for ages. He's taking me to the Halloween party."

"I'm so excited for you!"

She gazed dreamily ahead and sighed. "And, my God, that guy can snog."

"You kissed him?"

"Oh, it was so yummy. My lips are still tingling." She giggled. "Would you listen to me? I sound like *such* a pleb."

"I'm not sure what a pleb is, but I'm sure you don't sound like one. It's sweet."

Up ahead our bus was pulling into the stop. Laughing, we ran the last couple of yards, jumped on, and made for the backseats.

Once we sat down, I noticed Caitlin looked a little sheepish. I nudged her. "What's up?"

"So, the Halloween party next Saturday, it starts at eight thirty. Would you mind terribly if, instead of walking together, I meet you there? It's just that . . . well, Killian wants a little rendezvous beforehand. I don't have to meet with him, but I'd love to. Don't hate me," she added.

"Why would I hate you?" I laughed. "I'll be fine."

"Are you sure? It'll be dark."

"It's Kinsale, not the Wild West. Here, lemme show you what I bought to wear."

"Oh, that's divine," Caitlin said, holding my new top out in front of her. "You'll have him walking into trees wearing this."

"Who?"

"Oh, don't play innocent. You know very well who."

"Do you think he'll be there?"

"Of course he'll be there. He's always lurking somewhere when you're around."

My stomach fluttered a little. Saturday night couldn't come quickly enough.

My stomach was in knots as I opened the door to my house. I'd been playing out different scenarios in my head on the walk up from the bus. I wasn't sure how I was going to do it, but I had decided I was going to make a move on Adam.

I took some frozen chicken pies from the freezer, threw them in the oven, and set the timer. Then I ran up to my room, surrendered myself to the comfort of my bed, and dozed off.

The oven's beeping woke me up. Still disoriented, I jumped up and ran down to rescue dinner. I was halfway down the stairs when a memory came flooding back. Full and detailed. It smacked me in the face with such force that I slumped down onto the step.

The monk with the long beard had been standing behind my dad in my room in the hospital, after my mom died. As I saw the scene once more, I knew it wasn't a dream. It happened.

Who . . . no . . . *what* the hell was he? And why was he here?

My eyes began to sting and I coughed. The high-pitched beeping of the smoke alarm eventually snapped me out of my daze. Still a bit wobbly on my feet, I went into the kitchen, opened the windows, and dumped the contents of the oven into the sink. I ran the water over the charred remains. The burned pies hissed and then fell silent.

"Megan? Is everything all right in here?" Dad said, walking cautiously into the kitchen.

"Just a disastrous attempt at dinner, Dad. Sorry, but it looks like takeout again tonight."

"I have a better idea! Let's go down to the Lobster Pot." He looked delighted with himself.

"Sure, why not," I replied, even though it was the last thing I wanted to do. Now I'd have to watch Dad mooning over Petra for the evening. I was happy for him, but I needed to think, not make small talk over dinner with Dad's girlfriend. "Dad, this is going to sound a bit weird, but . . . do you know any monks?"

"Monks . . . like the Friar Tuck variety?"

"Sort of. I just thought I remembered one from the day in the hospital, you know, when I woke up after Mom . . ."

"What has you thinking about that, Meg? Is everything all right?"

"Yeah, Dad, I'm fine. It's just that I saw a monk the other day and it sparked a memory, and I was just wondering."

"I'd remember a monk in your room, Meg. I'm sure it was just you and me." He furrowed his brow. "Look, we can stay in and talk if you want to."

"No, no, I'm fine. I must have gotten it wrong," I said, pasting on a cheery smile and hooking my arm through his. "Dinner at the Lobster Pot sounds great."

Eight

HALLOWEEN

My dad was all dressed up and ready to go to the big Halloween bash in the yacht club. It had a royalty theme, and my dad was going as King Henry VIII. He looked hilarious in his pantaloons and smock outfit, but Petra, dressed as Anne Boleyn, seemed to think he looked dashing.

We had been seeing more of Petra this week. My dad never mentioned it to make it official, but it was fairly obvious what was going on. It was weird, my dad dating. It had just been me and him since my mom died. Even so, I was feeling pretty okay about the situa-tion. Maybe it was easier to deal with because he wasn't making it into a big issue.

My clothes were picked out and laid over my desk chair. Nothing fancy, but flattering all the same. Our party was going to be in a mucky field, which hardly called for a skirt and heels. I picked out my favorite jeans and my red Converse and the new top that I'd bought in the city. It was a purple V-necked sweater that enhanced my skin tone and made my hair seem rich and glowy. It was clingy, and the vee was a little more plunging than what I'd usually wear, but Caitlin and Jennifer had both told me that I had to use every weapon in my arsenal.

I'd decided to leave my hair down, wavy and natural. I dusted a little bronzer over my pale cheeks and nose, just to highlight my face, and carefully applied lots of black mascara to my eyelashes, curling them upward. I took one last look at the mirror. *Well*, I thought, *that's as good as it gets.* I smacked my lips at my reflection, then jumped back from the mirror and whirled around.

I could have sworn I'd seen the monk's face behind mine. I shivered and glanced around the room. No one was there, of course.

Since that conversation with my dad, I'd tried to block the creepy old man from my thoughts, and I had been doing pretty well. Until tonight. *Oh, well. Maybe it's just because I'm nervous about seeing Adam.*

I set off, wrapping my arms around myself. It was definitely colder tonight. And my raincoat was only that, a raincoat. It held no heat, but I didn't have time to go back for a warmer jacket. I continued on, wrapping my arms tighter.

A snapping sound made me look up. I knew it was my crow even before I saw him. I smiled up at him, welcoming his presence. Whatever his reasons for becoming my shadow, I felt no menace from him. In fact, I had kind of gotten used to having him around. And on a cold night like tonight, he felt like a real comfort.

I walked past the school and turned up the lane that led to where the party was being held. I could hear the whoops of laughter in the distance. The smell of bonfire hung heavy in the air.

With each step, I could feel my courage fade. I had no idea what I was going to say to Adam, or even how I'd approach him. I had just reached the turnoff when I noticed my crow was gone. A new noise replaced his familiar caw. Laughter.

I looked behind me and saw two boys approaching quickly. They seemed a little unsteady and they were talking loudly. I ignored them and kept walking, but they came nearer, laughing uproariously. Something cracked at my foot and I glanced down, startled. It was an egg.

"Idiots," I muttered under my breath, but quickened my pace.

Another egg sailed through the air, landing on my jacket. Now they were cheering.

"Hey, Miss U.S.A., where are you going in such a hurry?"

The voice sounded vaguely familiar, but I couldn't see their faces in the dark.

"Hey, I'm talking to you; don't ignore me!" One of them grabbed the back of my jacket.

His speech was slurred, and his eyes looked like they weren't focusing. I struggled to get out of his grasp as his friend pulled on his arm.

"Tom, give it a rest," his friend warned.

"No." He smiled menacingly. "It's Halloween. Let's have fun."

I felt my legs tremble and willed myself not to look as scared as I felt. His friend lowered his voice and bent in toward Tom.

"That's Caleb Rosenberg's daughter. If my mom finds out I messed with her, I'll be killed. Let's get out of here." He pulled on Tom's jacket. "Come on, Blánnaid is waiting for you."

"Just a little fun," Tom said, shaking off his friend. "Blán can wait."

The smell of alcohol on his breath made me feel queasy. He dug into his pockets and staggered forward. I saw an opportunity to escape and I slammed my foot down on his boot.

He yelped in pain, and glared at me.

I didn't know what to do. He looked like he was

thinking about hitting me, and his friend didn't seem like he was going to be able to stop him. I began to panic. Should I run? Should I scream? Suddenly, a freezing-cold gust of wind flew past us. It whooshed by my legs and swirled up around me, taking my hair with it. A chill ran through my body, from my toes right up to my head.

I screamed and tried to grab at the hair that was obscuring my vision. Finally, I pushed it out of my face in time to see the guys being picked up by the wind and tossed into the briars behind them.

"Jesus Christ! What the hell?" Tom yelled. I could hear the other guy moaning from the undergrowth, calling for help.

"Tom. Help me, I can't move," his friend called from the bushes. "Someone help me!"

Suddenly a voice spoke directly into my ear. "Megan, are you all right?" Startled, I spun around to see Adam standing right behind me. Instantly the wind stopped.

"Did you see that?" I gasped. "It was like a tornado or something."

"Hey, are you two okay?" Adam called to Tom and his friend as their pale faces emerged from the briars.

"What the hell?" Tom shouted at Adam. "You'd better not have been doing any of your voodoo shite on me, DeRís." He stumbled onto the lane and rubbed his hand over his face where the thorns had snagged his skin. The blood smeared down his cheek and neck.

"Don't talk crap, Tom. Anyway, I only just got here," Adam said. "You should cut out the booze; it plays havoc with the mind."

Tom's friend tried to climb out after him, but snagged his foot in the undergrowth and fell flat on his face, right onto one of the broken eggs. He hastily jumped up, wiping the blood and egg across his forehead with his sleeve.

"Tom, let's get out of here," he whispered, and stumbled away.

"Wait for me," Tom called, hobbling after him.

I watched them leave. My limbs ached, though the pins and needles were beginning to wear off.

"Hey, guys. What's going on? What's up with those two wasters?" Áine came into sight.

"I don't know. Something really weird just happened. Actually, I think I might puke," I said, lowering myself to the ground and putting my head between my knees.

"Is she all right?" Áine called to Adam, and I heard her footsteps speed up.

"She'll be fine." Adam put a reassuring hand on the back of my neck and rubbed his thumb along my hairline. The heat from his hand sent a spine-tingling pleasure through me. It worked its way down my back and limbs until even my fingers and toes relaxed. As the last of the tingling wore off I got such a rush of elation that I gasped.

Wow. Feeling amazing, I raised my head and looked

into his eyes. "Thanks."

"No problem," he said, stretching out his hand to help me up.

"Are you guys going to the party?" I asked, looking from Áine to Adam.

"We thought we'd check it out," Áine replied.

"Do you think it will still be going on? That wind was crazy," I said, surveying the damage around us.

"I'd say it was pretty localized, by the looks of it," Adam said with a smile. "Do you still feel up to going?" he asked, raising his eyebrows.

"I'm okay," I said, still buzzing.

"You might want to, uh, check out your hair." Adam smirked.

"Here, allow me." Áine reached over and started pulling leaves and other debris from my hair.

So much for my full arsenal, I thought, cringing.

"There, you're as gorgeous as ever," Áine said, smoothing out the last stray hairs.

"Thanks," I muttered.

When we got to the party, most people were hanging out around the huge, blazing bonfire. Caitlin and Killian were snuggling on some straw bales, and Jennifer was standing behind them talking to Darren. As soon as she saw us, she nudged Caitlin and pointed at me. Caitlin's eyes opened wide and her mouth dropped slightly. I gave her a quick wave and a smile.

"I'll be back in a while," Áine called excitedly over her shoulder, as she walked toward the bonfire. I started to head toward Caitlin and Jennifer, but Adam put one hand under my elbow and directed me over to a log in the shadow of a big tree.

"We need to talk," he said.

I looked up at him. It was a mistake. His eyes smoldered down at me. They were brighter than ever, as the light from the distant bonfire flickered up into his face. I could feel my heart pounding in my chest as my breath caught in my throat.

It seemed like he was fighting some sort of inner conflict. I had seen the look before, but this time he softened. Whatever the battle was, I think he had just won it.

"I apologize in advance for what I'm about to say. I don't want to scare you off, but I need to be honest with you."

"Okay," I whispered.

"This is going to sound crazy, but . . . from the moment I first set eyes on you I haven't been able to stop thinking about you."

I was stunned. I remained silent and let him continue.

"Since you arrived here I've been going crazy. I can't get you out of my mind. The more I try to distance myself, the more I find myself drawn to you. You might find that hard to believe, considering what an idiot I've been."

The honey-smooth tones of his voice caressed my face, as if it were his hands that had touched me and not his words. I opened my mouth, still not sure what to say, and he put his finger on my lips.

"I was warned to stay away from you. They told me from the very beginning that it wasn't safe to 'consort,'" he said, slightly wincing at the word, "with you. But I'm not strong enough to stay away. I think our destinies are too closely linked to be diverted to a different course."

He glared back toward the gate we'd come through and I followed his gaze. Rían was standing there, leaning against his motorcycle. Watching us.

"You feel it too. I can tell. It's more than just attraction." His finger that was caressing my lips moved slowly to my cheek. He let it slide gently up my jawbone toward my ear, stopping there to twirl a lock of my hair in between his finger and thumb. I lifted my hand to where his rested on the side of my face and I leaned into it. I rubbed my cheek slowly back and forth over his palm as I managed to get my breathing under control. I looked right at him, staring deep into his eyes.

"Yes. I feel it too," I admitted, barely able to breathe. "Since the first day I saw you I've felt it."

He brought his other hand up to the other side of my face and held it there, as if memorizing it. Slowly he bent toward me and kissed my left cheek, then my right. His breath was so warm it sent tingles down my spine. I sat perfectly still, delighting in every sensation. He moved up to my forehead and kissed it gently. His neck was tantalizingly close to my lips. He smelled warm, spicy even. My whole body tingled with pleasure.

He moved back down toward my nose and paused there for a little kiss before reaching my lips, where he stopped and pulled away slightly. Was he waiting for my permission? I moved into him, pressing my face into his hands, leaving him with no doubt as to what I wanted.

He bent in again and pressed his lips against mine. They were soft and full and everything I had imagined them to be. The kiss became deeper and more meaningful. The flow of electricity, of power, of passion between us was hard to contain. It was as if nobody else existed.

I put one arm around his back and left the other holding his palm against my face. His free hand raked through my hair. He pulled back gently.

"Wow," he said.

"Wow," I agreed.

"That was . . ."

"I know. What now?"

"Now things get very interesting." He looked back toward Rían, who climbed onto his bike and sped off back down the lane.

I put my hand on Adam's face and felt along his cheek and down along his jaw, reveling in the softness of his skin in comparison to the light stubble. He closed his eyes.

"You have no idea how good that feels," he murmured.

"Oh, I think I do," I replied with a smile. I felt slow, like I was moving through syrup. Everything around me seemed to glow.

"Megan," Caitlin called from the direction of the bonfire.

I looked away from him reluctantly. "Over here." A little embarrassed by my intense feelings, I pulled my hand away, but Adam held it to his lips, letting his tongue lightly caress my palm. My eyes closed in pleasure.

"There you are," Caitlin said, ducking under the boughs of the tree that were half hiding us from view. She stopped short, catching sight of the two of us.

"I, uh, I just wanted to check and make sure you were all right." She was already backing away. "So . . . you're okay?"

"I'm fine," I reassured her.

"It's all right, Caitlin," Adam said. "We were just coming to look for you." To my surprise he stood up and pulled me up from the log. "Let's go join the fun."

Caitlin glanced at me, wide-eyed. I just smiled. I would tell her some edited details later, but not everything. There was something entirely private about our moment.

As we approached the bonfire, a figure caught my attention. Standing by the hedge, just visible through the flickering flames, was the monk. I stopped walking and stared at him. His watery gray eyes smiled back at me, and then he just dissolved.

Adam tugged on my arm. "Are you all right?" He followed my gaze through the bonfire, squinting off into the distance. "What are you looking at?"

"Nothing," I said, moving toward the fire.

"Are you sure?" He looked back over his shoulder.

"I'm sure. Come on; let's join the others." We made our way over to Caitlin and the gang. When we sat down he whispered something to Áine, who jumped up and ran off into the darkness. She returned a few minutes later, shaking her head, and sat back down beside us.

The rest of the night passed in a blur. I sat by the fire with the most exquisite arm in the universe securely around me for all to see. I could tell people were whispering about us, but I didn't care. The bonfire was just a heap of softly glowing embers when we got up to leave. Killian was going to walk Caitlin home, so we said our good-byes.

"I'm just going to drop Áine off first and then I'll get you home. You all right with that?" Adam asked.

"That's fine." The more time I got to spend with him, the better. I didn't want this night to end.

Áine sank into the back of the car. "That was brilliant! We should try to do fun stuff like that more often," she said. I smiled in the darkness. I couldn't agree more. We stopped at an entrance to a house with large iron gates and Áine jumped out and waved to us.

"You're not going to drive her to the door?" I asked. I couldn't see the house up the long, dark driveway.

"Áine takes care of herself," Adam replied, turning the car.

We set off back in the direction of town. "You okay?" he said, looking over at me and taking my hand.

"I'm great. Perfect," I answered, gazing at our entwined fingers.

We pulled up outside my house. Dad was still out. My hand felt so right in his, like it belonged there. I didn't want to let it go.

He bent his head down to me, breathing in my breath, before he gently kissed my lips again. Slowly and reluctantly he pulled away. "Can I see you tomorrow?"

"I'd like that," I said.

"Can I pick you up in the morning?"

"Sure," I murmured.

"I'll need your number," he said, handing me his phone.

Feeling light-headed, I typed my cell number into his phone and gave it back to him.

"Thanks." He lowered his head for one last kiss.

Finally, I got out of the car and waved him off, still reveling in the memory of his touch. As I made it to my room, tiredness overwhelmed me. I flopped down onto the bed and fell right to sleep.

Nine

INTRODUCTIONS

When I woke up, my head felt fuzzy. I didn't know what time it was, but I knew it was Sunday and I was sure it was early. I opened one eye and moved the quilt just a little to look at the clock on my bedside table.

Ten thirteen. "Ugh," I groaned. Not nearly as early as I had hoped.

I rolled onto my back and looked up at the ceiling. Then, very slowly, last night started to play out in my head. I felt warmth radiate through my body, and I lay there luxuriating in the sensations that tingled at my fingers and toes.

"Megan, are you getting up at some point today?" My dad's muffled voice came from the other side of the door.

I had to break the beautiful spell to answer him.

"Yeah, Dad, I'm awake," I said with a grunt.

"Want some breakfast? I'm making pancakes."

"Sounds great." I stifled a groan. "I'm just going to take a shower; I'll be down in a little while, okay?"

"Sure," he said, and whistled his way down the stairs.

I crawled out of bed and walked to the window. It was another gray, damp day, with the clouds hanging low in the sky. My phone vibrated on my desk. I walked over to it. Five text messages and two voice mails.

Caitlin, I thought to myself, shaking my head. I scanned through the texts.

> Hi! Tell all, what happened?
> Stop holding out! Text me all the gossip.
> Hello! I'm still waiting.
> Good morning, beautiful, call me when you're awake. xx
> Adam

I did a double take and read the last one again. *Oh, my God.* I saved his number to my phone. Then I scanned to the next message.

> Friendship on the line here!

The two voice mails were from Caitlin too. I rolled my eyes and hit the redial key. It rang once and she picked up.

"Megan!" she exclaimed. "Where have you been? You know the rules! You should have let me know when you got home safely! Not to mention spill all the details on what all *that* was about last night! What happened?"

I didn't feel like telling her even an edited version at the moment. I needed to clear my head first. "It's a long story," I hedged. "Sorry I didn't call; I literally fell asleep the second I got home. Look, I'm hanging out with Adam today. Can we get together tonight for coffee? I promise I'll spill my guts. Deal?"

"Oh, you dirty hussy, you're holding out on me," she exclaimed.

"No, no, it's not that! Anyway, I'm sure you also have a lot to tell me about your night with Killian," I prompted.

"Oh, I do," she replied. "Okay, text me when you get back and we'll meet up in town. I can't wait. Just tell me one thing: Did you snog him?"

"Yes!"

"Oh my God," she shouted into the phone. "This is amazing! I can't wait to talk later."

"Neither can I. Bye."

I read the text from Adam one more time. I had spent

so long daydreaming about this moment. My finger hovered over the call button. I took a deep breath and pressed it. He picked up immediately.

"Megan." Just hearing him say my name sent shivers down my spine. "I'd hoped you would call. How are you?"

"I'm fine," I said, trying to sound relaxed.

"You slept well. Are we still on for today?"

"Yes, definitely." How did he know I had slept well?

"Great." I could hear the smile in his voice. I imagined the way he would look, how his eyes would crease up and crinkle at the sides. It scared me a little to realize how well I knew his face and his expressions, when I knew so little about the person behind them. "I'll pick you up at eleven thirty."

"Great, I'll see you then."

"Oh, and . . ." He paused. "I meant everything I said last night."

I flushed. "Me too," I breathed. "See you soon."

I sat down heavily on the bed. *Shoot.* Now I had to somehow work out how to tell my dad about Adam. And fast, since Adam was coming in less than an hour. I also had to find something to wear; my favorite jeans from last night were totally dirty.

First things first, I said to myself, and headed for the shower. I let the hot water flow over my body and put both hands on the tiles in front of me, leaning forward and allowing the water to power down on my neck and back. It felt so good, so relaxing.

My dad would just have to deal with this. He was lucky enough to have avoided me dating for this long. Besides, my dad already knew and liked Adam. So that was one hurdle over with, at least.

When I was finished, I stepped out of the tub and reached over to grab a big fluffy towel. I wrapped it around me, tucking it in firmly under my arm, and brushed my teeth meticulously, followed by a round of flossing and mouthwash. This mouth would hopefully be seeing some action today. Nothing but pristine condition would do. I leaned into the mirror to get a closer look at my front teeth and caught the reflection of the window in the mirror.

"Are you a peeping Tom now?" I said to the crow, who was peering in at me. *Oh, man.* I was definitely certifiable. As if talking to animals wasn't bad enough, now I was expecting them to answer.

"Megan! The pancakes are ready. Come on down."

"Coming!" I threw on a clean pair of jeans, a navy shirt, and the red Converse I had worn last night. I gave my hair a good rub with a towel, then ran my brush through it, praying to the hair gods for a good hair day.

"There you are," Dad declared as I walked into the kitchen.

"What's the big occasion?" I asked, taking in the kitchen table set with knives, forks, cups and plates, and—oh, my God, were those napkins? I sat down at my seat and helped myself to a warm pancake.

"I need to talk to you," he said nervously, clearing his throat.

I looked up from my pancake into his red face.

"I noticed you have settled in very well here, Megan. I've settled in myself and, well, there might be some changes in the future. . . ."

I looked up at him, panic-stricken. "Oh, Dad, no, please tell me we're not leaving. . . ."

"No, no," he said, putting his hand up. "It's nothing like that. You know Petra, from the Lobster Pot." He sat down and poured us each a cup of tea. "She and I are sort of . . ." He cleared his throat. "Well, dating."

I looked at him in mock surprise. "Wow, Dad, I never would have guessed."

"You're not mad?"

"Mad? Why on earth would I be mad?" I asked, putting a forkful of syrupy pancake into my mouth.

"Well, there hasn't been anyone since your mom. I wasn't sure how you would react," he said, relaxing a bit.

"Dad, I think it's great." I put a spoonful of sugar into my tea and stirred it.

"Oh. I was ready for arguments. I even had a whole speech prepared."

"Give me some credit, would you? I'm seventeen, not nine." I paused. "And . . . while we're on the subject,

I have a date myself today." I took another bite of my pancake, then slowly sipped my tea, giving him time to digest the news. There was a range of emotions running across his face.

"Well, I guess I should afford you the same level of maturity you gave me," he said with a reluctant smile. "So who is he? Is he in your class?" I could tell he was making an effort to sound calm and cool.

I smiled into my tea. "Actually, yes. In fact, you know him."

"I do?" He raised his eyebrows, his fork pausing on the way to his mouth.

"It's Adam DeRís." I tried to sound totally casual, but failed. Anytime I said his name, I couldn't help a tone of reverence from sneaking in.

My dad looked at me thoughtfully. "Really? Is it serious? He seems very mature for his age."

"He is mature, but isn't that a good thing? He's very responsible. Anyway, don't worry; it's early days."

"So where are you going on your date?" he asked, clearly trying to go back into Casual Dad mode.

"I'm not sure. He mentioned bringing me to his house to meet his family. He's picking me up in"—I looked at my watch—"ten minutes." I stood up and shoved the last of my pancake into my mouth. "Thanks for breakfast, Dad. It was nice. And I am totally happy for you and Petra. I have to run upstairs and finish getting ready, though."

"Okay. I'll let him in when he gets here."

I stopped walking. "Dad, please don't give him the third degree."

"Would I?" He raised his hands, the picture of innocence.

"I mean it," I said, and ran up the stairs.

My hair, unfortunately, was not behaving itself. I was tying it back into a shiny ponytail when I heard the doorbell ring downstairs.

"Let's do this," I said to my reflection.

I walked down the stairs and there he was, in all his stunning glory. My memories of his face did not do him justice. He was even more gorgeous in reality. He was dressed in jeans and a black sweater, the sleeves of which were pushed slightly up, revealing his tanned, muscular forearms. Everything about him screamed effortlessly beautiful, even his clothes and his slightly messy dark hair. He was talking to my dad like they were old friends. He smiled and they shook hands.

"Thanks for that, Mr. Rosenberg."

"Call me Caleb," my dad replied warmly.

"Thanks, Caleb," he repeated, then allowed his gaze to shift toward me. "Megan," he breathed, looking delighted to see me.

"Bye, Dad! I'll see you later. I won't be late." I turned to Adam. "Will I?"

"No, of course not, we're staying local. I thought we might have dinner with my family at my house. I'll get you home, safe and sound, straight after." He looked toward me for approval, and I nodded enthusiastically. There was a small awkward moment as we stood there; then I directed Adam to the door and gave my dad a reassuring smile.

Adam stood by the passenger door, holding it open for me. I took another deep breath as I walked toward him. I sank into the car and he closed the door firmly behind me. Adam slid into the seat beside me and smiled. My stomach fluttered in response. He pulled away from the curb slowly.

"Sorry about my dad. He can be a little overprotective."

"I can understand that," he said, looking at me. "But I thought he was quite cool about us. He just told me to be extra careful with you, as you were precious to him. I told him you're precious to me too. Anyway, you haven't witnessed my family in action. Wait until you see *them* in all their protective glory."

I looked over to see if he was joking, but there was no hint of a laugh on his face. "Now I'm worried."

"Oh, you just haven't met Fionn yet. He can be a bit . . . unsettling."

"Your guardian?"

"Yeah. Now, he is the epitome of overprotective." He put his hand down and took mine. "Look, don't worry about it. They're going to love you."

Doubtful. I believed Áine liked me and that we could be friends, but I wasn't sure about Rían. My only interactions with him thus far had been the tense stare-downs across the school. And this Fionn character sounded weird.

Adam drove along the Bandon estuary, over the low bridge, and around the bend, following the road up the river. We turned right over a tiny humpback bridge and then up through a wooded area where the road got very narrow. I vaguely remembered it from last night. He turned in through an entrance with big, heavy iron gates that looked like they had frozen in their current position years ago, and we traveled slowly up a long gravel lane that had grass growing up the middle of it. Farmland stretched out toward the horizon on either side. We finally drove under a huge stone arch in a wall and pulled into a farm yard that was walled on all four sides. "Are you ready?" He looked a little nervous, and that scared me.

I squeezed his hand. "If you are." I smiled up into his face.

"With you here, I'm ready for anything," he said quietly, and kissed me softly on my mouth.

I reeled from the sensuous touch. Closing my eyes, I leaned into him.

He pulled away, looking a little flushed. "Best to keep a clear head. Come on. Let's get this over with."

I felt a new confidence building. I could take on the

world with him by my side. Taking care on the cobblestones, we made our way to the back of the house, which had a stable door with the top half open. Adam reached inside and unlatched the bottom section.

"Ladies first," he said, swinging the door out and stepping to the side.

I stepped into the gloom of a back porch with low beamed ceilings and a dark flagstone floor.

"This is just the scullery," Adam said, following me in. He pushed another door, which opened into a huge kitchen. All the stone walls had been painted white, and the kitchen was filled with various freestanding counters and tables. In the middle of the room was the biggest kitchen table I'd ever seen. It had massive carved legs that looked like they'd remained on the same patch of flagstone for centuries. There, sitting on one of the benches that ran along each side of the table, was Áine.

"You came!" she exclaimed, and pushed her cereal bowl to the side.

At that moment something flew over my shoulder. Startled, I ducked and watched incredulously as a crow— *my* crow—landed on the table by Áine. He tottered over to the discarded cereal bowl and started helping himself.

"Hey, what are you doing here?" I blurted out, addressing the bird. Then I caught the mood in the room. Adam had turned a little pink, and Áine didn't quite meet my eyes. "Hang on a second," I said, catching on. "Is he your bird?"

"Well, technically he's Fionn's, but he loves me the best. Don't you, baby?" Áine replied, turning to the big black bird. She started making cooing noises at him as she rubbed his head and neck. I swear he smiled as he leaned into her.

I looked at Adam suspiciously. "That bird has been following me around since I got here. He's always peering in at me."

"I didn't think you'd notice," Adam said, his voice heavy with guilt.

"What do you mean, 'notice'? What's going on?"

Adam looked at Áine, but she stood up and edged backward. "Don't you dare pin this one on me!" She turned to me with a smile. "I'll see you later, Megan," she said, and the crow flew after her and perched on her shoulder as she stepped out into the yard.

"What's up with the bird?" I asked, turning back to Adam.

"I don't know if I'm ready to tell that story yet," he said, not meeting my eye.

"Well, I'm ready for you to," I continued, a little bit irritated. "That bird has been spying on me in the shower!"

"The dirty dog! He never told us that."

"What do you mean the bird never *told* you that?"

"Look, can I give you the details about the bird later? I promise I will tell you everything. Let me show you around first. Please?" He looked at me with pleading eyes.

"Okay, fine. But don't think for one second I'm letting this go. You have a lot of explaining to do," I said, thinking suddenly of last night's mini-tornado.

"I know." His face turned serious. "More than you can possibly imagine."

The floorboards creaked underfoot as we made our way into the beautiful front hall.

"This house is amazing," I said, looking up at the high ceilings and dusty chandelier. There was a withered decadence to the faded wallpaper and chipped moldings.

"It once was, but it's fairly moth-eaten now," Adam said, picking up a bit of the heavy drapes that hung over a window and pointing out a big hole. "It's such a shame."

I didn't know what to say.

"Someday I'll fix this place up and return it to its former glory," he said, smiling at the wall and giving it a gentle pat. "Come on; I'll show you my room."

He took my hand and led me up a creaky staircase. Halfway up, on a landing where the stairs changed direction, there was an arched blue stained-glass window. The beautiful leaded pattern cast shimmering reflections on the walls and across Adam's face as he turned to smile at me.

"Pretty, isn't it?" he said, taking in my enraptured expression.

I watched the magical reflections flicker on Adam's face. "Yes, very pretty," I murmured, feeling my heart flutter.

At the top of the stairs, Adam led me into his room. After the elegant hall downstairs, his room was a bit of a shock.

Adam laughed, stretching his arms out to the gaudy orange floral wallpaper. "I know what you're thinking. It's horrible. Back in the sixties some bright spark 'updated' the bedrooms. So now we have dilapidated retro land up here."

"It's not too bad. It's just . . . not what I was expecting," I hedged, looking around. "I never put you down as the floral type."

"Hey, if you think this is bad, you should see Rían's room."

I sat down on the edge of the sleigh bed in the middle of the room, my heart pounding. *I'm sitting on Adam's bed!* Not knowing where to look, I picked a knot in the floorboards and stared at it.

He walked over to me. "If you're uncomfortable, we can go back downstairs."

Drawing in a deep breath, I allowed my eyes to move up from the floor to his legs, pausing at his chest before glancing at his face.

"I want to be here."

"Good," he said, bending down and dropping a gentle kiss on my lips.

He sat beside me and placed a cushion behind me. Then he pushed me gently down onto it, until my back came to rest on the quilt. "You take my breath away."

"As much as I love hearing you say things like that to me, it does make me wonder about your mental stability," I joked.

"Don't you believe me?" He sounded offended.

"I'm just not good at taking compliments."

"Well, I think you're beautiful, and I think I'm mentally stable." He laughed, then made a crazy face.

"Oh, very nice."

"So, why can't you take a compliment?" he asked, tucking a lock of hair behind my ear.

I shrugged. "I guess I'm just not used to it."

"Surely other boyfriends have told you."

"That would be hard, considering there haven't been any other boyfriends."

He looked shocked. "Why not?"

"I don't know. We moved around a lot. Anyway, I never wanted to date just for the sake of dating. I thought that when I met the right guy, I would know, so there was no point in wasting my time until then."

"And now?" he prodded. "Me?"

I flushed a little. "Well, I guess this is 'then.'"

He beamed down at me. "I can accept that."

"And what about you? Any gorgeous exes I should be aware of?"

He let out a little laugh. "Not really. We moved around a lot too, and our lifestyle doesn't lend itself to forming relationships. I'm sure you've heard what the locals have to say about us."

"I have. Is there any truth in the stories?"

He rolled to one side, lay down on his back, and laughed again. "Why, are you scared?"

I threw a pillow at him. "No, but I'm curious."

"Don't worry; the stories are nonsense."

"Oh," I said, a little disappointed.

Adam let out a contented sigh. He took my hand and raised it to his mouth to plant a kiss on it and then left it resting there. I lay quietly by his side.

This felt so real. It seemed like my future was suddenly very clear. I had a whole new purpose—and it all revolved around this boy by my side.

A hard rapping on the door snapped me out of my reverie.

"Heads up, Adam." Áine popped her head in the door. "Fionn's home."

I felt Adam's body stiffen slightly.

"Time to face the music," he said with a groan.

"Oh, come on; how bad can it be?" I said.

Adam and Áine looked at each other, strained. *Crap.*

I guess it could be very bad.

The three of us headed down the stairs together, Adam walking in front of me as if shielding me from what was to come. Even in the face of Adam's discomfort, I couldn't help feeling like this was a bit ridiculous. Fionn wasn't even Adam's dad.

"Fionn." Adam's voice rang out against the silence of the kitchen. "This is Megan Rosenberg."

"Yes, Adam, I know who she is."

Adam's guardian had his back to us. He seemed reluctant to turn around and he was rubbing his hair in irritation, his hand running up and down over the back of his head. He was a very big man, strong and lean, with a broad, defined back. His hair was cropped very short; he looked more like a bodyguard than a father.

"Fionn." Adam's voice broke through my thoughts. "You're going to have to get over it. She's here now, just as she should be. You know that as well as I do. You're in denial," he said, raising his voice.

Huh. This seemed kind of intense for a first-time introduction of a girlfriend. I was no expert, but I was pretty sure these things should be a little more relaxed.

"You're endangering her as well as yourself," Fionn snapped as he spun around.

Endangering! *What?* I looked up nervously at Adam, but he was glaring at Fionn, his jaw rigid.

"I specifically told you to keep your distance and not

to engage with her," Fionn said.

Well, I reflected, *at least now I know who warned Adam not to "consort" with me.*

"Your judgment is impaired, Adam. You should have listened to me," he growled.

"I tried to keep away, but I couldn't," Adam said. "I explained this to you; you just wouldn't listen. And you of all people should understand what I'm going through."

"The forces drawing you together are more powerful than attraction, Adam. You know that. And we decided as a family not to involve her," Fionn said through gritted teeth.

I stood there, red faced. "Adam, what's going on?"

"Megan, I'm so sorry. I shouldn't have brought you here," he said gently, still staring at Fionn.

"Forces? Is this about . . . magic?"

Fionn turned to me with a stunned expression. My scar was burning, hotter and more intense than ever before. I began to feel sick.

"What does she know about the powers?" Fionn snapped.

"I swear I told her nothing," Adam shot back, looking from me to Fionn.

The atmosphere in the room was smothering me. I could hardly breathe. I needed to get out. I stumbled toward the door leading to the yard, but it was too late. I slumped to the ground.

"Megan!" Adam called out, but I couldn't respond. Everything seemed muffled, many voices rolled into one dull roar. As I started to come around the voices got a little clearer. Adam and Rían were standing over me, shouting at each other.

"You idiot! What the hell were you thinking?" Rían yelled.

"Rían, shut up. Just get out of here." Adam's voice was sharp, and I heard footsteps pounding out of the room.

"Is she going to be okay, Fionn?" Áine asked. "She's as white as a sheet."

Something cold and wet dabbed at my forehead. My fingers and toes had pins and needles. They stabbed at me, my limbs numb and aching. I could feel the blood start to flow back into them. I groaned aloud and tried to sit up.

"Whoa, there," Fionn said. "Now just lie down for a few minutes. It will pass."

Adam started rubbing my hand and turned nervously to Fionn. "Is she going to be all right? I'm so sorry. I know I shouldn't have let this happen. I just couldn't help myself."

"Stop blaming yourself, Adam. I would have done the same thing," Áine said, rubbing Adam's hunched shoulders.

"It's nothing. She's just had a growth spurt. Having you all here together must have triggered it." Fionn sighed. "I guess we were going to have to face this sooner or later; I would have liked some warning, though!"

"You knew how I felt," Adam replied, his eyes downcast.

I still had no idea what was going on—and what was all this about growth spurts? It was time to muster whatever dignity I had left and peel myself up off the floor.

"I'm okay now," I said, grabbing Adam's hand. "All that's been bruised is my ego . . . and maybe my neck. Ouch." I rubbed my stinging scar.

"Megan, I'm sorry about this," Fionn said. "But you must tell me: How do you know about the powers?" He indicated that I should go sit on the bench beside him.

Áine looked a little sheepish. "Um, I think that might have been me," she muttered, and put her hands up. "It was an accident, I swear. I didn't know she was there."

"It wasn't just you, Áine," I said, glancing up at Adam apologetically. "I saw what Adam did to the water, and with the wind on Halloween."

"That wasn't me," Adam said, smiling softly. "Wind isn't my thing."

"But I saw it with my own eyes. You were standing right behind me."

They stayed silent, looking at me sympathetically.

"If Adam didn't make that wind, then who did?"

Fionn looked me square in the eye. "You did."

Ten

ORIGINS

What? That's not . . ." I gave Fionn an uncertain grin. "Ha, ha. Very funny."

Fionn sat down across from me. "I wish I were joking. Listen, Megan, before we go any further, you need to know the story that has brought you to us." I suddenly saw that behind his tough exterior there was a deep sadness. What could have happened to him to leave such memories in his eyes? I scratched my neck in thought.

"Megan," he began. "That scar on your neck. It tingles when you're nervous, scared, or under pressure, right?"

I looked at him, surprised. How did he know about my scar?

"How did you get it?" He held my gaze.

Tears sprang into my eyes. "In a car accident, eleven years ago," I whispered. Adam moved to stand behind me. He put his hands on my shoulders reassuringly, but stayed silent.

"The twenty-sixth of June?" Fionn asked.

"How do you know that?" I gasped.

"That was the day Adam, Áine, and Rían lost their parents and their unborn baby sister." Fionn faltered over the word "baby."

"That was also the day my mom died," I said.

Fionn nodded. "Áine, come over here, will you?" he said, still looking at me.

Áine walked obediently to his side and turned her back to me. With her right hand she lifted her hair off the back of her head, revealing her neck. "Look at this." Fionn indicated a spot on Áine's neck.

I peered closer. Then I saw it. A mark—it looked almost like a birthmark, but it was made up of three interlocking circles, with an arc to one side that looked like the beginning of another circle.

"Rían," Fionn called into the hall, where Rían had retreated.

Rían didn't look at me as he strode into the room and walked over to Fionn. He turned to the side, pulled down the collar of his jacket, and pushed back some of his dark, wavy hair from his neck. The birthmark on his hairline was plain to see. It looked just like Áine's.

I looked at Adam. He turned his head to the side and pointed to the mark in exactly the same spot as the others. I knew I still must be missing something. "What does this have to do with me?"

Rían stalked back to the hall and leaned against the door frame with his arms crossed. Áine perched herself on the end of a bench, curling her long legs in under her.

"Megan, like Adam, Áine, and Rían, you are Marked," Fionn told me. "You are intrinsically linked to this family and have been since the day you received your Mark. The day your mother died. The day *their* mother died."

My eyes flicked from one to another, trying to grasp what Fionn was saying. "But I just have a scar."

"Look again," Fionn said, pointing to a mirror above the fireplace.

I got up slowly and stood on the tips of my toes to see into the mirror above the giant fireplace. I craned my neck around and pulled at my skin to look at my scar. There it was, the slightly raised semicircle. But then I did a double take. Surrounding it and interlocking through it was a very pale mark, just like the one on Adam's neck.

"That was never there before, I swear."

Fionn rubbed his hand down the side of his face. "You didn't get your scar in an accident; it's the scar of an activated Mark. The remainder of your Mark only started growing when you came into contact with the other Marked. These guys." Fionn pointed at Adam, Áine, and Rian. "When the fourth arc of their Marks started growing we had no idea what was going on. We just knew that it was a reaction to you. We thought you might be a threat, and I made these guys promise to keep a safe distance until we could be sure. And I admit, I wanted to stop the growth. But nothing I did could stop it. Once it takes hold, there is no going back."

Shaking my head, I turned back to them. ". . . I'm Marked? But what does that even mean?"

Fionn exhaled heavily. "The Marked Ones are vessels for the four elements that create equilibrium and balance on Earth. The four elements have existed in human form for thousands of years, passed down from generation to generation through a royal bloodline."

I couldn't help laughing out loud. "Wait, what? This makes no sense. First of all, trust me: I'm not royal."

"I'm sorry, Megan; I know this is a lot to take in, but let me try to explain. Have you ever heard of the Celtic goddess Danu?"

I shook my head and leaned forward on the bench.

"She predates all histories. She was the divine creator, and she embodied all the main elements: air, earth, fire, and water. She managed the elements, keeping them aligned to maintain the perfect balance. Now, Danu loved humans above all things on Earth, so she created her Tuatha de Danann, her children of human form, and gifted each with one of her powers—"

"One of her powers meaning each child got one of the elements?" I interrupted.

"Yes, exactly." Fionn smiled at me and continued. "Danu raised her children carefully, training them in the ways of their powers and making sure they understood the importance of balance and the delicate nature of the earth. Then in their eighteenth year, she completed the transfer of power to them during the summer solstice.

"But what Danu had not accounted for was the weakness of the human mind. Surrounded by corruption, greed, and jealousy, the Tuatha de Danann started misusing their powers."

Fionn's deep voice had a hypnotic effect on me. I wondered what exactly they did to misuse their powers, but it was much easier to sit and let Fionn tell the story in his own way. And I figured I'd have plenty of time to ask him questions later.

"Danu was angry at her children for succumbing to the weakness of the human mind, and she left the earth and returned to the realm of the gods, vowing not to return until her children could learn to live in harmony. Until they learned to set aside their differences and come together, the four elements would not be united, and Earth would remain imbalanced. However, even though they had disappointed her so gravely, Danu didn't want to abandon her children entirely. So she gave them a

Sidhe—a spirit guide of human form—who would help them on their path to the elemental alignment."

Fionn paused and looked up at me with sadness in his eyes. "But that never happened. The Tuatha de Danann fought endlessly with one another, and the more they exposed their power, the more others hungered for it. Battles were fought; many died. Only one Tuatha de Danann survived the first wave of aggression. She became known as the Carrier of the Mark."

"So let me get this straight. You're telling me that you're descendants of one of Danu's children?" I stared at Fionn in disbelief. "How is that even possible? And what does my mom's dying have to do with any of this? And . . . hang on, we're not related, are we?" I turned to Adam, alarmed.

"No, no, the bloodline is complicated," Fionn reassured me. "Thousands of years separate you all from the original bloodline. Megan, what you have to understand for now is that you are a Marked One. We had three before. Earth in Áine . . ."

Áine picked up a sunflower seed that the crow had dropped by the cereal bowl. She held it in her fist for a few seconds, then turned her palm up and opened it. Nestled there was a tiny green sprout. My mouth fell open as it grew before my eyes.

"Water," Adam said softly behind me. He raised his hand from my shoulder and grabbed at the air. A perfect sphere of water made its way from the sink like a delicate bubble and hovered over the table.

"Fire," growled Rían.

Before I could turn to look at him a flame shot through the air, engulfing the sphere of water and evaporating it with a loud hiss. I slowly turned in my seat and looked at each of them in turn. Áine and Adam smiled reassuringly, but Rían just stared at me with eyes that burned like embers.

Fionn spoke again after a moment. "The forces that guide the Marked have brought you to us, which leaves us with an interesting and unprecedented situation. A situation I'd hoped to avoid. We have the fourth element."

"Air," Áine said with a flourish.

"I'm air? Are you telling me I have magic too?"

Rían thumped the wall. "This is crap. If she was the real deal, the Sidhe would have guided her to us years ago," he growled at Fionn. "And even if she *is* the fourth, her power would be weak—and let's not forget her time is nearly up. If we bring attention to her now we draw attention to ourselves. We can't put ourselves in danger for *her* sake."

"Shut your mouth!" Adam shouted.

"Why don't you make me, little brother?" Rían shouted back, squaring up.

"Enough!" Fionn roared. "The significance of this cannot be ignored, and I am bound to protect the Marked

Ones. All *four* of them!" He glared at Rían.

"Rían," Áine said gently, "her power is strong. Adam and I have seen it."

"That was a fluke, a one-off. She didn't even know she did it."

"Rían, she found us. She must have been guided," Áine said.

"I've heard enough of this crap. I'm out of here," Rían muttered, and stormed out.

"Stay close," Fionn called. "We have to be extra careful until we're sure of the lay of the land."

"Don't mind Rían. He doesn't react well to change." Adam rubbed my back gently. "Your head must be spinning."

"What did Rían mean about a 'shee'? What is that?" I asked, trying desperately to keep up with everything. "Fionn mentioned it too."

"The Sidhe is the spirit guide of the Marked," Adam answered. "He watches over us. He guided you to us." He raised his eyebrows. "Looks like a monk with a long gray beard."

"The monk is the Sidhe?" I gasped.

"You've seen him?" Adam asked.

I nodded. So the old monk was a spirit guide. It sort of made sense . . . at least, some kind of sense when spoken in the same breath as everything else I was hearing.

My hand wandered up to my scar—*no*, I corrected

myself, my *Mark*—and traced the faint pattern. "Was my mom Marked?"

"No, but either she or your father must be of royal blood, a descendant of a Marked one," Fionn replied.

"So why me? Why did I get the Mark?"

Fionn shook his head. "When or why the Mark comes to royal bloods of indirect descent, we're really not sure. When the direct bloodline is broken suddenly, like in the case of their mother, the Sidhe makes his selection and guides the new Mark to the others."

"So I'm air," I whispered quietly to myself.

"Yes." Áine smiled encouragingly.

"What can I do?"

"Air is a very powerful element," Adam said softly. "You can pretty much do anything you want."

"What do you mean?"

"Think about it. You can manipulate air. You can move things with a single command. At full strength, and with training and experience, you'd be capable of controlling the air and anything existing in it."

"So you've known about me and my Mark all along?" I looked him straight in the eye.

"No. At first we weren't sure what you were. But then all of our powers started acting up and the fourth arc appeared on our Marks. Even then, we weren't positive. But I was so drawn to you. My element knew you were the fourth before I did."

"Is it just the Mark that draws you to me?" I blurted out. Was what we had even real? Or was it just some weird mystical force at work?

He studied my face and then shook his head. "It can't be just the Mark. What I feel for you is real. It has to be. I tried to stay away, but I couldn't. It would hurt when you were close and I could see you, but not touch you." He looked sincere, but I could see the same fears in his eyes. I realized he was trying to convince himself as much as me.

"So I made that tornado thing happen last night? How did I do it?"

"Your power is deep within you, looking for an outlet. You have to tap into it to be able to release it," Fionn said, standing up. "Fear or stress can trigger your power unwittingly. That is why we must act fast. If your power is starting to manifest, you must learn to control it. The Sidhe could have orchestrated your move to Kinsale years ago. There must be a reason why he waited until such a late stage in your development to bring you here. We just need to figure out what that reason is."

"So it was the *Sidhe* that got my dad the job at the yacht club?"

Fionn nodded. "It must have been. There's no other explanation. Listen, I'm sorry to leave you like this, but I have to get Rían on our side."

"Fionn, wait. What did you mean before when you

said that this was a situation you'd hoped to avoid? Is it the same reason Rían is so against me?" I asked, dreading the answer.

Fionn's face softened. "Rían, Adam, and Áine are my life. I'd do anything to protect them. I'd hoped that the elements would not call on them. But it seems destiny has other plans. With the arrival of the fourth it looks like an alignment is necessary."

"Alignment? What is that?"

"The true purpose of the Marked Ones. It's a ritual that aligns the elements on Earth. It has to be performed on the Summer Solstice."

"But surely that's a good thing?"

"It should be, but I don't like the dangers it presents to my family. It's selfish, really. I should be thinking of the greater good." Fionn smiled gently and walked outside to find Rian.

I turned to Adam. "Dangers?"

"Let's talk more about that when Fionn comes back. First things first: Are you okay?"

"I think so. But . . . I really don't feel like I have any power in me."

"Oh, you do; I've seen it."

"Last night?"

"Not just then. You use your power all the time. You just don't notice. I've been watching you . . . stalker style, even when I couldn't see you."

"He even had me hounding you," Áine interjected. "As you surely have guessed by now . . ."

"The crow!" I looked at her in astonishment. "He *was* watching me."

"Not so sly, huh?" She laughed and held out her hand, looking toward the window. A moment later my crow flew in and landed on her arm. "He's actually a rook. This is Randel," she introduced us. "Randel," she said, addressing the bird, "you already know Megan." He bowed his head toward me in recognition and then jumped up onto her shoulder.

"I had poor Randel and Áine working around the clock watching you," Adam said softly.

"Which, by the way, you owe me big-time for," Áine said to him.

"I know, I know, name it." He sighed.

"Oh, don't worry; I will! But right now I'm going to go help Fionn with Rían; he's really worked up." Áine started to head out, but I said her name and she turned back to face me.

I took a deep breath. "So you're telling me you can speak to Randel, and that he can speak to you?"

"I can speak to and understand all animals, and I have a few other earthly tricks up my sleeve too." She winked at me.

"My head's fried at the moment," I muttered wearily, "but remind me to ask you about them some other time."

"Sure, we have the rest of our lives. I can't tell you how happy I am that you have joined our family. Finally, I'm not the only freaky Carrier of the Mark; it takes the pressure right off. Perhaps Adam here will oblige. . . ."

"Get out of here," Adam told her lightheartedly, throwing a cushion in her direction. She easily ducked out of the way and danced from the room.

Adam turned to me. "Want to go for a walk?" He stood and pulled me up into his arms.

"Yes. I just . . . I need some time to sort it all out in my head." I stood there in his arms quietly for a moment.

"Come on, let's go for that walk. I know a place that will make you feel *much* better," he said. He grabbed my jacket and wrapped it around me. "Let's get out of here."

We climbed into his car and drove in silence until we got to James Fort, an old ruin set on a grassy headland. Then we set off on foot. The grass was long and damp. It soaked my jeans a dark blue around my feet, but I barely felt it. The fresh sea breeze hitting my face felt so good, blowing away the fears and the panic. The raw beauty of this place made the magic seem almost believable.

Adam took my hand and held it firmly. We walked in silence until we came to the abandoned ruins of the fort. Only the ancient exterior walls of the original structure remained. Thick battlements with huge arched windows overlooked the water, facing a sister fort on the other side of the harbor.

Adam lifted me up into one of these windows and tucked me in on one side, with my back to the curving stone frame. Then he pulled himself up and sat on the other side, so we were face-to-face, our boots touching. It had started to rain lightly, but we were well sheltered in the wall. Adam raised his arm and pointed over to the other fort across the water.

"Have you been to Charles Fort?"

"No. I've been meaning to since I got here, but never quite got around to it." I gazed around the crumbling walls of James Fort, with trees growing out of walls and floors blanketed with brambles and grass. "This place is like the poor relation to her rather fine sister over there," I said, eyeing the well-preserved walls and manicured grass of the other fort.

"Yes, but I prefer the real thing. This place has sat here undisturbed all these years. It feels alive. The other fort has been restored for the tourists. It's lost its soul."

I could see his point. It was comfortable here, deserted; the only sound was the rain hitting the leaves and the damp earth, and the waves breaking on the rocks far below us. I wrapped my arms around my knees and hugged them to me.

"I love this place. It feels so like Newgrange," he murmured softly.

"What's Newgrange?"

"It's a temple in the Boyne Valley, in Meath, built for the Marked Ones, back in the beginning. It was perfectly positioned for the winter solstice and, of course, the alignment. It's never been used by us, since there has never been a successful alignment, but the tourists and archeologists get a kick out of the winter illumination. There's a magical serenity to the place. I get that same feeling here. Do you sense it?"

"I think I do. Everything seems to make sense here." I paused. "Isn't there some sort of ghost story attached to this place?"

"Not here. The White Lady haunts Charles Fort. Her husband was killed on her wedding day, so she jumped to her death, mourning her lost love, and now she walks the battlements each night."

"Well, that's cheerful."

"Ah, yes, these stories usually are." He smiled over at me. "Would you like to hang out and see if she appears?"

"I think I've had my fill of the supernatural for one day."

"I guess you have. How are you feeling now?"

"Weird and . . . a little scared." I looked up at him. "And happy, actually. I feel like I could take on the world when I'm with you." I got up onto all fours and crawled over to him and he took me in his arms.

"Try not to feel too overwhelmed," he said into my

hair as he hugged me tight. The warmth from his body gave me goose bumps and sent shivers down my spine.

"You should know," he began softly, "that if this is all too much for you, if you don't want this, you don't have to accept the Mark. If you don't evoke the element before the summer solstice, it will skip you and move on to the next generation." He paused, and let his words sink in. "I wouldn't blame you. I wonder what any of us would have done, given the choice."

"Is that what Rían meant about my time running out?" I asked, trying to remember the details of the conversation.

"Yeah. But you don't have to worry about that right now." He rocked me back and forth. "Let's see if we can spot the White Lady." He put on a ghoulish laugh.

I snuggled in closer to him. I don't know how long we sat there, but the sun was on the other side of the battlements when he nudged me awake.

"Wake up, sleepyhead," he said softly in my ear. "Fionn called. It looks like Rían's been talked down. We'd better get back."

Eleven

THE ORDER OF
THE MARK

When we got back to the house they were waiting for us in a sitting room off the main hall. Two threadbare sofas faced each other in the center. Fionn sat on one with his elbows on his knees and his hands cradling his face. Beside him, Rían slouched into the corner, his long legs stretched out in front of him. Áine came in behind us and shut the door. She walked past Rían and curled up in an armchair by the ornate fireplace.

"Megan, welcome back," Fionn said as we walked into the room and sat on the couch opposite him and Rían. "I want to apologize for our reactions earlier. You are, of course, very welcome in this family, and from now on, you will be thought of as one of us." His pleading eyes met mine. "Can you accept our apologies?"

"Um . . . sure," I said. "We were all under a lot of pressure."

He smiled. "Thank you for being so understanding."

The warmth of this smile caught me off guard. I had turned this man into a hard military type in my head; I now struggled to unravel my opinion of him.

"I've been in contact with the Dublin Order—" Fionn started.

"What? I thought we were going to keep them out of this until we'd assessed the situation," Adam interrupted with an irritated edge to his voice.

"It's time to act, Adam," Fionn said. "It's obvious from what we've seen that Megan is ready."

"What am I ready for? And what is the Dublin Order?" I asked, looking from Fionn to Adam.

"Megan," Fionn began, "I'm a member of an ancient order, the Order of the Mark. We have been in existence for millennia and we exist for one reason: to hold and protect the secret of the Marked. We originated from a group of druids who came together in an attempt to guide the world out of the chaos it was left in after Danu went back to the realm of the gods. When the first three Marked Ones perished, the Order put the remaining Marked One into hiding to protect her from those who sought her power.

"Her Sidhe—who was a mortal monk back then—died sometime later, leaving us alone to figure out the secrets of the Marked. The Order had to ensure the continuation of the bloodline, but for a long time they were not very successful. It turns out the Marked gene is recessive. Pairings rarely produced Marked children. The Order managed to maintain one or two Marked over time, but it was hit-and-miss. Then some children who were descended from royal Marked blood started growing Marks in their teens. The Order could not understand what was happening until the children spoke of an old monk who appeared to them. It soon became clear that the Sidhe was continuing his calling from the spirit realm.

"So the elements were maintained, but in order to perform elemental alignment, the Order needed four elements fully evoked at the same time. The strength required of the four elements to connect and balance Earth is substantial. A failed alignment is more harmful to Earth's delicate balance than no alignment at all."

"I still don't really understand how that's possible . . ." I said, but Fionn smiled at me, and the look in his eyes made me realize that this was another question that he would be able to answer later.

"The royal blood spread out across the world," Fionn continued. "There was no way of knowing which royal bloodline the Sidhe would activate and when and if he would at all. It was rare for the Sidhe to activate the royal bloods, and they were always male, which didn't help. The Order needed Carriers. So the Order abandoned the royal bloods and concentrated on the children of the direct lines, hoping to aid the creation of new Marked Ones. They sought out neutral gene carriers as matches for the Marked Carriers, in order to allow the recessive Marked gene to pass to the next generation—"

"Hang on," I interrupted Fionn, feeling like my head was about to explode. "So royal bloods are descendants of Marked ones, but don't bear the Mark."

Fionn nodded.

"And they didn't get the Mark because . . . ?"

"They were either born to an unmarked mother and Marked father *or* to a Marked mother and a father who did not carry the neutral gene," Fionn finished for me.

"So who carries the neutral gene, and how do you know?"

"This isn't all hard science, Megan; there is an element of magic here. Danu never thought her Tuatha de Danann would fail; she never intended for the line to continue. So she didn't exactly leave a user manual. Through trial and error the Order discovered that it was a recessive gene, and that it only manifests in certain families, so the Order paired the female Carriers with partners from those lines. But getting the right combination does not guarantee Marked children.

That's what made the DeRís family special."

"You mean because all of the children were Marked?" I asked, looking around the room.

"Because they had a Carrier of the Mark for a mother and a father who carried the neutral gene. So now Áine is a Carrier of the Mark and Adam and Rían are Marked royal bloods." Fionn waited for me to continue.

"Adam is water, Áine is earth, and Rían is Fire, so their mother must have been . . ."

Fionn smiled sadly. "Air."

"Like me." I swallowed nervously. "And you said the Sidhe only activated male royal bloods. What does that make me?"

"It makes you unique," Adam said slowly.

"First and foremost it makes you a Carrier of the Mark," Fionn added. "It also makes you less detectable. Nobody would suspect you of being an activated element. I believe the Sidhe was trying to protect the fourth element by hiding it in a female."

"What does it need protecting from?"

"The world is a very different place now," Fionn said, rubbing his forehead. "Things have changed over the centuries, and the Order has been forced to retreat into a very secret world. Knowledge of the Marked tends to be handed down through families of the Order, all educated in their history and power. Order members are based around the world now, in small pockets, living normally in communities with families and jobs. We do stay in contact, but we meet only when necessary. Ireland is the ancestral home of the Mark. We have hidden chambers under Trinity College in Dublin. The three members of the Dublin Order watch over our archives and artifacts there."

"But the Order has an agenda. We don't have many dealings with them," Adam interjected.

"What's the agenda?" I asked.

"Let me tell the story, Adam, please." Fionn gave Adam a warning look. "As Adam says, the Order has an agenda, and quite rightly so. Its ultimate goal is to perform the alignment ritual. It is, after all, the very reason for your existence—and the reason that Danu created the Marked Ones in the first place."

"You said before that alignment was dangerous," I said, thinking back to this morning.

"Yes, the ritual itself is very draining. That's why all four Marked Ones need to be at full strength in order to even *attempt* an alignment. They've attempted the ritual throughout the ages, sometimes with three elements, sometimes with elements at varying stages of development. They all failed, doing more harm than good—"

"But what do you mean?" I interrupted. I wanted a straight answer here; my head was still swirling.

Fionn gave me an apologetic look and went on. "I mean the attempted rituals threw off the balance in the world even more, sometimes at the expense of a Marked One. But quite honestly, even beyond the dangers of an alignment ritual, there are more immediate dangers that the Marked Ones face. There are those who want the powers of the elements."

"Seriously? There are people still fighting over the Marked?" I asked.

"Yes, and they are as determined now as they have ever been. That is where my loyalties divide. My first priority is to my family." Fionn looked around the room. "The Order would gladly sacrifice any of the Marked if they thought they could perform their alignment. But I will never allow that to happen. Not with me as your guardian. I'd forfeit the alignment in a heartbeat if it meant keeping you guys safe." Fionn fell silent for a few moments, and his eyes glazed over. He looked far away in his thoughts. "When they had four Marked Ones the last time, the Order got sloppy. They became obsessed with the alignment and let their guard slip. The Knox found us. They were after Rían, Adam, and Áine, of course. They had little interest in the children's mother and father, and they were unaware that their mother was pregnant at the time. I escaped with the children, but their parents, Emma and Stephen, and their baby sister perished. We couldn't even attend their funerals."

The silence in the room hurt my ears.

Fionn pinched the bridge of his nose and continued.

"We moved around for a while, outrunning the Knox, and we eventually found safety and a home here. Emma came from the most successful line of Carriers, and this was their ancestral home. It's protected and keeps us safe. But the Knox is still looking for these three. They don't give up. I swore to protect their mother and I failed her. So I pledged my life to protecting her children."

"The Knox," I said, mesmerized by the story and hungry for more information. "Who are they?"

"The Knox," Fionn began darkly. "Well, there were always those who coveted the elements, who wanted to take the powers for their own use and benefit. But they were disorganized, untrained, and unskilled. Then, in the sixteenth century, all that changed. The Order had a female Carrier of the Mark—Éile Knox. She produced three Marked children. The fourth child was a girl, Anú Knox. Anú wasn't Marked, as there were already four elements. She was obviously born of royal blood and, like all other royal bloods, had the potential to be Marked, but she would not receive her Mark unless Éile renounced her power and released it to Anú. Ideally the four elements should be from the same generation, where their powers are of similar age and strength. Anú—being of direct descent—was the rightful heir. But Anú was a strange child who leaned toward the darkness, and the Order feared that she would not use her power as it was intended. It was decided that Éile would retain her power and perform the alignment with her three children when they were evoked to full strength, in the hope that it would be balanced enough to achieve a full alignment.

"Anú resented the Order for their decision and craved the power that she believed was rightfully hers. Bitterness ate away at her sanity. On the eve of the summer solstice, when the alignment ritual was to take place, Anú killed Éile and claimed the power. However, having no experience with the element and unable to control its strength, her power, fueled by anger, wreaked havoc on the Order. She killed indiscriminately. Her brothers perished, but the Order managed to save her sister. At that point, the members of the Order were forced to do the unthinkable. They stripped Anú of her power."

"They can do that?" I gasped. "The Order can remove the power?"

"They could back then because they had the Amulet of Accaious. Before the goddess Danu ascended to the realm of the gods, she gave her children the amulet and the Cup of Truth to help them in their task. The amulet enabled any Marked One to renounce his or her power and pass it on to the next generation. But the amulet could also be used to strip a Marked one of his or her element. The catch was that with it, their life essence would also be removed."

"You mean they'd be killed?" I was stunned.

"Not quite, but close," Fionn said. "The Order had

no choice. They couldn't kill Anú—the Order is bound to protect the Marked. But Anú's element was out of control, and the only option left was to strip it from her.

"They fled with the last Carrier. Three Order members stayed behind to perform the ritual. They watched in horror as the process began. Anú went from a sixteen-year-old girl to an old woman in minutes. She lashed out at the three men, killing two, but the bearer of the amulet was immune to her failing power. In her final throes she ripped the amulet from his neck and broke it into pieces. She grabbed a shard of the amber stone from the amulet, swore vengeance, and fled.

"With the Order's numbers diminished and their number one priority being the last Carrier, they let Anú go. Most of the Order left Ireland after that, leaving only a small group to watch over their crypt. They set up bases around the world, tracking down the lost royal bloods in the hope of discovering the three lost Marks.

"Anú bided her time. She recruited an army of followers to do her bidding, all hungry for the power of the elements. They called themselves the Knox, after their leader. Anú also realized she could use the amber shard from the amulet to track the Marked, as the amber was sensitive to the elements and glowed when they were near. Since then, the Marked have been going missing."

I flinched. "You mean . . ."

Fionn shrugged. "We have never found a trace of any of the missing Marked. Ever. These days, the Knox is a complex and well-funded organization. Stop and think of the power one would have if he or she controlled the elements. The food sources of the world could be controlled. And who would need weapons of war if he controlled fire? Whole countries could be wiped out if you can control the water. And then there's air." He looked directly at me. "What is the world without air? A dead, lifeless planet. If the Knox held the power, they'd hold the world to ransom."

"How have they not found you here?" I asked.

"This land is protected. It's what we call 'echoed' lands. I'm sure you've heard the stories," Adam said. "There were no witches, of course, but there were the Order members, descendants of the original druids. You see, land touched by Danu holds echoes of her power. The druids searched Ireland for the echoes. They were strong here, so they took control of the land. It protects the Marked from detection, but only within its boundaries."

"But the Order knows where you are?" I asked.

"Only the Dublin Order," Áine said from across the room. "The other Orders aren't safe."

"What does that mean?" I turned around to her.

"The Order is riddled with traitors. How else do you think they got my mom and dad?"

"That's not entirely accurate, Áine," Fionn interrupted. "The Order is hardly *riddled* with traitors. But yes, the Knox has infiltrated the ranks of the Order. Unfortunately we don't know who we can trust."

"But the Dublin Order is on our side. We can trust them," Áine said, smiling reassuringly.

"Yes, they are the good guys. We need them," Fionn said, looking at Rían, who was staring at the floor. "Which brings us back to you, Megan. The Dublin Order members are eager to get you into training. If you choose to follow your Marked path, you need to evoke your power before the summer solstice in June."

I turned to Adam. "Did you ever think about not accepting it?"

He shook his head. "I didn't have a choice. I was born with my Mark, and my mom was a Carrier. I evoked my power well before I could have even comprehended stopping it. You've been selected, and your power has only been growing since the selection. If you acted quickly, you could suppress it."

My head was spinning. Terror mixed with a magical feeling of being part of something . . . huge. I could walk away from this. Have a normal life. But did I want that? I looked over at Adam and a warm feeling wrapped around my heart. "I don't want to suppress it. I want this."

"You can't want this!" Rían exclaimed, letting his

eyes drift up from the floor. "Haven't you heard a word Fionn has told you? It's dangerous. There are people who want to capture you, torture you, and use you for your element. Do you really want that?"

"Rían," Fionn growled. "We talked about this."

"What? You're the one who wants her to know all the facts. Well, here are some facts." Rían stood up and pulled his T-shirt over his head. An angry red scar ran down his back from his shoulder blades right down to his waist. "This is the reality we live with."

"How did you get that?"

"Having these powers isn't all rainbows and moonbeams. We've had our run-ins with the Knox."

"They found you? When?"

"Four years ago, just before we left the U.K.," Fionn jumped in. "It happens, but we've been safe here."

"And if you think Rían looks bad you should have seen the other guy." Áine smiled a little. "Or what was left of him," she said, scrunching up her face.

"You have your chance to walk away," Rían said quietly. "If it were me, I'd take that chance and start walking now."

I looked at Adam's face and felt the warm glow radiate through me.

"Thanks for the warning, Rían. I get what you're saying, but if this Sidhe guy guided me here to you, he had good reason. Something about this feels right."

Rían stared at me for a few moments, then looked defeated. "All right, then, crazy girl. Just remember, you were warned."

"Good. I'm glad to see you setting your differences aside, Rían," Fionn said, standing up. "Because the Order has put you in charge of her training."

"What?" Rían and Adam said in unison.

"They feel that Rían is the most qualified when it comes to control. I tend to agree with them. Training will begin next week."

"But—" Adam began.

"But nothing, Adam." Fionn held up his hand. "You know that Rían is the man for the job. I'll need you on the ground watching out for her. We can only guarantee her safety on the estate, and we can't keep her here. She has to maintain her normal life. I want you, Áine, and Randel running watches. Keep your ears to the ground."

I stood there watching them discuss the plans that were taking shape. "What will I do?" I said quietly from the couch.

They all looked at me.

"You stay safe," Adam said.

"And you learn," Fionn added. "You have two weeks to put your element to the test before you meet the Order. You have some serious work ahead of you."

With that, the family meeting seemed to be at an end, and everyone stood up and started to walk away. I held out my arms and Adam pulled me into an embrace. "Is that it? Don't I need to hear the rest?"

"You have enough to mull over for now. I think part two of your induction is scheduled for Tuesday," Adam said into my hair.

"What about tomorrow?"

"Fionn's going to Dublin tomorrow. We have to wait for him to get back." He pulled back and looked at me. "You're very eager."

"Do you have any idea how amazing all of this sounds? And to think I'm part of it! I want to know everything."

"You will; I promise. But now I need to get you home. I told your dad I'd have you back after dinner. Oh, *crap*. Dinner." He gave me a rueful look.

I laughed. "Don't worry. I couldn't eat now even if I tried."

Twelve

GOING PUBLIC

I was wide-awake the next morning at six a.m. After tossing and turning for fifteen minutes I finally gave in and got dressed for school. I couldn't stop thinking about how much had happened in just one weekend.

Adam was picking me up at eight forty-five. That way my dad would be gone, and we would get to school at the last minute, with as little fanfare as possible. Too bad it was still only seven fifteen.

Dad was up; I could hear his shower running. I went downstairs and poured myself a bowl of cereal. I ate it slowly, one flake at a time, and watched the minutes tick by. I couldn't wait for Adam to get here. It was weird how much more in control I felt when he was with me.

Yesterday, everything had made perfect sense. Well, sort of. But during the night, the logic had gotten messed up. My head was all over the place. I also felt guilty about blowing Caitlin off after I had promised her I would fill her in. I could not—and would not—jeopardize that friendship.

My dad came down whistling.

"You're chipper this morning," I said, glancing up from my cereal bowl.

"Well, life is good." He tapped his stomach. "What's for breakfast?"

"Cornflakes," I deadpanned.

He cringed and poured himself a cup of coffee. "You're up early."

"There's a lot going on at school today. I wanted to make sure I was on top of it all."

"Anything exciting?" he asked, flipping open his laptop.

Well, actually, I can control air. "Nope, nothing too exciting. Just lots of schoolwork."

"Don't overdo it," he said, frowning. "You have plenty of time until exams." He checked his e-mail, and then gulped down the last of his coffee. "I'm off," he said, grabbing his coat. "See you later."

"Later," I called out after him.

I cleaned up the breakfast dishes and got my bag ready. Finally eight forty-five rolled around and Adam's car swung into my driveway. My heart flipped. I walked out to him and locked the door behind me.

"Adam." I smiled as he got out of the car and walked up to greet me.

"Megan," he breathed, and pulled me into an embrace.

"Hello! You kids want to break it up so we can get to school sometime today?" Áine said out the back window.

Adam pulled back and rolled his eyes. "You ready?"

"As ready as I'll ever be."

He opened the passenger door for me and ran around to the driver's side and jumped in.

"I've been relegated to the backseat," Áine announced with a big grin.

"We can swap if you like," I offered, turning to look back at her.

"God, no," she declared. "I'm happy to hide out back here. You have your weird connection vibe going on, and it's uncomfortable to be between you two. No . . . it's nauseating, actually." She laughed, stuck her finger in her mouth, and fake-gagged.

When we arrived at the school, Adam pulled into one of his regular parking spots. I looked nervously out the window toward the school gates. Caitlin wasn't there. *Shoot.* She must be really angry.

"What's up?" Adam looked at me thoughtfully.

"I think Caitlin's pissed off at me." I sighed. "I blew her off last night—completely forgot I was supposed to meet up with her."

"She'll come around. She's a good friend," he said softly.

"I hope so. I never meant to hurt her feelings."

Áine got out of the car and crossed the road, and Adam squeezed my hand.

"We'd better follow her lead and get in there before I drive off and keep you captive for the day."

"Feel free," I said, laughing.

A smile crossed his face, but his focus was beyond me, out the window toward the school.

"Looks like Caitlin's a better friend than you imagined. I'd say she's ready to forgive and forget."

I followed his gaze and saw Caitlin standing inside the gates on the green. "Caitlin," I squeaked.

We got out of the car and he took my hand again as we walked toward the school. People were looking at us, but I couldn't care less. I went straight up to Caitlin, grinning at her wide eyes.

"Hey," I said. "I'm so happy you're here. You're the best."

"I know," she replied, never taking her eyes off Adam.

"I'll see you in class," Adam said, giving me a quick kiss. He turned to Caitlin with his most captivating smile. "Thanks for understanding."

"Sure," she mumbled as Adam walked away.

I turned back to her with an apologetic look. "I'm so sorry about last night! I got carried away and didn't realize how late it was."

"Don't worry about it. I'd have dumped me too if I was on a romantic date with *that*! But I need details! You owe me that much."

"That I do," I agreed, laughing, thrilled to be forgiven.

"Thank goodness we have maths today, since I have you all to myself in that class. Too bad I have to wait through three other classes! Now come on or we'll be late," she said, grabbing my sleeve.

We ran to our first class and made it just in time. Adam was there sitting in the second row with two seats beside him. He surreptitiously tapped the one closer to him and I rushed to claim it. Caitlin gave me a meaningful look and sat in the seat on the other side of me. Jennifer turned around and took in the seating arrangement with wide eyes. Then she half smiled and flicked her hair over her shoulder as she turned around to face the front of the class again. Adam seemed to be enjoying the attention.

Finally, fourth period rolled around, and Caitlin and I headed to math. I couldn't wait to tell her everything. *Well*, almost *everything*.

Caitlin was eager to get me to class early, so we could talk before we had to resort to writing notes. She ushered me into the back row. As I sat down, my stomach twisted a little. I wasn't looking forward to lying to my best friend. It was made so much worse when her excited eyes looked at me and she smiled her gorgeous, open smile.

"Well?" she prompted, waiting for the floodgates to open.

"I don't know where to start," I replied honestly. *I guess lying by omission isn't as horrible as all-out lies.*

"Start with how on earth you ended up arriving at the party with Adam!"

After everything that had gone on yesterday, I had completely forgotten about the egg attack on Saturday night. I retold the story about the boys, of course carefully edited, leaving out the part about me actually creating the tornado that ripped through the lane.

She started laughing. "I heard Blánnaid Flynn telling a story about her boyfriend, Tom O'Donnell, and his friend Mick. Apparently, they were found walking around the town all bloody and windswept, saying Adam used voodoo on them." Suddenly she stopped laughing. "He didn't, did he?"

"Definitely not. Adam arrived after that freakish wind kicked up."

"It's weird. There was no wind like that down at the bonfire."

"Yeah, really weird. I couldn't believe it myself," I said, not quite meeting her eyes.

"Tom and Mick had been drinking cider since dinner, the idiots." Caitlin frowned. "They must have been smoking something stronger too, if you ask me, with the stories they were telling. They made such eejits of themselves, everyone's laughing at them, and Blánnaid even broke up with Tom over it. If her dad heard about what happened, she would be in serious trouble. Did they scare you?" she asked, concerned all of a sudden. "I shouldn't have let you walk on your own."

"No. Don't worry about it. They were just acting like drunk morons," I reassured her.

"Well, they won't be bothering you ever again. They're so freaked out."

Just then Miss Moore, the math teacher, walked into the room along with the stragglers late for class, and Caitlin and I moved our conversation to paper.

Well? More!

When we got to the party, we sat around and talked. It turns out we have a lot in common.

That was totally true. I'd let her take from it what she liked.

And the kiss?

I flushed and caught her eye. She took the paper back.

That good, huh? So what happened on Sunday?

He came over to my place and "met my dad," even though of course they already knew each other. Then we went to his house, to meet his family.

167

Wow . . . What did you guys do?

Time now for some serious editing. I thought for a moment, my pen hovering over the paper.

We hung out in his room . . . kissed some more . . . Mmmmm, very nice.

I felt like that sounded casual enough. If I told her the truth about how intense our relationship was she would think I was crazy.

And then, after all the kissing?

We went for a romantic walk to James Fort and talked all afternoon. Then he dropped me off at home. I should have called you. I'm sorry. I still feel awful about it.

Don't worry. I had <u>amusement</u> of my own!!!

Tell!

Oh, I will! Killian and myself are hotting up. Wait until I tell you the juicy details!

"Caitlin, have you something you would like to share with the class?" Miss Moore inquired, peering over her glasses.

"No, Miss Moore," Caitlin said sweetly, as she hid the sheet under her book.

We both tried to look suitably interested for the rest of the period.

As we walked to geography class, Caitlin gave me a play-by-play of her weekend. Killian joined us at one point and Caitlin nearly exploded with happiness. I was so excited for her, and I was thrilled the spotlight was off me for a little while. It was a relief to have a break from lying. Then, when we got to the door, there stood Adam leaning against the wall, smiling at me. I had to use every ounce of my willpower to stop from diving into his arms. I seriously had to get control of my emotions—and fast; otherwise I was going to flunk my exams. I forced myself to pay attention to the teacher, but I couldn't help feeling hyperaware of Adam's very warm and muscular thigh right next to mine.

After class Adam turned to me. "Was that as hard for you as it was for me?" he asked with a cheeky smile. "Lunch?"

Lunch. *Shoot.* Adam and Áine normally went home for lunch. I felt my mood plummeting, though I told myself I was being silly. After all, he'd be back in an hour, and I'd survived one class period without him already.

"Oh, right. I guess I'll see you later," I muttered, trying to hide my disappointment.

"Actually, I thought I might join you and your friends. If you don't mind, that is." He fumbled around in his bag and pulled out a lunch box. "Fionn made me a sandwich," he added with a smile.

"You're kidding." I laughed. "Fionn? Sandwiches?"

"I swear," he said, opening the lunch box. There was a limp-looking cheese sandwich in it with a big handprint stamped into it where Fionn had held it down to cut it in half.

"Wasn't that sweet of him?" I grinned. "Come on, then," I said, standing up. "Let's do lunch." I held out my hand to him, he took it, and I pulled him up. I wished, not for the first time, that kissing weren't against the school rules.

After the bell rang at the end of the day, I headed out to meet Adam. Lunch had been wonderful, but I hadn't seen him since then, and my mind was swirling with questions that I needed answered.

"Is everything okay?" he inquired as I approached him.

"I need to talk to you," I said. "Alone."

"Sure. Let me just ask Rían to pick up Áine." He took out his phone and quickly called his brother, who I could tell from Adam's end of the conversation wasn't very happy with Adam's request.

When Adam got off the phone he turned to me again and took my hand. "Thanks," I said. "So, Rían doesn't like me much, does he?"

"It's not that," he began thoughtfully. "Rían has a tough time accepting who we are and our purpose. He blames the elements for our parents' death and he resents his particular power most of all." He looked at me. "We had to move quite a bit before we settled here and Rían

170

had to work very hard to learn how to control his power. When we were younger it ended in a lot of houses being torched. I think he's just finding it hard to accept that you would opt in when you have the chance to walk away."

"Wow. That explains a lot." I wondered how Rían had learned to master his power, since it seemed like the hardest one to control. Maybe if he ever let his guard down I would ask him about it.

Adam and I walked in silence to his car and drove to my house. I didn't want to bring anything up while he was driving—I wanted to have his full attention for all of my questions. Once we got inside, I made two cups of tea, grabbed a box of cookies, and led Adam up to my room. We sat down on my bed and he put his arms around me and hugged me, bending his head to mine for a lingering kiss.

"I can't be distracted," I said, breaking away, but then kissed him again. "Okay, I guess I can be distracted, but I don't want to be."

"You want to talk element stuff?"

"Yes. Seriously, I need to know everything."

Adam looked thoughtful. "I don't know everything, really, but Fionn does. I'll tell you what I know, but we'll have to talk to him again about it too, okay?"

"Of course. But I want to hear what you know first." I handed him a mug and faced him, ready to drink in the stories behind my ability.

"You're more Irish than you know," he said, indicating the tea.

"Well, this tea-drinking habit is totally addictive."

"I got quite fond of it myself when we first moved here." Adam smiled, looking like he was lost for a moment in the memories.

"How old were you?"

"Fourteen."

"So you've only lived here three years?"

"Nearly four." He lay back on the bed. "So where do you want to start?"

"With the whole 'my time running out' thing," I replied firmly.

"Thought you might." He scratched his head. "Well, Rían, Áine, and I were born with our Marks. And, of course, we were born into a family that was groomed in the way of the Order. Our powers were apparent almost from birth, and they were fostered and cared for by people with extensive knowledge of the elements. We never had to evoke, in a manner of speaking, because we had done so without knowing, when we were children. We were bound to, really, since the elements grow stronger when they're together. You, on the other hand, received your Mark when you were six, and while your power may have surfaced at times since then, you were too young to understand what was happening, and there was no way it could have been recognized by those around you."

I racked my brain, trying to think of other weird windstorms or minitornadoes that I might have caused, but couldn't come up with anything concrete. Adam paused as though he could sense that my focus had wandered, but as soon as my eyes met his once more, he picked up where he had left off.

"Anyway, your element has only really started growing since you came into contact with us. And from what I've seen so far, it's growing fast, so you need to learn how to harness your power right away; otherwise you could do a lot of damage, and even possibly hurt yourself or other people. As for the possibility of the power passing you over, the element hits maturity just before we turn eighteen. If you don't perform the evocation ritual before then, the element will pass you."

"So if I don't evoke the power before my birthday, it'll be gone forever?"

"Well, technically it's not your birthday; it's the summer solstice in the year following your seventeenth birthday. But yes, that's the general gist."

"The summer solstice? When is that?"

"Next year it's June twentieth," Adam answered patiently. "You have a lot of time to make your choice."

"What's the evocation ritual like? Does it hurt?"

"It doesn't hurt. It's simply surrendering yourself to

173

your element, so that you coexist. Your element is being suppressed at the moment and the ritual helps you free it. But your element needs to be strong first, in order to evoke. That's why you'll be training."

"Training with Rían, you mean."

"Yeah." Adam shrugged, making it clear that while he still thought the arrangement was far from perfect, he didn't think he could fight it. "Fionn has been working with the Dublin Order to work out a schedule for your work with Rían, and to try to estimate a date when you'll be ready for evocation."

"The Dublin Order. They're the guys up at Trinity College, right?"

Adam nodded. "We call them Watchers, and there are three of them who are based in Dublin: Hugh McDonagh, William White, and M. J. O'Dwyer. They lecture in theology and philosophy at Trinity and they protect a crypt there where much of our history is stored." He put down his empty cup and wrapped his arm around my shoulder.

"Any more questions?" he asked.

"Yeah, one more thing. I think I understand the whole Carrier of the Mark genetic line thing now, but Áine said something about not being the only '*freaky* Carrier of the Mark.' What did she mean by 'freaky'?" I watched as a pink tinge worked its way up his neck to his cheeks.

"So you understand that as a male Marked, I can't pass on the Mark?"

"Yeah, I think so. You just pass on the royal blood, right?"

He nodded. "So the continuation of this line has always been dependent on Áine. I guess you share that responsibility now."

Suddenly I understood what Áine meant when she said "Perhaps Adam would oblige."

Flushing wildly, I pressed my face into his shirt, and only looked at him again once I was sure my face had returned to its normal color.

"So all the babies that a Carrier of the Mark has will be Marked?" I asked.

"Well, not necessarily. It all depends on timing. There can only be four elements at any given time. If there is an opening, a baby would get the Mark. If not, the baby is born a royal blood, but first in line for the Mark. It's actually just like any royal structure, really. In the event where the direct line of royal blood comes to an end, like in the case of what happened to us, the Mark has nowhere to go, so that's when the Sidhe steps in and makes his selection from the royal blood pool out there—someone just like you."

"So let's say for argument's sake that Áine got pregnant now by a partner who carried the neutral gene. That baby wouldn't be Marked?"

"No, because there are already four elements. But the child would be royal blood of direct decent and first in line for the Mark. One of us would have to die, or give up our element. But if neither of those things happens before the child's seventeenth birthday, then that child gets passed over in favor of the next in line."

"My head hurts," I said, snuggling back into his arms.

"I know it's a lot to take in. But it's something we don't have to worry about. There are four Marked ones. We are all alive and well. It's not even an issue right now."

"Yeah, I know. I just need to understand. What happens if a Carrier of the Mark falls in love with someone who isn't from a gene-neutral line? What then?" I felt Adam tense.

"It doesn't really work like that."

"What do you mean?"

He pulled me closer. "The Order hand-selects gene-neutral males to . . . you know . . ." He cleared his throat uncomfortably. "They pick who the Carriers will marry. It's basically like arranged marriages."

I turned to face him. "What? That's crazy!"

"I know. We don't talk about it much—it freaks Áine out."

"Will she have to do what they say?"

"She won't be forced to, but there's a deep-rooted sense of responsibility in her, just like in my mother."

"I can't even begin to understand that kind of

pressure," I said, and then I noticed the clock on the nightstand. "Uh-oh. My dad will be home soon. I'm not sure how happy he would be finding you lying on my bed."

"You're quite right, O wise one. Best not to fall out with the in-laws so early on in our relationship." He laughed. "Anyway, I'm going to go." He stood up. "Can you ask your dad if you can come over for dinner tomorrow?"

"I will." I stood up and fell into his outstretched arms.

"Sleep tight," he whispered in my ear.

"You too."

"I'll see you in the morning."

After Adam left, I started putting dinner together. Spaghetti Bolognese. It was quick and easy. A few minutes later, my dad came in.

"Hi, Meg," he called, as he hung up his coat.

"Hey! Are you hungry?"

"Starving."

"Spaghetti's almost ready." I smiled at him as he came in the door.

"Did I see Adam DeRís coming down our road just now?"

"Yup. He dropped me off after school."

"Hummmm," my dad mumbled, as he peeked into the saucepan simmering on the stove. "So what's the story with you two?"

"Dad." I groaned, embarrassed.

"You really like him."

"Yes, Dad, I really like him. Now, no more questions, please."

"It's just . . . I worry about you," he continued in a softer tone. "I wish you had a mother to talk to about, you know, girl stuff."

Oh, no. I could hear it coming.

"You were never one for boyfriends, so I got away without needing to have the Talk with you, but that doesn't mean I'm not concerned."

"Dad!"

He held up his hand. "No, Megan, this is my job. We need to do this." He took a deep breath. "Now, there is much more to sex than mere mechanics."

I cringed into the boiling pot of spaghetti.

"There's nothing wrong with sex, and I don't necessarily believe in saving yourself for marriage, but sex is precious and should only be shared with a person you love. Just bear that in mind, please, for me? I don't want to see you get hurt."

I glanced up after a few seconds. He seemed to be finished. "Thanks, Dad, but honestly, you don't have to worry about anything like that yet. It's a long way off. Speaking of which, should I be giving you the same lecture?"

He flushed.

"Oh, I see. I'm too late," I said, a bit shocked. His

flush deepened. I was thankful the timer started going off, and I ran to drain the pasta. "Saved by the bell," I exclaimed. I wasn't sure whether to laugh or be horrified. My father? Sex?

Yikes.

After dinner I got up to clear away the plates. "Dad, can I have dinner at Adam's house tomorrow?"

"Sure, just don't come home too late."

"Thanks!" I said, dumping the plates in the sink.

"Dinner was good, Meg. There's a movie starting at eight if you want to join me."

"I'd love to, Dad, but I have a lot of homework to do."

"Okay. It's good to see you so focused; we should start checking out what the colleges have to offer here."

Thanks for the segue, Dad. "Funny you should say that. Adam and I were just discussing Trinity College in Dublin."

"Wow, Trinity. That's like the Harvard of Ireland."

"I know how to pick 'em." I smiled.

As I made my way up the stairs, I thought about what my future could hold. I hadn't really thought much about college before, but with the Dublin Order based in Trinity, it seemed like a logical place to set my sights on. I could learn about my heritage while studying for my future. I broke into a grin. The future looked exciting.

Thirteen

TRAINING BEGINS

The next day after school, Adam and I headed over to his car, where Áine was waiting, leaning against the door with her arms crossed, rubbing the tops of her sleeves.

"Come on, guys," she called. "It's freezing."

"We're coming!" Adam answered. He opened the doors with a click, and we all jumped in.

"Well, did you tell her yet?"

Adam stiffened. "Áine when we get home, will you remind me to kill you, please?"

"Tell me what?" I looked from Adam's face to hers.

"It's nothing," he said quietly, pulling out of the

parking space. "Well, I guess it's not *nothing*. It looks like we might be going to Dublin sooner rather than later. The Dublin guys are eager to set a date for a trial evocation."

"Isn't that great?" Áine declared from the backseat. "I haven't seen the lads in ages, and think about all the major shopping I'll be able to do!"

"Áine, don't be stupid. This is a big deal for Megan. Actually, it's a big deal for all of us."

"Fionn never lets us into the cities; I'm finding a way to make good use of this trip." She folded her arms and looked out the side window with a pout on her face.

Adam rolled his eyes and gave me his full attention. "Fionn wants to talk to you about the Order, and the setup in Dublin."

"This is awesome!" I exclaimed. "I can't wait to meet the Order. And I don't even mind that you didn't tell me right when you found out," I teased, jabbing him with my finger. "But what's with the trial?"

"It's just a test to see how far you can take the power. It will give them a rough idea of when to schedule the *actual* evocation. And there's something else you need to know," Adam said, pulling into the yard.

"Oh, yeah," Áine said. "You're starting your training today." She jumped out of the car and ran to the back door.

Adam rolled his eyes again.

"Today? I thought we were still on day two of induction?"

"Yes, but you need to start training immediately. Rían will be starting slow. Don't worry; you'll knock 'em dead."

"That's what I'm worried about."

He gave me a wry smile. "Do you think I would hand you over for training if I didn't think you were up to it?"

I gave him what I hoped was a confident smile in return. "Of course not."

"Megan, hello," Fionn's voice called from the hall as Adam and I walked into the house. "I'll be with you in just a second."

"Okay."

Adam turned to me. "Hungry?"

"Um, sure."

Áine was already in the kitchen, making some crackers and cheese. She smiled at us as we walked in. "Want some?"

"That would be nice," Adam said. He put the kettle on and took down some cups from a cupboard.

"I'll have one of those if you're making it," Rían said, as he sauntered in and sat down on the bench at the other side of the table.

"Hi, Rían," I mumbled, sitting down opposite him. I stared at the back of Adam's head, willing him to turn around and rescue me. As if on cue, he brought four cups over.

Rían took his cup and started drinking. Why on earth was he sitting here? Was this his idea of making an effort?

Thankfully Randel flew in, distracting me from Rían. He landed on the table and started pecking up the cracker crumbs. "Randel! How are you?" The big black rook looked up at me. "Have you given up on spying on me in the shower?"

Áine laughed. "I had a word with him—told him it was a tad inappropriate."

I put out my hand to stroke the bird. "May I?"

"Go right ahead." She scratched his head. "He loves the attention."

I ran my fingers over his glossy black feathers. "Well, aren't you a gorgeous boy?" I asked as he eyed me appreciatively.

"Watch it, Randel; she's mine," Adam warned the bird. "Don't go getting any ideas."

Randel stretched out his wings and cawed at Adam. We all burst out laughing, easing the atmosphere.

"Right." Fionn walked into the kitchen. "All of you. Come with me."

We followed him into the sitting room. I sat down on one of the couches and Adam joined me. Áine curled herself into an armchair. Rían flopped on the other large couch opposite me, beside Fionn. As soon as we were all settled, Fionn cleared his throat and began talking.

"Megan, the visit to Dublin has been moved up and we're going to begin your training today. I need you to understand that this will be an exhausting and potentially dangerous process."

I squeezed Adam's hand. "I understand."

"I will also have to make arrangements with your father so you'll be able to travel with us to Dublin next week. Do you see any problems there?"

"It should be fine. I've been talking about colleges with him, so I'm sure I can work something out."

Fionn's tone turned even more serious. "Megan. Please understand that you cannot tell your father anything about the Mark. The situation is still very fragile, and we can't risk anyone knowing of our whereabouts or your existence. It is absolutely imperative that we stay hidden. The Dublin Order is not even going to tell the council about you, not until we discover whether you are able to evoke your power. There is no point in drawing attention to ourselves before we need to."

"The council? What's that?" I couldn't believe there was yet *another* group of people involved in this.

"It's basically the 'voice' of the Order. The council is made up of senior Order members from around the world. But you don't need to worry about them for now."

I took a deep breath. I could not, and would not, let Adam and his family down.

"We will start training immediately," Fionn continued, "and then travel to Dublin this Saturday."

I looked over at Áine, who was nearly jumping up and down in her chair in excitement.

Rían, on the other hand, sat quietly with his head slightly drooped. He leaned his elbows on his knees with his hands under his chin, apparently lost in thought.

"Megan," Fionn said, pulling my attention back to him. "We will all be helping with your training, but Rían will be your main teacher. He has had to employ specific measures to channel his excesses, and we feel we can use this knowledge to help you find your trigger."

"Where will we do the training?" I asked.

"Here. It's isolated enough not to bring attention to ourselves and, more important, it's safe. If need be, we can move to a more remote location."

I nodded. "So what do we do first?"

"I was thinking we could start out gently," Fionn replied. "Maybe Adam, Áine, and Rían can give you a little demonstration and see if you pick up on anything." He smiled at me encouragingly as Adam pulled me up and kissed the top of my head. The five of us walked to the yard and continued down past an ancient turret and out a small gate into the fields beyond.

"Go on, Áine; show us your stuff," Adam said.

Áine dropped to the ground, digging her nails into the earth. "Watch this," she said.

The sun had just about set. The last glow of its fading light illuminated the turned earth of the field that stretched out before us. A cold, gentle breeze blew down the valley, catching Áine's hair and lifting it slightly from her face. She closed her eyes and started humming a little tune. At first nothing happened. I looked around from face to face, to see if they were seeing something I didn't, but they just kept looking at her. Then I felt a vibration under my feet and nearly lost my balance.

"What was that?" I asked, righting myself.

"It's okay. Look." Adam put his arm around my waist to keep me steady while the earth shook beneath our feet. The rich brown soil that stretched out before us seemed to quiver. Suddenly, a haze of green moved up the valley, like a swarm of locusts charging toward us. I took a step back.

"Keep watching," Adam whispered.

The green haze crept closer. It wasn't insects. It was seedlings, millions of them, popping out of the ground at amazing speed. They moved past us and back toward the house. I looked over at Áine again. The seedlings were curling their way around her, entwining themselves in her hair; they seemed to caress her entire body.

"That tickles! Stop that." She laughed, opening one eye and untangling a sprout that had worked its way up to her ear. She looked up at me. "Well, what do you think?"

I looked at the field of lush growth in amazement. "You did that?"

She nodded and gently removed the sprouts that were still hugging her. Then she stood up and came back over to us.

Adam smiled at me. "She's quite something, isn't she?"

I was awestruck. "That was seriously cool. How did you do it?"

She shrugged. "I'm not sure. I feel warmth in my chest and in my head; then it gets warmer and it just sort of *flows* from me. I let my energy know what I want, and . . . well, it does it." She put her arms out and swept them from side to side, then dropped down onto her knees again. She pushed her hands with the palms facing down into the earth. As she did, the entire field of seedlings retracted and disappeared under the soil.

"What did you do?" I asked as the green field turned back to brown in a wave flowing off into the distance.

"It's not their time. They need to sleep until spring," she said, smiling fondly over the field before returning to her feet.

I looked at this girl; she had such a strange and awesome power. How could I ever come close to that kind of beauty and effortless control?

Fionn looked to me. "Did you feel anything? Any strange sensations?"

"I don't think so. But I don't know what I'm supposed

to be feeling or even what to expect."

Adam rubbed my arm. "Don't worry. It will probably come to you when you least expect it." He looked over at Rían. "You want to give Megan a demo?"

Rían shrugged. "Sure." He closed his eyes and held out his hands to the sides, his fingers splayed and curling upward, as if he were holding something in each of them, gripping it tight. Suddenly his eyes flashed open. They glowed an unusual color, like the green had been tainted with orange. Then twin balls of a strange blue-and-green flame ignited in his hands.

Frightened, I took a step back. He strained out his hands and pushed them up into the air like he was lifting a heavy weight. The fire shot up and out of his hands, then danced in the air in an erratic pattern around him, leaving glowing trails in its wake. His strange burning eyes followed the flames' every move. They worked their way around us, then filled out until we were surrounded by a roaring, crackling circle of fire. I could feel the sweat running down my skin.

"Rían, that's enough," Fionn shouted.

Rían scowled and pulled his arms in toward him. The flames condensed into balls and shot back into his palms. Then he squeezed his fists shut over the flames, and they were extinguished with a hissing sound.

I couldn't look away. The danger and the strength of Rían's power had me trembling. Áine's power was awesome, magical—pretty, even—but Rían's felt darker somehow.

Rían slowly opened his eyes. They had returned to their normal green color, dark and distant.

Áine walked over to her brother with her hands on her hips. "Impressive, Rían. You've been practicing, haven't you? Are you trying to outdo me?"

He smirked. "Shut up, little sis, or I'll incinerate your precious sprouts."

It was a joke, I knew, but I still shivered a little at his threat. If he wanted to, he could destroy everything that Áine brought to life.

Fionn walked closer to us. "Did you feel anything this time, Megan?"

I shook my head. "Sorry. I don't think so."

Adam, still holding my hand, took a step forward. "I guess it's my turn then. Just something small, to see if we can get your magical juices flowing." He smiled at me. "Try to feel what I feel. Focus on the connection in our fingers."

I tried to home in on the feeling of Adam's hand in mine. He lifted his left hand, held it out to the trees, and closed his eyes. Then he grasped at the air like he had just caught something. In that instant, all the individual droplets of rain that were hanging on the leaves and branches around us flew into the air. There were thousands of them, maybe millions. The delicate evening light reflected off them, making each one sparkle like a diamond. They hung in the air totally motionless. Then Adam moved his hand gently and the droplets danced. They stopped directly in front of me. I reached out my free hand to touch them.

I definitely felt something moving through me from Adam, but I couldn't identify it. Each droplet I touched was wet, but had form. It didn't burst or break ranks. It just bounced back into position.

"Now watch this," he said with a grin.

He snatched at the air with his hand. A wall of water shot up from the bottom of the valley. The water floated high above our heads, until it formed a dark and heavy cloud that made a low rumbling sound.

Adam grasped at the air again. This time a shimmering mist of water rose above the fields and trees. It looked like fog as it climbed steadily up to join the now loudly rumbling cloud high above us. Adam winked at me and snapped his fingers. The cloud shuddered a little and collapsed into a downpour.

"Adam, for Christ's sake," Rían shouted, before making a run for the yard.

Áine pulled a tiny umbrella from her purse, and with a quick click, her shelter was complete. She shrugged. "You live and learn," she said, walking over to Fionn.

I turned to Adam with my hair drenched and stuck to the sides of my face. "That was so awesome." Forgetting that we had an audience, I stood on tiptoe and kissed him while the rain poured down on us. "I think I felt something that time," I whispered.

The rain stopped. Adam held my face in his hands; then he ran them over my hair and down my arms. With his touch every drop of moisture evaporated, leaving me as dry as I had been before the downpour.

Fionn coughed. "Adam?"

Áine made a puking sound. "Yeah, if you could pass the bucket, we're trying to get her to evoke air here, and not our last meal."

I pulled away and looked at them excitedly. "I felt something that time, with Adam. There was definitely a sensation: a coolness that ran through me, like a chill deep inside. I don't know how to describe it."

Fionn moved toward us. "You're onto something. You need to focus on that feeling. Try to harness the sensation, learn to identify it. It will eventually become more obvious." He bent down and picked up a small leaf and placed it on my hand. "See if you can move this with your mind. Focus on the coolness you felt. Clear your head of everything except that feeling and the leaf in your hand. Try to remember how you felt at Halloween. Try to recapture the sensations you had that night."

I looked down at the small leaf, willing myself to believe I could do it. Adam squeezed my other hand.

I closed my eyes and tried to feel the chilling coolness

from before, to harness it. I visualized the leaf moving, blowing delicately off my hand. I pictured the leaf gone from my palm. Then I opened my eyes.

The leaf was still there. It hadn't moved at all.

"Damn," I muttered.

Rían jogged back over to us and stood right in front of me. He held out his hands for me to take them. I swallowed hard. I had seen what they could do.

He smiled. "Are you chicken?" He cocked his head to the side. "Trust me; take my hands. Let me show you."

I looked up at Adam and gave my hands to Rían. They were warm, but not scorching, the way I'd expected.

His face turned serious. "Close your eyes and feel the heat. Take a deep breath and hold it. Now let the coolness trickle down to your arms, to the heat you feel in my hands."

His voice was so calm and reassuring, hypnotic almost. I did as he suggested. I felt my hands getting hot and found the coolness inside me. I willed it to move to my hands and push the heat away.

"Now, breathe out, and with the air you expel, move the cool energy through your fingers."

I did exactly as he instructed. I felt the cool air move through me, and as I did Rían slowly let go of me. I felt like I was in a trance. I heard a gasp and I forced my eyes open. Rían had a small ball of fire in each of my hands and they were being gently pushed away from my palms.

He held his arms out and the flames shot back to him. He gave me a huge smile and stepped aside.

"You did it!" Adam picked me up and spun me around. "You repelled fire." He kissed me passionately.

"Again, we're right here," Áine said beside us.

Adam smirked. "Go away, then."

Fionn started walking toward the house. "Áine, Rían, let's go dry off and get dinner ready."

Adam smiled at me. "You repelled fire on your first go. You are going to be one powerful girl."

"Let's do it again."

He put his arms around me and laughed. "No, no more magic for you today."

I laid my head on his chest. "Speaking of magic, what you did before was amazing."

"Ah, that was nothing. I'll show you what I can really do, another day."

"I'll look forward to that. Come on; let's go for a walk until dinner is ready."

He put his arm over my shoulders and we headed off into the trees on one side of the field.

I looked up at him. "Rían was amazing too. Scary, but amazing."

Adam looked back down at me. "I told you. He has a talent. He'll really help you. But just remember whose girlfriend you are." He stopped and turned to me with an expression of mock horror.

I fluttered my hands to my chest. "Well, Rían is devastatingly handsome, with that whole smoldering, brooding-eyes thing he's got going on. Maybe I picked the wrong brother."

He grabbed me and pushed me up against a tree. "Oh, I have ways of convincing you that you chose right." He kissed me with such passion it left me breathless. I felt my legs starting to give way under me.

"Yeah, that could do it." I gasped, breaking away and smiling coyly at him. "Could you convince me some more?"

He leaned his body in closer and put his hands around the tree, holding me. He slowly kissed my throat, then up my neck to my ear and back to my mouth. I melted into him. I never wanted this moment to end.

"Megan, Adam . . ." Áine came into sight and she looked at us in disgust. "Guys, Fionn says dinner is ready, but it looks like you two have already eaten." She started back through the trees toward the house, giggling.

I flushed with embarrassment, but Adam just laughed. "Come on; let's go get some dinner." He held out his hand in front of him, then grasped the air and closed his eyes for a moment. I heard Áine screaming off in the distance.

I looked up to him. "What did you do?"

He grinned. "You'll see." As we walked toward the house I could see Áine standing in the yard, soaking wet and glaring.

"You know the rules! We're not allowed to use our powers on one another. You're an absolute git!"

I tried hard to keep a straight face, but she looked so funny standing there in a pool of water, with her hair stuck to her face. Beside me, Adam had tears streaming down his cheeks, he was laughing so hard.

"Fine! An eye for an eye." She closed her eyes and waved her arms. Randel appeared from the house. He landed on her hand and she whispered something to him. He launched himself into the air.

Adam grabbed my hand and started running toward the house. "You didn't!" he roared.

"What? What did she do?"

"Just run!"

Something hit him on the head with a loud *splat*. Adam stopped dead. He had a load of bird poo dripping off his hair onto his face. I burst out laughing. I couldn't help it.

"You think this is funny?" He grabbed me around the waist and tried to rub his head on me.

"No, no!" I finally broke his hold and ran for the protection of the house, making it inside just in front of Áine and Adam. They both headed upstairs to clean up, heckling each other as they went. I walked into the kitchen to help Fionn and Rían set the table. We worked in silence for a few minutes; then Rían looked at me.

"You were quite good, you know. You're very strong. I'm looking forward to working with you."

I hadn't been expecting such a nice compliment from Rían, and at first I didn't even know what to say. Finally, I just mumbled, "Yeah, me too."

He handed me the glasses to put on the table. "I'm sorry about how I acted when you first got here. I was obnoxious."

"It's okay; I think I understand. I'd probably have acted the same way."

Rían gave me a small smile and I felt a huge weight lift off my shoulders. Maybe working with him would turn out all right after all.

Fourteen

TRAINING WITH
RÍAN

It had been decided at dinner that Rían and I would train every day after school, to get as much practice as possible in before our trip to Dublin the following weekend.

I ran the trip by my dad when I got home, telling him that we were going to check out Trinity, since it was Adam's college of choice and Rían would be going there next fall. Luckily, he thought it was a great idea for me to check out the school, and only asked that the DeRíses pick me up at our house so that he could meet Fionn.

During the week, I spent every moment that I could

working on my power. Caitlin and I covered for each other. We had more free rein when our parents thought that we were hanging out with each other instead of with the boys. She told her mom and I told my dad that we were spending time in the stables helping out Killian. For her it wasn't stretching the truth *too* much—she really was spending her evenings with Killian, but very little cleaning was going on. I, of course, was spending my time with Adam and Rían. Caitlin could never know what I was really up to, but she thought she was in on the big plan, so she was happy. I still hated lying to her, but it had to be done.

My relationship with Rían had altered dramatically in just a few days. While he was still a dark character, and I knew it would take a long time for him to really let me in, he was making a tremendous effort and I appreciated it. We mostly focused on working together with fire. It seemed to be the one power that helped me recognize where my element was and what it felt like.

Adam would always sit on the scullery steps, out of the way, watching, but not getting involved. I would gaze up at him every now and again, my mind wandering, imagining how much nicer it would be to run my hand down his gorgeous face, how his tall, lean body would feel under my fingers. I had to pinch myself constantly to remind myself that this wasn't just a dream. Adam was mine.

At the same time, I was constantly stressed about my power. I still hadn't been able to accomplish anything notable, and I needed to evoke as soon as possible. Fionn told me about previous air Marked and the power they possessed. Some even had the ability to manipulate the air around them so that they appeared to be able to fly. I had gotten a taste of my power on Halloween and I was hungry for more.

By the time Friday night rolled around I was starting to feel exhausted from exerting myself. I glanced back up to Adam, sitting as always on the steps, patiently observing from a distance.

Rían followed my gaze and rolled his eyes. "Adam, any chance you would sod off for a while? Megan can't keep her eyes off you for less than ten minutes, and it's interfering with her training. It's also making me feel like I'm going to puke."

Adam said nothing and quietly went inside. I was mortified. I had no idea I had been looking at Adam so often, or so obviously.

Rían looked at me sternly. "Look, I'm sorry, but I need you to focus. This is our last training session before we meet the Dublin Order tomorrow."

It suddenly occurred to me that this was as important to him as it was to me. Maybe even more. He had been picked to train me and apparently had a lot to prove. I tried to refocus. "Adam mentioned you're really good at control because of years of training with Fionn and meditation techniques."

"Did Adam mention why I had to become so good at control?"

I looked into his pained eyes. "No . . . well, not really. He said you had some problems with control when you were younger, but he didn't say too much."

Rían was quiet for a while as he looked out into the fields. "I assumed he would have told you. I owe him my life; we all do."

I didn't know what to say. This was obviously very hard for him to talk about. I sat there in silence, giving him time to continue when he was ready. He eventually took a deep breath and went on.

"I was eight when my mum and dad were killed." His eyes darkened. "I loved them both so much. And . . . I never got a chance to say good-bye. I wasn't even allowed to go to their funeral. I got angrier and angrier about what had happened, and the more bitter I became, the stronger my power got. I couldn't control my emotions, and as a result, my power became more erratic and difficult to manage. I'd wake up at night having a nightmare, only to realize my bed was on fire. I'd scream and scream until Fionn came in and extinguished it. It got so bad that Fionn had to sleep in the room with me, so he was on hand to put out the fire before it took hold. We had to move constantly, since I kept damaging the houses and that would make people start asking questions. But the more we moved the more unsettled I became. It got so bad that if I was in a crap mood, things would just burst into flames around me."

He shook his head slowly. "One time, I was just outside my school and I was in a really foul mood, and I lost it. There were kids everywhere and parents and teachers and I burst into flames. I was endangering their lives and exposing us, but I couldn't control it. Fionn grabbed me and wrapped his body around mine, trying to extinguish the fire. He clung to me, burning, without so much as crying out. I eventually calmed down when I realized what was happening, but by then Fionn was badly burned. He has horrible scars all over his chest, but he has never complained, not once."

I cringed. I couldn't believe all that Rían had been through. He caught my expression and sighed.

"That isn't the worst of it. When I was fifteen, I was a little git. I was sick of all the restrictions forced on me and I tried to rebel. Fionn once caught me lighting a cigarette, you know, with my hand, without a lighter or anything, where people could see. He dragged me home and freaked out on me, told me I was risking exposing us. I just saw red; I didn't even feel it coming."

He was talking so low now I had to strain to hear.

"Áine was in her room listening to music; Adam was outside in the garden mucking about. I just exploded in anger and the element took over. I completely engulfed the house in flames. It was like nothing we had seen before. They radiated out of me with such force, I had no time to try to control them. Fionn couldn't get to me and neither of us could get to the stairs. We could hear Áine screaming for someone to help her. We were all trapped. Then Adam saw what was happening. He managed to evoke his full strength there and then. He was amazing. He used power I had never seen before, and somehow he was able to pull water from the pools, the ponds, the rivers, and the clouds themselves. Everything that he could get. The house was doused inside and out in a deluge that put out every flicker of fire. Then he ran to get Áine."

Rían dropped his head down into his hands, reliving the agony of that day.

"The Knox found us within hours—they don't miss 'phenomena' like that. So that was my fault too. That's when we came back to Kinsale, and when I started my meditation and control training with Fionn. It's been hard, but I've managed to contain my element since then. My family will never suffer from my hands again." He balled his fists up tight. "I guess when you arrived I was worried that the power of the fourth being here might trigger the instability again. But so far, so good." He smiled at me, holding out his hands and inspecting them.

"So does my element being here affect you at all?"

"Well, since you've arrived all of our powers have intensified. It's been harder to keep them suppressed. Adam mentioned that you noticed how the water reacted around him at the marina."

"That was because of me?"

"Yes. We had our powers well under wraps until you showed up. Áine delights in the new strength, but for me and Adam it's a little bit harder to hide it in public. Why do you think I'm loitering around Kinsale and not in Dublin at Trinity? I was due to start the week you arrived."

"Oh, no. Rían, I'm so sorry."

"Forget it. It's not your fault." He looked at me thoughtfully. "You know, our powers, they're triggered by emotions as well as a conscious action. Maybe focusing on that will help?"

"I'll try anything at this point."

He smiled. "You were pissed off at those guys on Halloween, right? Let's get really pissed off and see if that does anything. So, Meg, what really pisses you off? Think about it."

"I guess I'm pissed off that my mom died."

He stood opposite me. "Okay. Focus on the sadness, the pain of her loss. Then grasp the chill you feel."

I put everything into it—but there was nothing.

Rían was getting impatient. "Try harder."

I focused on my mom's face, but Rían started shouting

at me, telling me to focus, to feel something. I knew he was trying to get me angry, but the shouting just wasn't helping.

"Megan, you're holding back—let it out. She was your mother! Don't you feel anything?" He threw his arms up in the air. "You're not trying hard enough, for Christ's sake! Megan, push yourself. Just do it; you're wasting my time!"

Then Rían put his face close to mine. "Megan. She's dead. You'll never see her again."

Tears ran down my face, but my power just wasn't reacting.

"I can't." I sobbed.

"Yes, you can!"

He was shouting so loud that Adam came outside to find out what was going on. When he saw Rían shouting at me, he started running toward us.

"Rían, shut the hell up and lay off her before I make you."

I started to tell Adam what Rían was doing, but Adam stopped me. He stood in front of Rían, squaring up to him.

"If you so much as raise your voice to her again, I'll smash your face in." Adam stood protectively in front of me. "I agreed to this as long as I could keep an eye on things, and I said it would stop if it seemed like she was in any danger. I will not have you within a million miles of her if you go supernova on us."

Rían lost the amused look on his face. "You might want to rein it in and shut your face, Adam; I was only trying to help her."

Adam gritted his teeth. "Don't you tell me to shut my face."

"Or what, little brother—are you going to drench me with a bit of rain?" Rían's eyes flickered orange.

Adam looked furious. "Don't push me," he growled, as a swirling mass of clouds started to form overhead.

I could see the fight brewing and felt powerless to stop it. "Enough!" I cried, pushing my arms out to separate them.

I felt a strange surge of power run though me. The cool feeling ripped through me like electricity, and Rían and Adam were flung through the air. They landed on their backs twenty feet apart.

I stood there in complete shock. What had I done? They both scrambled to their feet.

Adam stared at me. "What the hell was that?"

"I don't know. I just wanted you both to stop fighting. I didn't want you to get hurt and . . . I panicked." I looked down at my hands in awe.

Rían brushed off his clothes and walked toward me, laughing. "Well, I guess we've figured out what pisses you off real good. I'll have to remember that for the next time."

Adam looked confused. "Next time? You mean you were doing that on purpose? Why didn't you tell me?"

Rían laughed into Adam's astonished face. "We tried, but you weren't listening, little brother. Anyway, who cares? It worked." Rían had a satisfied smile on his face.

Adam put his hands up and approached me slowly. "Are you okay?"

I rolled my eyes. "Enough of the drama, Adam. I won't hurt you. I don't even know if I could do that again."

He looked at me, awestruck. "I've said it before and I'll say it again: You are going to be one hell of a powerful girl." He put his arms around me and leaned in for a kiss.

Rían had already turned to walk back to the house. "Guys, at least give me a chance to get into the yard before you go getting all pukealicious," he called. His chuckle floated back to us. "Wait until I tell Fionn what just happened."

Fifteen

TRINITY

At exactly six thirty a.m. on Saturday morning, Fionn's Land Rover pulled into our driveway. He got out of the car and walked up to the house. I opened the door before he knocked and led him into the kitchen, where my dad was having coffee.

"Dad, this is Fionn Christenson."

Dad stood up and reached out his hand to Fionn. "Nice to meet you, Fionn. You're Adam's guardian?"

Fionn took his hand and shook it firmly. "Yes, I'm Adam, Áine, and Rían's guardian. It's nice to meet you, Mr. Rosenberg."

"Call me Caleb."

Fionn let go of his hand. "Caleb it is. I'll take good care of Megan this weekend. I won't let her out of my sight."

I could see from my dad's face, as he eyed how lean and muscular Fionn was, that he didn't doubt that for a second. "Thank you, Fionn." Then Dad looked at me. "Be good and listen to Fionn, and make sure you bring back a copy of Trinity's brochure for me."

I gave him a hug, grabbed my bag, and ran outside to the Land Rover. As soon as I got into the backseat, Adam picked up my hand and raised it to his lips.

Oh, yeah. This is going to be a nice weekend.

When Fionn finished talking with my dad, he came out to the car and climbed in.

"So, how long is it to Dublin?"

Fionn looked at me in his rearview mirror. "It's about three hours, longer if we stop."

It was a warm and bouncy ride. Áine was listening to her iPod on headphones, and Fionn and Rían were in front, guessing at what might come of our visit. That meant I was free to snuggle into Adam's shoulder and relax. I had been stressing about this trip and all I had to learn, but here in Adam's arms I felt safe and sure and very sleepy. I put my arm across his chest and fell fast asleep.

When I woke up he was tracing patterns across my face.

"Morning, beautiful."

I started to sit up and looked out the window. "How long have I been out?"

He stretched, raising his arms above his head. "About two hours."

I moved away to give him more room. "I'm so sorry! You must have been so uncomfortable."

He chuckled at me. "I was more comfortable than you could possibly imagine."

Áine leaned over him. "You were snoring like a rhino; I could hardly hear my music." She shook her iPod at me in annoyance.

I blushed. "I was?"

Adam started laughing. "Don't mind her; it wasn't that bad, and it only lasted for a few minutes."

I was absolutely mortified.

Rían turned around and looked at me with a grin. "Remind me to talk about this during our next session; it's bound to get you ticked off. We could see some serious stuff—maybe even a tornado!"

Everyone burst out laughing. I made a face. "I'll get you all back someday."

When everyone had calmed down, Fionn told us what he was planning for the day. "We will go straight to Trinity and meet up with Hugh, Will, and M.J. We can have lunch with them and then we'll go check into the hotel."

Áine eyed him suspiciously. "And my shopping?"

Fionn tried to look stern. "Shopping can wait until Sunday. We have far too much to focus on today." He stared pointedly at her in his rearview mirror.

She smiled sweetly at him. "Righty-o."

When we pulled into Trinity, Fionn had to give his name to the security guard at the gate. The barrier was lifted and we were waved through. We parked, and I was happy to get out and stretch my legs.

Fionn led us purposefully across the cobbled drive and through the campus. It was beautiful, but the others, who'd all seen it before, continued without a glance. We turned down a little road into a vast square of grass and trees with what looked like a bell tower at the center. The square was surrounded on all sides by impressive stone buildings. Fionn made his way to one of them and approached a door tucked away in a corner. As we got near, a small man with white hair and a beaming smile walked toward us, his arms outstretched.

"Welcome, old friend. It is so good to see you again," he said, hugging Fionn and straining the seams of his brown tweed suit.

Fionn smiled. "Hugh, it's good to see you too. Where are Will and M.J.?"

"In the crypt, buried in books. I haven't been able to get them out of it since we heard the news."

Hugh turned to us. "You're all looking so well. And

this must be the elusive Megan. My, aren't you the rare find." He tipped his head to me. "It's an honor and a privilege. Welcome." He took a handkerchief from his breast pocket and dabbed at his shiny pink face as he turned toward the door. "Come, let's go to the crypt and see if we can prize the others out of there, so we can get some lunch."

We followed him through the ornate wooden door and into a grand office. He closed the door behind us and locked it. We made our way to the back of the room where Hugh unlocked a small door and held it open for us. Inside, a rickety staircase led down into a storeroom full of old books and broken equipment. Hugh came in behind us and went over to a bookshelf. He pulled back a panel, and turned something. Suddenly one of the old flagstones shifted and revealed a wooden hatch in the floor. Hugh pulled it open and stood back.

"After you." He indicated the hole in the ground.

He had to be kidding. I wasn't going down there. But the others started off without hesitating. Adam, sensing my reluctance, went before me, stepping down onto old stone stairs that were very narrow and curved around, so that you couldn't see the bottom of them. They were lit only with very dim wall lights. Adam was already nearly out of sight, so I scurried to catch up with him and grabbed his hand. There was no way I was letting go of it down here.

Hugh, who was behind me, gasped. I glanced over my shoulder at him and saw his smile had disappeared and his brow was furrowed. Weird.

The farther down we went, the smaller the steps got. They eventually led into a tunnel with an arched stone ceiling. At the end of this tunnel was a big wooden door. Hugh walked past us and knocked on it twice. We heard the sound of a huge metal bolt being pulled back, and the door swung open. It was bright inside and my eyes struggled to adjust to the light.

"Welcome, welcome! Come in," a voice from inside called to us.

Adam turned and smiled at me. "You ready?"

I was still a bit dubious, but I squeezed his hand. "I think so."

A tall man with a gray beard walked toward us.

"Fionn, good to see you again so soon." He shook his hand firmly. "How is my favorite family?"

He smiled around at Adam, Áine, and Rían. He hugged them all individually, stopping to talk briefly with Áine. I looked over for Hugh and noticed that he was standing behind a desk speaking in hushed tones to a rotund man. They each looked from me to Adam. I held Adam's hand tighter and tried to tuck myself in behind him.

Adam looked at me. "What's up?"

I pulled him closer so I could speak into his ear. "That

Hugh guy keeps looking at me weird."

Adam glanced over to where Hugh stood, but just then the tall man approached me from the other side.

"And you must be Megan. It is wonderful to meet you. I have so much to ask you."

Fionn came over. "M.J., I think Megan is a little overwhelmed. You can ask her all the questions you like, but let's have lunch first and give her a chance to get to know you."

M.J. was obviously reluctant to wait until after lunch. "I'm sorry, Megan; it's just that we have so much to learn from you." M.J. looked over to where Hugh was still talking to the other man. "Will, come over here and meet Megan."

The fat man with the half-moon glasses stood up. "I'm on my way." He shuffled over, eyeing Adam's hand in mine before greeting us. He led us to a huge mahogany table in the center of the room. "Why don't you all make yourselves comfortable here. We will be ready to go in a few minutes." With that, he rushed back to Hugh.

The table had ten high-backed chairs around it, made of the same shiny dark wood. We all sat down and M.J. immediately started talking with Fionn. I looked around, drinking in the room.

It was like nothing I had seen before. The arched ceilings were supported by vast stone pillars. The walls on all four sides had floor-to-ceiling bookshelves made of the same dark, glossy wood with ornate carvings. Some of the shelves were behind locked metal grilles. There were six huge chandeliers hanging from the central point of each of the arches. In the back of the room two large desks with green leather tops had been pushed together. Brass lamps with green glass shades illuminated piles of books.

"What is this place?" I whispered to Adam.

"This is the crypt," he answered.

I looked around nervously. "Does that mean there are bodies buried here?"

"No, no, nothing like that," he assured me. "It was built as a storage facility and meeting place for the Order of the Mark. This used to be a monastery called All Hallows. It was built on echoed land given by the Order to the All Hallows monks. They protected the crypt and its contents until the monastery fell into disrepair. Then in 1592, when Trinity was founded, the monastery lands were given to the college, but All Hallows ensured that the crypt would be secure. When building commenced on the site, the crypt and sections of the old monastery were hidden beneath the college foundations. The crypt's existence was wiped from all records. Over the centuries there have been many different keepers of the crypt, all working here in Trinity. Very few people know of its existence, so now you're part of a privileged group." He beamed down at me. "Welcome to the club."

Will and Hugh were leafing through their books on the big desks. Hugh glanced up at me nervously again, but looked away quickly when he saw I was looking at him. He and Will were still in the middle of a heated discussion under their breath.

I leaned into Adam. "Adam, I get the distinct impression that Hugh doesn't like me."

He looked up at them suspiciously. "M.J.," Adam interrupted M.J. and Fionn's conversation. "What's up with Will and Hugh? Is there a problem or something?"

M.J. looked over to the two men at the desk. "What are you two fussing about over there? Everyone's hungry. Let's go have lunch. We have reservations," he reminded them.

I couldn't just sit at the table any longer, so I got up and walked over to a bronze statue that was mounted on a marble pedestal. It was a nude of a rather voluptuous woman.

Adam came up behind me. "It's funny that you're drawn to her." I turned to face him. "That's Danu, mother of the original Tuatha de Danann."

I looked back at the bronze and studied her features. "She's very beautiful. What an amazing history your family has."

He put his arms around my waist and kissed the top of my head. He leaned his chin on my hair and rested it there. "It's your history now too."

"Can we get out of here?"

"Sure. The others can follow us." Adam took my hand and we started toward the door we had come in through.

Hugh, Will, and M.J. were standing in our way, staring at us.

Adam half smiled at them. "What's going on?"

Hugh walked to the door and locked it. He turned to face us. "Adam. We need to talk."

Sixteen

REVELATIONS

Fionn stepped up beside us. "Is there a problem?"

The three men looked uncomfortable. Hugh's pink face was now a bright red. He took a step forward with his hands in the air. "We just noticed, er, that Adam seems to have developed a *personal* interest in Megan." He cleared his throat and pulled at the collar of his shirt. "And it appears the feelings are reciprocated."

"And?" Fionn inquired impatiently.

Hugh trembled a little. "I'm so sorry, but this cannot be allowed to continue."

Adam snorted incredulously. "What! What does my relationship with Megan have to do with any of you?"

Will moved beside Hugh, his skin visibly paling. "How long has it been going on?"

Adam laughed. "That is none of your business."

Hugh peered at Fionn. "Have they been intimate?"

"How would I know?" Fionn said. "What is all this about, M.J.? You had better explain yourself before I take my family and drive out of your lives forever."

M.J. pointed at Adam and me. "They cannot be together. A physical union between two Marked Ones is completely forbidden. The result of it could be apocalyptic."

Fionn looked at him scathingly. "So you're telling me Megan and Adam can't be together, ever?"

Hugh was visibly worked up. "Don't underestimate this, Fionn! A physical union between two Marked Ones is unforgivable—the results of such a union are terrifying. Who knows what events—or creatures, for that matter—would follow?"

"Creatures?" Áine's voice piped up from behind us.

"Yes, creatures. If Adam and Megan were to produce a child, it could spell the end of the world. The strength and power of two such parents would produce something of immense force that could not be controlled."

A flush of embarrassment passed through me. I couldn't believe that three strange old men were talking openly about my nonexistent sex life. I'd only known Adam for six weeks—we'd only been together for two!

And they were talking about some monster baby that I was destined to produce. Wanting the shadows to swallow me, I tried to hide myself behind Adam.

"I can't believe you're spouting this crap!" Adam snorted. "We're seventeen, for Christ's sake! Even if any of this rubbish turned out to be true, children aren't exactly on the agenda right now."

"Adam, just you two being together when fully evoked will trigger the imbalance," M.J. said.

"How do you know that?" Adam asked.

"It's in the Druid Scribes. Transcriptions tell clearly of a fire element and a water element who ignored—"

"Stop right there." Anger seemed to flare up in Adam. "This is rubbish. Everyone knows the Druid Scribes are full of crap; they're all fairy stories and folklore."

"What are the Druid Scribes?" I asked. As mortified as I was, if there was something that held information about my relationship with Adam, I wanted to see it.

"It's a testament of the Marked history. It's been passed down through the generations of the Order, with each one adding entries of significance. It's here, in the crypt," M.J. said.

"Can I read it?"

"Most of it is written in a druid script, which can only be deciphered with a key. And even the knowledge of *that* has been lost. It's only been partially transcribed," Adam said.

"How was the knowledge of the key lost?" I gasped.

"Anú. When she wiped out half the Order she took out the senior transcriber," Adam explained, rolling his eyes impatiently.

"I need to see it." I looked back at Adam.

Adam's eyes narrowed. "You can't listen to them! This is all rubbish."

"Adam, even the partially transcribed sections give us enough to know the consequences." M.J. said, glancing from Adam to me.

"What consequences? What happened?" I asked.

M.J. went to his desk and picked up a vast leather-bound book and flicked through pages until he found what he was looking for. He put the book down on the huge table and tapped wildly at the page. "It was recorded here, in 1303. A male fire element called Áed fell in love with his cousin Bébinn, a water element. The results were dire. Their powers combined—they fed off each other. The Order tried to separate them, but their elements took over. The seas of Northern Europe froze over as the elements played havoc with the climate, and an ice age struck. Áed and Bébinn would not listen—they couldn't be stopped. The entries recording the phenomenon are difficult to translate, but we've been able to capture snapshots."

I stared at the pages of strange script that looked more like hieroglyphics than any language I'd ever seen.

"In 1315 there was rain that fell for more than one hundred days, and crops failed all over Europe," M.J. continued. "By 1319 there were epidemics and even reports of cannibalism. Then in 1322 Bébinn became pregnant and Áed died within days. The scribes tell of a twenty-five-year pregnancy, which devoured Bébinn as the creature within absorbed her element and every drop of life she had in her. Then it launched itself on the world in the form of a plague—a plague that wiped out half of Europe."

"Crap, crap, and more crap," Adam spat. "Those are your interpretations of the entries. They're just legends written to explain historical events. What about the entry about the *other* Marked pair? The one that came after Áed and Bébinn? You can't pick your tale to suit your agenda."

"Neither can you, Adam," Hugh replied, stepping forward. "The record of another couple only proves the point that the elements attract each other so much that serious considerations like consequence and obligation get ignored. The second pairing wasn't even named, and their relationship hasn't been translated."

"Which proves there wasn't anything worth translating!" Adam shouted in irritation.

"Adam, there's also the Fifth Prophecy to consider," Hugh added, putting his hand on Adam's shoulder. "You know that. The Order revolves around keeping the bloodlines clean to avoid such a situation."

Adam shrugged Hugh's hand off. "Of course I've considered the Fifth Prophecy. It would be reckless not to! But the Druid Scribes, ugh. Don't even go there," Adam warned through gritted teeth.

I wanted to ask about the Fifth Prophecy, but I suddenly realized that Adam was dangerously close to a meltdown. He was shaking, and beads of perspiration had formed around his hairline.

"Megan, step away from Adam," Fionn urged.

"Why? What's wrong?"

"Just come over to me." Fionn stretched out his arm and stepped forward.

"Adam, what . . ." I looked up at him, then froze. Adam stared forward. His eyes had darkened into huge blackened pupils surrounded by a swirling vivid blue.

"Megan, listen to Fionn. Come over to us." Rían beckoned me toward him.

"What's happening to him? What's wrong with his eyes?"

Rían slowly moved closer to me. "His element is taking over; you need to—"

Adam pulled me closer and glared at Rían. "I need to get out of here," he said in a gasp.

"Adam, don't do this," M.J. said. "Look at yourself! Your element is overreacting to the potential separation from Megan and her element. The dependence has already begun. I know the elemental pull is strong, but don't confuse this with real human emotion, because it's not and it's dangerous."

"I'm not talking about this now!" Adam shot M.J. a murderous glare. "I need to think. Now open the door."

None of them moved.

"If you don't open the door, I'm sure Rían will," Adam growled.

"I'm right here for you." Rían stepped forward with two balls of flames in his hands.

Hugh moved to the door nervously. "Please calm down, everyone; I'm opening the door."

Adam stalked out, pulling me with him.

Before we could get out, though, Hugh grabbed Adam's sleeve. "Adam, please think about what you're doing. This is only going to get worse."

"Let go of me," Adam said in a hiss.

We walked back out to the great cobbled square, followed closely by Rían, Áine, and Fionn.

Fionn ran to catch up with Adam and me. "Adam, try to control it. Take deep breaths."

Adam kept on walking.

"Adam, hold up. You need to listen to me. We have to get back to the hotel and talk."

Adam spun around to Fionn in a fury. "My relationship with Megan is not open for discussion!"

Fionn looked at him sympathetically. "I'm not saying

I agree with them. But for now you need to control yourself."

"Adam, you've got to focus, man. You nearly lost it in there," Rían added. He put his hands on Adam's shoulders and steadied him, forcing Adam to meet his eyes. "Bro, are you listening to me? We can work this out, but you need to keep it under control, for Megan's sake." He looked at me, then back to Adam. Above us ominous gray clouds were gathering at a ferocious speed, darkening the sky and blocking out the sun. "Quick, talk to him, Megan; he'll listen to you."

I put my arms around Adam's waist. "Adam, look at me, please." I reached up and put a hand on either side of his face and tilted his head toward me. "Look at me." The black and swirling blue of his unfamiliar eyes focused on my face. Suddenly I felt aware of an icy sensation in my chest. It pulsated, reacting to the darkness in Adam's eyes. Hiding my anxiety, I smiled at him. "You should listen to Rían and Fionn. I don't like this either, but they're on our side; they will help us."

His eyes flickered green for a moment as he fought for control.

"Adam, you're stronger than this. You control the element—it doesn't control you."

Large splatters of rain started falling around us. Everyone in the courtyard was running for cover.

"Come back to me," I pleaded.

"You're right," he said, exhaling a big breath. "Of course you're right." The cloud that hovered angrily above us shuddered a little before falling in a torrent. His soaked hair clung to his skin where the rain ran down his pale face in rivulets. Slowly, his pupils contracted and his irises returned to their usual green. "I'm sorry," he said, shaking a little. "That's never happened to me before." He slumped into my arms and I held him. "What I feel is real; I just know it is," he whispered. "Please believe me?"

"I believe you," I whispered back to him. The pulsating iciness in my chest dulled, but I was still conscious of its presence.

"Adam, let's get you out of here," Fionn said, approaching us slowly.

Adam nodded. "I'm sorry, Fionn. I lost control." He looked down at his shaking hands.

We got back to the car and all climbed in. The tension was unbearable. As Fionn started the engine, the news blared out from the radio:

"Despite Met Éireann's forecast of clear skies today, sudden torrential rain in the past few minutes has stopped play at the Republic of Ireland's friendly with New Zealand. Spectators claimed that—"

Rían flicked off the radio and we rode the rest of the way in silence. We parked the car and collected our bags, then waited for Fionn to check us in. Áine looked particularly upset. I'd have liked to say something to make her feel better, but I was just trying my best to keep it together for Adam's sake. He still looked dangerously close to snapping. My hand ached where he held it tightly, apparently unwilling to let it go.

Fionn walked toward us. "Right, Áine and Megan, you're sharing." He gave us our key card and room number.

"Adam, you're with Rían." He held out the key card to Rían. "I'm in two oh five. Go up and get yourselves settled and meet in my room in ten minutes, okay? Adam, you come with me; we need to talk."

We walked to the elevator in silence. When we got out on the second floor and walked up the carpeted corridor, Áine stopped. "This is us."

I looked at Adam. He still hadn't let go of my hand. Fionn kept walking past us.

"Come on, Adam," he said over his shoulder. Adam looked at me again, then let go of my hand reluctantly. I could feel the blood start flowing through the veins that had been constricted before. He watched me walk into my room. Áine closed the door on his troubled face.

She walked in, chucking the key card on the dressing table and her bag on the floor, then grabbed a towel from the bathroom and flung herself on one of the beds.

"Wow. That was so intense," she said, rubbing her hair absentmindedly.

I walked over to my bed, took off my soaked jacket, and sat down heavily. "Will he be all right?"

"He'll be fine. Fionn will make sure of it. . . . And I thought *I* had problems."

"What do you mean?"

She smiled. "I'm sure you don't want to hear all my woes today, of all days."

"Oh, please tell me; I could really use some distraction."

She looked at me thoughtfully for a few seconds. "Well, as you know I was the only female Marked One, until you appeared. So when I was born, the Order picked a male for me, an intended, my 'perfect partner.' He'll eventually be my husband, and he and I will be in charge of producing children in hopes that we will be able to have four Marked Ones." She shuddered visibly. "To think there is an eighteen- or nineteen-year-old boy somewhere being groomed to be my husband, to marry me! Ugh! I'm sure he's probably lovely and all that, but the idea of being forced to marry a complete stranger, the way my mom did, is so awful." She gazed off into space for a moment, then glanced up at me. "You know, she never loved my dad."

I groped for words, shocked. "I'm sure she did."

She shook her head. "She was in love with Fionn, and Fionn was in love with her. But she did her duty and married the one chosen for her. And in doing her duty, she broke her own heart and devastated poor Fionn."

Áine smiled wearily at my disbelieving face.

"Fionn doesn't talk about it much; I think it's all too painful for him. Anyhow, I was hoping that you would be the answer to all my troubles. You're so in love with Adam. I was sure, up to today, that you would eventually get married and have loads of Marked babies and I would be off the hook. But now that's looking less and less likely."

My face fell; I was devastated by the outlook she had just given me a glimpse of. Today was supposed to be about the four elements and my evocation ritual. But now it was all about Adam and me and our future . . . and babies. All that felt so far-off. But what scared me more was the thought that what I felt might not be real. Was it just my element reacting strongly with Adam's? If I gave up my element, would Adam stop wanting me? Would his attraction die with my power?

"Oh, crap, I didn't mean to upset you," Áine said sadly, coming over to sit next to me. "Look, we'll come up with something and it will all work out. Please, Megan, don't cry." She wiped away my tears. "You have no idea just how much he needs you."

I turned to her. "What if it's just his element that needs me?"

She looked at me seriously. "Megan, he only started living when you came into his life. I know my brother. This is not just elemental attraction; this is the real deal.

You have to believe him."

"I do. I feel the same way," I whispered. I believed Adam's feelings to be true, but I couldn't convince myself of where those feelings originated—from him or his element.

"I know you do. I only slag you and wind you up because I'm dead jealous. I wish I could experience that intensity, feel that kind of attraction. I just don't see it in my future."

I hugged her. "Don't say that. It will happen for you. I'm sure of it."

There was a knock at the door.

"I wonder who that could be," Áine said, rolling her eyes.

I ran to the door, needing to see him. I pulled the door open and fell into his arms. I breathed a sigh of relief. "Adam."

"Hi," he whispered into my neck. "Are you all right?"

I nodded my head close into his chest. "I'm fine. Are you okay?"

"I'll be fine." He kissed me tenderly. "I'm so sorry about earlier. I don't know what came over me."

"Don't worry."

He looked over my shoulder to Áine. "Are you ready? Let's get this over with." The three of us walked to Fionn's room, where Rían was waiting for us.

"Right, we're all here," Fionn began. "I'm sorry it has

come to this. The last thing I want to do is interfere in your lives, but it has to be done. Will, M.J., and Hugh are our friends. And they are genuinely concerned about the effects your relationship will have on this world, as unlikely as that sounds."

"But, Fionn, this is all speculation!" Adam protested.

"You're right; there is no hard evidence, but nonetheless, if there's one thing I've learned over the years in the Order, it's that prophecies and fables have a habit of becoming fact. We would be wise to observe a little caution until we have more details."

I stood there listening to them discussing the rights and wrongs of our relationship and its effects on our world. It soon became very clear to me that there was only one course of action. After hearing Áine's tales of her mother's sacrifice and Fionn's heartache, I knew what I had to do.

"Couldn't I just stop training?" I interjected. "I could give up my element."

"No, Meg," Adam said. "You don't know what you'd be giving up."

"Adam's right, Megan; you can't do that," Rían said. "You have to look at the bigger picture."

"This only becomes a problem after I evoke my power. I could try to delay it and buy us more time," I pleaded.

Fionn put out his hand. "Regardless of what we want

and don't want, you must remember that your first priority here is to the alignment. As much as it pains me to say it, for now your personal life comes second to your calling. Megan, trust me; I know how you're feeling, but for the greater good you need to see this through." He looked from Adam to me. "Look, Adam's right. The Druid Scribes are pretty flaky and the translations are seriously flawed. While we can't ignore them, we can take comfort in the fact there is a chance the Order has it wrong. The untranslated story of the unnamed pair may even hold the answers to your problems. Let's proceed with caution. I take it that you two weren't planning on starting a family in the near future?"

I flushed with embarrassment, but Adam's strained face broke into a little smile. "Not just yet."

"Good. Let's keep it that way; cool your relationship down until after the alignment. In the meantime let's get our hands on the Druid Scribes. If they hold the answers we are looking for, we'll find them. Okay?"

We nodded in agreement and Fionn went on. "Adam, how are you feeling? Have you got your power under control?"

Adam nodded.

"Okay, then. I think we should go meet Hugh and the others for lunch." With that, Fionn, Rían, and Áine got up to leave.

I tugged Adam's hand, pulling him away from the

others. "I don't want to choose between you and the power," I whispered.

"You won't have to," Adam reassured me, running his finger down the side of my face. "Fionn will find something in the Druid Scribes."

"And if he doesn't?"

Adam didn't reply.

"The Order says we can't be together if I evoke. And I can't imagine not being with you. But I feel this pull in me—I want the element too. I can't help feeling like you, me, and the elements are all connected somehow, and I don't know if I can choose one over the other." My heart was pounding as I rushed on. "And what if they're right? What if our attraction *is* based on the elements? If I decide not to evoke, I might lose you anyway! There has to be a third option. There *has* to be a way I can keep the element and you too. How can I separate the two things that make me feel whole?"

Adam cupped my face and looked into my eyes. "You won't have to; I promise. I'll find an answer. I will never give you up."

"If we don't find a solution, I'll do my best to stop the evocation—at least that will give us a chance."

"Don't do that."

"I'm going to try." I turned away from Adam and called after Fionn to get him to come back.

"No!" Adam said, raising his voice.

"You're not sure, are you? You're as scared as me!"

His strained eyes met mine. "I'm not scared," he protested. But I saw it in his eyes—the fear that his feelings *were* tied to my element.

"Fionn," I called again, feeling light-headed with the implications of Adam's resistance.

"Yes?" Fionn said, coming back into the room.

"I don't want to evoke yet. We need you to get the Order to wait until the last moment possible to perform the ritual."

Fionn looked at me for a second, then flicked his eyes over to Adam. "Are you sure about this?"

I nodded.

"This will solve nothing, Megan. Don't do this," Adam said.

Fionn sighed. "I don't know how much time I can buy you, but I'll see what I can do."

"Fionn!" Adam pleaded.

"It's her decision, Adam."

Seventeen

DELIBERATIONS

The Dublin Order was waiting for us when we got back to Trinity, and we gathered at the huge table and sat down. Áine sat across from me, a picture of desolation. I felt terrible for her, but I knew she would understand my decision. Rían sat beside her, dark and silent. He had been entrusted to train me and had been doing so well; it had given him purpose. Now his scowl had returned, his eyebrows back in that flat line above his dark eyes. Then there was Adam, sitting by my side.

Everything else paled in significance. I could not live without him. As much as it upset me to hurt the others, it was nothing compared to the stabbing pain I felt when

I thought of being parted from him. What we had was powerful. Forces beyond our understanding brought us together and held us there. How could anything as beautiful and pure as that be dangerous? But I wasn't about to take any chances. This decision might be the wrong one, but I had to try. It would buy us time for Fionn to find a solution, and for Adam and me to figure this out.

Fionn stood at the head of the table. "Today was not the day we were all expecting, but I don't think we should forget the reason we're all here. Megan has found her way to us." He smiled at me. "Now, new information has come to light about a serious issue regarding Adam and Megan's relationship, but let's not get caught up in the technicalities of that for the time being. Our main purpose for meeting was so that Hugh, Will, and M.J. could meet Meg and talk to us about how best to train her and prepare her for evoking her full power."

I started to interrupt Fionn, but he held up his hand to silence me.

"Megan appears to have immense power. She has surprised us all at how well she has embraced her element. It now seems very likely that Megan will be able to evoke her power before the summer solstice."

Adam was still sitting rigidly beside me. His face was like stone, his eyes narrowed into two slits and his jaw set in a stiff line.

"We were going to do a demonstration today," Fionn

continued, "but in light of our new circumstances, I feel it's best not to put Megan under any more pressure."

Will removed his half-moon spectacles and fiddled with them nervously. "Fionn, can you give us some details of Megan's powers to date?"

Fionn sat down and leaned back in his chair. "Well, she can repel fire, and she physically moved Rían and Adam simultaneously."

M.J. leaned forward, rubbing his beard in excitement. "She did what?"

Fionn nodded in M.J.'s direction. "Yes, Megan will be very powerful. However . . ."

"However?" repeated Hugh.

Fionn looked over to me and back around the table. "After today's big 'reveal,' Megan has decided to slow training in a bid to delay evocation."

Hugh went all purple in the face. "She can't! We have been waiting so long for a fourth. It's a miracle she's here at all! She has responsibilities. You all do. You can't shirk them so lightly."

Fionn shook his head. "As I understand it, their being together poses no threat until after evocation. They deserve an opportunity to find a solution before it comes to that."

Will looked pleadingly at Fionn. "But she must be made to understand the importance, the significance of what she is."

Adam was staring at the table. Now his gaze rose slowly. "Stop speaking about Megan like she isn't here. If you want to say something to her, then say it."

He looked around the room, his glare making Will, Hugh, and M.J. shrink back into their seats.

Adam had tremendous presence. I saw in that moment that they all respected him, even feared him. In all the time I'd spent with the DeRíses, I'd only ever thought to fear Rían. I realized now that there were three incredibly powerful people here today, people who could wipe out everything in this room—in this college, even—with the flick of a finger. They wouldn't do it, but the potential was there, and the three men of the Dublin Order seemed acutely aware that Adam was teetering on the edge.

"Megan, I'm sorry." Will cleared his throat and looked nervously at Adam. "I'm just not used to having another member of the family. In some ways you still feel fictitious to me." He smiled kindly. "But please understand. The Order has waited thousands of years to perform the alignment ritual. We could never get the four elements at full power at the same time. Now we're so close. You have the ability to transform the world, to align the seasons, the weather, and seismic activity. You could help end droughts, plagues, and famines, and alter billions of people's lives for the better. Don't you want to be part of that?"

I felt guilt rising up inside me, but I stood firm.

"I am going to continue working on my power, but I'm just going to tone it down a little, temporarily. Fionn is going to help us find a solution. I still want to evoke before the time is up. But just not yet."

"Evocation can be difficult; it might take several attempts. What if you misjudge your abilities and don't develop the strength required for the ritual? Adam, speak to her," M.J. pleaded with him. "She needs to be fully evoked by March at the latest. Otherwise she'll never be ready for the summer solstice alignment."

Adam took my hand firmly. "We'll make sure she's ready for the ritual when the time comes. What is important is just that she evokes before the solstice. The alignment can wait until the next summer solstice, and you know it. You've waited this long—another year won't make a difference. For now, I'm supporting her decision."

Áine sat forward. "I'm with Megan. I'd do it too, given her circumstances."

Rían shifted in his chair and put his hand on the table in front of him. "This is what Megan wants. She's strong. I'm confident she can do it."

"And I'm with them too," Fionn added. "So there is no debate. Anyway, I'm not entirely convinced of the danger posed by Adam and Megan's being together. I propose that we continue training, but very carefully.

Megan will maintain her power until she's ready for the next level. Megan and Adam are very responsible, and I'm confident they won't put the world in any danger in the next six months. In the meantime, we'll dissect the Druid Scribes for the truth and unlock the secrets of the unnamed pair." He looked around the room. "Are we all in agreement?"

There was some mumbling and nodding of heads.

"I suggest we set a tentative date of . . . February twentieth," Fionn continued. "That's exactly four months to the solstice. That gives us time to schedule another ritual, just in case the first one fails."

My heart fluttered as I mulled over the implications of my decision. I knew I was being selfish and the guilt made my head spin. I rested my cheek on the table, letting the coolness of the glossy wood ease the heat from my skin.

"Are you okay?" Adam asked, bending down to me.

"I'm fine. I think I need some air," I whispered.

Adam stood up. "I'm going to take Megan out for a while. We'll meet you back here later."

"Sure," Fionn said. "We'll see you outside."

Adam nodded and we left the room quietly, making our way up the tunnel and the winding stairs, out of the hatch, locking doors as we went. Finally we emerged into the evening light.

I went into his arms. "Thank you."

"For what?" he asked gently. "What have I done that deserves thanks? I put you in this situation."

"For letting me do it my way."

"I can't stop you." He shook his head slowly. "I know that you're worried about my feelings for you, but they *are* my own. Not my element's. I'm sure of it. I just don't want you to sacrifice your gift because of me. I don't know what to do. I'm potentially denying you your power by not giving you up, but I'm too selfish to." He looked down at me sadly. "I always thought I was the strong one in the family. I see now that I'm the weakest link."

I hugged him fiercely. "You are not weak. I'm the selfish one." I smoothed my hand down his face, trying to wipe away some of the worry around his eyes. "You never know; it might all work out." I nodded back in the direction of the door we had just come through. "They might find the answer."

Adam shook his head. "I can't believe our fate is being dictated by the Druid Scribes."

I took his hand and started pulling him toward one of the greens. "Will you show me around?"

He faltered a little. "I guess."

I laughed at him. "Come on; you can do better than that." I stood on my toes and kissed him gently.

"Well, okay," he said. A small smile broke across his face. He picked me up off the ground and kissed me long and hard right there in the middle of the square. People who passed by stared at us, but I didn't care.

"Come on; we'd better get that brochure for your dad," he said as he came up for air.

"That would be wise," I agreed, laughing. It seemed so trivial, given everything we had learned today, but it was kind of nice to think about something besides the elements.

Adam showed me all around the campus. It was too late to get in to see the famous Book of Kells in the library, but he showed me the beautiful buildings: the Campanile, a stunning bell tower, and Parliament Square and the very pretty chapel. We even walked around a bit of Dublin, with its beautiful architecture and little streets. Under any other circumstances, it would have been a magical evening, and even with all that was hanging over our heads, I still felt the joy of simply being with him.

It was almost eight p.m. when we reluctantly started heading back to the gates at Trinity. The closer we got, the tenser Adam seemed.

They were all waiting for us outside. Áine saw us first and ran up to intercept us. She hooked her arm through mine. "Are we all good?"

"I'm not sure," I said, looking over at Adam.

We started walking in the direction of the restaurant the Dublin Order had originally chosen for lunch, but they had since changed the reservations to dinner. Áine looked at Adam, who was gazing off in the other direction. "I know he looks like he's going to snap, but he won't. He just needs some time. I'm so sorry about this stupid Druid Scribes thing," she said under her breath.

"I'm sorry too. I know how much all of this means to you; I just wish there were something I could do to make everyone happy."

She looked at me kindly. "Don't stress yourself out. This has always been my path, my burden. I envy you, though. You get a chance to opt out. I wish I had that choice."

"I'm not going to opt out now. I'm just buying some time before I have to make that decision." I squeezed her arm reassuringly. "We're in this together, but I need Adam, and Adam needs me."

She nodded in agreement. "Look, let's forget about it for tonight. I want to enjoy myself while I still can. I got to go to a few shops this evening. You want to see what I bought?"

Adam excused himself and caught up with Fionn, where he got into a deep conversation. Áine then proceeded to tell me all about every shop she had been in, giving me every last detail about a pair of killer heels she had bought. I listened, feigning interest, but kept a close eye on Adam. He glanced at me now and again, giving me a forced little smile or a wink.

When we reached the restaurant, Adam sat down on my right. Áine was just sitting down on my left when Will called to her.

"Won't you sit with me, Áine? I'd love to catch up with you."

"Sure," she agreed, moving over to the other side of the long rectangular table. Hugh came up and took her place beside me. "May I?"

"Of course." I pulled out the chair for him.

"Thank you," he said, sitting down. "Really, what must you think of us? I know that the way we acted was unforgivable. We were just so shocked. We're honestly not that bad." He paused, then gave me a shy smile. "Let's start again, shall we?" He held out his hand for me to shake it. "Hello, Megan, lovely to meet you. I'm Hugh McDonagh."

I smiled slightly. Hugh was charming, like a little old elf. I shook his hand.

Adam was straining to hear what we were saying. He was holding my other hand firmly under the table.

"Any chance you'll accept my apology, Adam?" Hugh inquired, leaning around me.

Adam raised an eyebrow. "I will." He shook Hugh's hand. "But tread carefully." He smiled, but I could see he meant the warning seriously.

The atmosphere around the table eased and the evening became quite enjoyable.

After the main course, Fionn, Rían, Adam, and M.J. were deep in conversation. Áine and Will were still catching up.

"Hugh, what actually happens during an 'alignment'?" I asked, turning to him. "I've heard so much about it, but I still don't understand what happens."

Hugh looked delighted with the question. "Ah, the alignment. It's a correction. The last full alignment was done by Danu herself. Since then, the four physical elements have been existing in their individual states, growing, moving, evolving, and being utilized by the people of Earth. Over time, the balance has been thrown into disarray, as the elements are constantly in a state of flux. The elemental alignment connects the holders of the elemental powers with the physical elements. All the strength and beauty of the four is allowed to flow through each of you, until each element is restored to its original and perfect state, a state that will correct all the imbalances that have caused misery and destruction in the world. Imagine the serenity of an aligned world—chaos turned to harmony. It's our life's work. It's hard to contain the excitement," Hugh said, clasping his hands together.

"Really? The world would be so dramatically affected?"

"It wouldn't appear dramatic to the casual onlooker. The damage from the imbalance will take some time to heal. But nature will begin to correct itself as soon as the four elements are synced."

"Wow. That sounds amazing."

"It will be. That's why it *must* happen." Hugh leaned into me and quietly said, "And on that note, I'd like to tell you a little story."

"What kind of a story?" I asked.

"I don't want to alarm you, but you need to know. Love and Carriers do not go hand in hand. As a Carrier of the Mark you have a great responsibility to the world, to every other human. You exist to protect them, and with that power comes great responsibility. You're not the first of your kind to fall deeply in love." He looked over at Adam to make sure he was still engrossed in conversation. "Adam's mother, Emma . . . she was a lovely girl, delightful. She grew up in the Order."

"Fionn told me about her."

"Did he tell you the full story?" he inquired. "I doubt it. Emma grew up with Fionn, and their friendship blossomed into love. There was no denying their connection, but when the council saw what was happening, they decided it was time to marry her to her intended, a young man by the name of Stephen DeRís. She was devastated to be separated from Fionn, but she knew her duty and married Stephen.

"Fionn knew his duty too. He vowed to protect them, as their personal bodyguard. He watched another man marry the woman he loved. And still he stood by silently, doing his duty. It was a life of sacrifice, but it was for the greater good. Remember, by denying yourself your power, you are also denying Adam his birthright, and Áine and Rían too. I don't want to force your hand or burden you, but please"—he put his hands on mine—"give your decision more thought before it is too late."

"But why do Carriers of the Mark have intendeds? Why can't the Marked pick their own partners?"

"The genetic process is complex, as I'm sure Fionn has told you. The Marked gene is recessive. We've only been successful in producing Marked children though blood-lines that we know are pure and carry the neutral gene that doesn't suppress the Mark."

"So Fionn and Emma wouldn't have had Marked children?"

"It's unclear. Fionn doesn't carry the neutral gene, and we couldn't take the chance that they would have unmarked children. Our Carriers are too precious, too rare. We only pair them with neutral carriers from proven genetic lines. Look, don't concern yourself with all this now. It's just something I thought you should know. You have to consider your *own* future as much as Adam's."

"My own?"

"Yes. The Marked line will need to continue. You and Áine hold that key."

My mind was reeling. Áine had spoken of her intended, but I didn't think for one second of the possibility of an intended for me.

Adam finished his conversation and dipped his head low to my ear. "Are you okay?"

"I'm fine," I said, and smiled at him though my heart was thudding in my chest.

After dinner, we said our farewells. It had been an exhausting day and we all felt the stress of the occasion. Adam kissed me good night and went to his room with Rían, and I went with Áine to ours. She was still babbling on about all her new stuff when she came out of the bathroom in her pajamas.

"Oh, I forgot to get my toothbrush from Adam's bag; I'll be back in a sec," she said, walking out the door.

I was already in bed, even though I knew it would be impossible to sleep. It had been a day of revelations, and now, after Hugh's story, I didn't know what to do. I wanted Adam more than anything else, but there was so much at stake.

The door of the room opened, letting in a beam of light from the bright hall outside. I sat up.

"Did you find it?"

"I don't know about *it*, but I certainly found what I was looking for," Adam's voice said softly in the darkness.

"Adam, what are you doing here?" I couldn't hide the elation in my voice.

He walked over to me and crawled onto my double bed. "Áine's little present to us. She thought we deserved a break." He smiled down at me.

"Áine. She's the best. Remind me to thank her in the morning," I said, feeling a little self-conscious in my pajamas.

"Do you mind?" He lowered himself down beside me.

"No, not at all," I replied, blushing into my pillow.

He pulled me in close to him. I luxuriated in his smell, his warmth, the feeling of his skin on mine. How could I ever give this up?

"So, should we be on the lookout for a great meteorite to crash into Earth, wiping out all life on the planet?" I joked, trying to break the fizzing of excitement that ran though me.

"I'd say we're safe enough for now." He laughed softly in my ear.

He kissed me gently and combed his fingers through my hair. He ran his hand over my body, caressing the skin where it was exposed.

Since meeting Adam, I'd imagined moments like this, but my daydreams were nothing compared to the tantalizing sensations I felt as his skin brushed mine. I gasped in pleasure.

Adam flicked his hand away. "I'm so sorry; I got caught up in the moment." I could hear the mortification in his voice.

"No, don't stop."

"No. I shouldn't have come in here." He sat up.

"Please don't go."

"It's just that my head gets so fuzzy when I'm with you."

"Adam, it's all right. Please stay," I said, pulling him back down beside me.

Relaxing a little, he turned me over and curled into my back. "You're sure?"

"I'm sure."

"You're amazing. I will never lose you," he whispered. "I mean it, so don't go trying to be all noble for our sakes. I know how Hugh works. I'm sure he's been spinning tales to you about your duty and self-sacrifice."

I turned back to him. "You mean your mom and Fionn?"

"Yeah, but I bet Hugh didn't tell you the whole story."

"There's more?"

"There's a lot more, but it's not my story to tell; it's Fionn's. I'll ask him to speak to you. In the meantime, don't go getting ideas. I'll make this work. All right?"

"Do you promise?"

"I promise."

I cuddled down into the crook of his arm. I felt so safe there, so sure, even with our future up in the air. Adam's fingers trailed up and down my arm; I closed my eyes and just enjoyed the caress that eased me gently to sleep.

I woke with a start. Adam was still fast asleep. I marveled at the way his eyelashes grazed his cheeks, his face smooth and stress-free. Daylight was coming through a crack in the curtain and it sent a thin beam of light across his cheek and down his torso. He opened his eyes a bit and smiled sleepily at me.

"Why, hello," I said, and gave him a kiss.

"Hello to you too. It's nice to see you in your morning glory."

"Is my hair all over the place?"

He reached up and stroked my cheek. "You're stunning."

I leaned down to kiss him again, but the phone rang and jolted us out of the moment.

"You'd better answer that," he said, "considering I'm not meant to be here."

I couldn't help giggling a little as I picked up the call. "Hello?"

It was Áine. "Megan, it's time to swap back. I think Fionn will be doing rounds shortly. I guess you two didn't get up to anything too serious last night, as the Earth hasn't imploded!"

"I heard that!" Adam grabbed the phone. "Áine, as much as I love you and appreciate last night, sod off and mind your own business."

I heard laughter ringing through the line as Adam hung up.

"I guess I'd better get going," he said.

"Last night was pretty great."

"Pencil me in for another sleep date soon." He grinned.

"Definitely."

He left, and a moment later Áine walked in. She jumped onto the unused bed and turned to me with wide eyes. "Well, how did you get on?"

I blushed. "Thank you so much for that. It was the best present you could have given me."

She beamed. "No problem—but I will be looking for you to return the favor one of these days."

I laughed. "You're on. Did Rían mind your bunking with him?"

She shook her head. "Not at all! It was his idea in the first place, actually."

We got dressed quickly and met the guys for breakfast. Then Fionn checked us all out and we headed out to the Land Rover. The ride back to Kinsale was quiet; we were all lost in our own thoughts. We got into town around lunchtime, and since my dad wasn't expecting me back until the evening, I decided to go home with the DeRíses.

As soon as we got into the house, Fionn went into the kitchen and put the kettle on, while Adam and I headed out to the backyard.

"Want a coffee?" he called.

"Yes! That would be great," I answered.

Soon Fionn appeared with three steaming coffees, and

we all settled down on the steps. "What is it, Adam?" he asked, looking concerned. "There's something on your mind."

"I think Megan needs to hear your story. Hugh tried to coerce her with a guilt trip last night."

"Christ, that's low," Fionn grumbled, looking more frustrated than I'd seen him in a while.

I started to tell him that he didn't have to give me the full story if he didn't want to, but he shook his head. "I don't mind telling you; I just can't believe they would stoop to pulling my story on you. I guess I underestimated their determination. How much did they tell you?"

I felt awful. I couldn't believe I had to regurgitate such personal information back to him. "Well," I began slowly, "they told me that you and Emma were in love, but you both knew that it was best to part, for the good of the Order."

Fionn laughed bitterly. "That sounds about right for them! What spin!"

"Wait, what really happened?" I asked, startled.

Fionn's eyes clouded over. "Oh, I loved Emma, all right. And she loved me. You and Adam remind me so much of us back then. But we always knew there was another man who had been chosen as her intended. Stephen DeRís. Stephen was a great guy, groomed for the role. Emma didn't love him, but she was fond of him. And she was under a lot of pressure to do her duty.

I respected her wishes and those of my superiors, but I demanded to stay with her as her guardian." His voice roughened. "Every day was a heartache; every touch was a stabbing pain. And when the children were born, I saw the babies that should have been mine. She felt the same, but remained faithful to Stephen and to the Order.

"After Rían, Adam, and Áine were born, the Order had the four elements. Stephen, having done his duty, wanted out of the marriage, as did Emma. But the Order would not allow it. They had some time to go until the children would be strong enough to perform the alignment with their mother, and the Order wanted to play it safe, just in case anything happened to any of the Marked Ones. They wanted another child of direct descent as a backup, and they wouldn't permit the separation until they had it."

I was shocked. I couldn't imagine feeling so trapped—and knowing that the person you loved was just out of reach. I looked over at Adam. He was as rapt as I was.

Fionn's eyes darkened as he continued his story. "Emma was distraught. She had sacrificed her life for the Order, they had the four elements, and still they would not free her. Emma and I were still passionately in love, and one evening it all became too much to bear. We couldn't be kept apart any longer. Emma told Stephen and he was fine with it. He knew that we should have been together from day one. So we continued the happy-family charade for the Order's sake, but Emma and I were together, as good as married. Then Emma got pregnant with my baby. We were overjoyed. The Order, thinking the baby was Stephen's, agreed to release Stephen and Emma as soon as the baby was born. But—" His voice broke off and he closed his eyes, fighting back whatever painful images filled his mind.

Adam went over to Fionn and patted him on the shoulder.

Fionn pinched the bridge of his nose and took a deep breath. "I respect your strength, Megan; I wish we had been as strong as you. Love is never worth giving up on. If I could do it all over, I'd tell the Order to stick it, and run away with her. We would have been happy. The Marked line would still have continued. The Order doesn't always know best. I will not have you and Adam suffer the same fate as Emma and me—or as Adam's father, for that matter. Three lives wasted over rules and old traditions. The Knox snuffed out the lives of Emma and Stephen before they could *really* start living, and a baby girl before she got the chance to live at all. I will not let that happen to you. We'll find a solution."

I was so moved by the story it took me a while before I could speak. "There was something else Hugh said, about your not being her match because you weren't a carrier of a neutral gene. He said the Marked gene is recessive—"

"They said my children wouldn't have been Marked,

right?" Fionn said with a twisted smile.

"He implied it. Hugh said they couldn't be sure."

"Hah! They think they have the whole genetic thing worked out, but they don't. They got lucky with Emma and Stephen. The recessive gene is still a mystery. I don't care what they say."

He stood up and hugged me. "You are as much a daughter to me as Áine. When the Sidhe selected you, you received Emma's Mark. You carry with you a little bit of her and the daughter I never got to meet." He ran his finger over my Mark. "I feel as if their spirit is in you." Tears sprang into his eyes and he turned to walk into the house, lost in thought.

"You see," Adam said, "whatever happens, we stay together. Fionn will fight to the death to protect you and what's best for you—which, incidentally, is me," he added with a sly smile. "Now, I think it may be time to take you back to your dad. He's probably wondering what we DeRíses are doing to you, keeping you away for so long!"

Eighteen

DAY TRIP

After we got back from Dublin we continued our regular training schedule, but we were much more cautious than before. I found it easier to trigger my power now. I could feel it—deep in my chest, an iciness served as a constant reminder that my element was always there, just below the surface. And my Mark was stinging again. Not all the time, but occasionally it would flare up. I hoped the power wasn't growing too fast. I let Rían think that I was finding training more difficult than it actually was—I didn't want anyone to know about the strength that I felt flowing through me. Not yet. I wanted to give Fionn and the Dublin Order time to find the solution. I was not giving Adam or my element up without a fight.

Adam was working on his control issues. It had been two weeks now since he'd lost control, but his element had grown inexplicably more erratic ever since Dublin. He reassured me that he would be able to resolve the problem, but it seemed like his power was acting on its own accord. Fionn had started working with Adam to help him manage it, using the same techniques that he'd used with Rían.

I made sure to make time to hang out with Caitlin when we were back, which felt easier now that I wasn't as focused on my training. I'd missed her over the past couple of weeks.

One Monday after school we went down to a little café on the seafront. We dumped our bags and ordered giant hot chocolates. "Fill me in," Caitlin ordered. "What have you been up to recently? And I want the *real* story. Not the school-lunchtime version."

"Things have been pretty intense."

"Really? Tell me!"

"I don't know where to begin. Adam is amazing."

"Yeah, tell me something I don't know! So . . . did you do it?"

"Do what?"

"You know . . . *it*." She raised her eyebrows up and down suggestively.

"What? *No!* Of course not."

"Awww, I thought that after the Dublin trip there might have been some steamy sessions."

"Oh, there was steam, and lots of it," I said, blushing a

little. "I've never felt anything like this before."

"I know how you feel. Me neither," she said dreamily.

"Hang on a sec; did *you* do it?" I asked.

"No! Definitely no *it*."

"Phew! It still feels a little early for all that, doesn't it?"

"I suppose so. All in good time." She winked at me. "So, any more freaky magic from the DeRíses?"

Keeping my eyes on my cup, I shook my head. "I think we were letting our imaginations get the better of us. It was probably all those hormones rushing to our brains." I forced a laugh, hoping I sounded suitably breezy, then cringed—disgusted with myself for the all-out lie. "They're just a little . . . unique. They're nice, though. I'll bring you up to their house with me some-day after school. You can see for yourself."

"I'd love to! I've lived here all my life and have never been inside."

"Well, I'll arrange it. You should see Adam's room. It's all sixties flower power."

"Seriously? That's too funny."

"I know! I didn't know what to say when he showed me." I grinned at her as I leaned down to pick up my napkin that had fallen on the ground, but when I put out my hand, the napkin fluttered up from the floor and jumped into my palm before I even thought about what I was doing.

"Did you see that?" Caitlin said. "It just floated into your hand."

"A draft must have caught it. What are the odds?" I tried to force myself to keep my tone light, and I quickly changed the subject. "So, what's going on with Jennif— Ouch!" My neck stung sharply.

"Are you all right?" Caitlin asked, leaning toward me.

"I . . . I think something stung me." I rubbed my Mark under my hair, trying to ease the pain.

"Do you want me to take a look?"

"No, no. I'll be fine."

I heard a mumbled whisper. "Sorry, Cait, I didn't hear that. What did you say?"

"I didn't say anything." She looked at me, concerned.

I heard the whisper again, this time right at my ear. I felt a shiver down my spine; goose bumps spread out across my skin. I spun around, but there was nobody there.

"Megan, are you sure you're all right?"

The pain started to ease in my neck. I waited for a few seconds to see if there would be any more whispers, but the air was clear.

"I'm fine . . . I think." I looked around the café. "I just . . . thought I saw a bee." A thrill of fear ran through me.

"I don't see one. Anyway, you were asking about Jennifer—wait until I tell you about the fight that she and Darren had over the weekend. . . ."

Caitlin's voice faded away. I needed to talk about this with Adam, but if I told him about my Mark stinging, he might realize how strong my element was. He couldn't know. Not yet.

Adam had stayed out of school all week. He still wasn't totally sure if he had his element under control and he didn't want to risk flooding out Sister Basil. I missed him fiercely, and on Saturday morning, while I trained, Rían banished him from the yard so I could concentrate.

By the afternoon I was exhausted and we called it quits. I went up to Adam's room, and he and I curled up on his bed. Adam lay behind me with his body curved around mine. I was so tired from trying to suppress my element. I'd been warned of the strength required for suppression, but I didn't think it was going to be this hard.

"So how's your meditation going?" I asked, keeping my eyes shut.

He sighed. "Meditation isn't really for me. I'm concentrating on managing the new strength."

"Well, how's *that* coming along?"

"Good. I'm going back to school on Monday. Fionn reckons I've got things under control again."

"Hooray. Last week was long without you there."

"I missed you too. Hey, now that I've been deemed safe, do you want to get out of here for what's left of the day?"

I opened my eyes and turned around to him. "I'd love to. What do you have in mind?"

"Well, I've been pining for the sea. I'd love to take the yacht out. Do you fancy a quick spin out in the harbor?"

I cringed, recalling my ill-fated sailing lesson. "Couldn't we go skydiving or bungee jumping or something else less likely to kill me?"

"Don't tell me you're afraid to go out sailing with me! You do realize that I control the water, right? You can't come to any harm. In fact, it's the safest place you could be. Anyway, you told me you weren't afraid anymore . . . remember?"

"Old habits die hard," I said reluctantly. "Are you going to go all black eyed on me again?"

He sighed and released his grip on me. "The black-eye thing looks like it's here to stay. Well, when I use my element anyway. It seems to be part of the power now. I guess it's like what happens to Rían. Do they freak you out?"

"I'll get used to them if I have to; don't worry." I ran my fingers under his eyes. "They're just so nice when they're green."

"Come on." He stood at the foot of the bed and pulled me up toward him, running his hand along my neck and over my Mark. I tensed for a second as he pulled back my hair for a better look.

"Has my Mark grown much?" I asked.

"No, it's pretty much the same as it was before. Why do you ask?"

"Oh. I just thought . . . It's been stinging a little this week, sort of flaring up."

"Really?"

"On Monday I was downtown with Cait and it was really acting up, but it's fine right now."

He caught my chin in his hand and looked at me thoughtfully. "I'm going to run this trip by Fionn. Want to get some food together for us? I'll be down to help you in a minute."

I headed down to the kitchen and found Áine at the table, petting Randel.

She looked up at me. "What are you up to?"

"Since I'm restricting the use of my power, I have been put to work in the kitchen making sandwiches."

"Let me help."

Randel shook out his feathers, hopped up over to the window, and flew away. I looked after him. "Is he off on patrol again?"

Áine wrinkled her forehead, her eyes clouding in concern. "He's been a bit anxious for the past few days, but I can't figure out what's bothering him." She shrugged and then looked at me with suspicious eyes. "So what are these sandwiches for? Am I sensing an outing? A picnic? Ooh, can I come?"

Suddenly Adam's voice rang out loud and clear behind me. "Absolutely not."

She stuck out her tongue at him but he ignored her

and came up behind me, putting his lips at my ear. "Let's get going before anyone else tries to join us. Oh, and Áine," Adam said, turning to her. "Fionn needs to see you in his office."

Áine raised one inquisitive eyebrow at Adam before leaving the kitchen.

When we got to the marina, Adam punched in the security key code and opened the gate wide for me to walk through. He guided me down the gangway, nodding to the odd person here and there on their boats. We came to the club's yacht, a large white-and-blue boat with graceful sails all neatly tied up. I didn't know much, but even I could tell that she was a beauty.

Adam helped me aboard and then jumped on himself. He went below deck to store away our lunch and then came back up and handed me a life preserver. I rolled my eyes. "What happened to my being completely safe with the controller of the oceans?"

"It's to make you feel psychologically safer. Besides, it's club rules."

"Fine. If you insist."

As Adam prepared to set sail, I found myself a comfortable seat and relaxed. It was nice to be around water but not have any lingering feelings of fear. As soon as we had gotten a safe distance from the marina, Adam cut the engine and got to work unraveling ropes and clicking catches. With a whizzing noise the main sheet ran up the mast and billowed out. Then it fell silent as the wind caught it. The beautiful sails strained at the lines as we moved out of the harbor.

We followed a southwest heading for about two hours. Finally we got to where Adam wanted to be. He dropped the sails and tied everything in place. "Now," he said, doing a full three-sixty. "We are most definitely on our own."

That was certainly the truth. There was nothing but sea in every direction. The sky was blue and very clear, with a pale, winterlike quality.

"First things first," he said. "Let's eat."

"Good idea! I'm starving." I ran down the steps, grabbed the picnic bag, and made my way back up.

"Do you mind if I take a quick dip before we eat?"

"Ummm . . . swimming in November? Fine with me, but you do realize that it's absolutely freezing in there, right?"

He smiled. "That I do." He kicked off his shoes and removed his shirt in one fluid movement. I caught my breath. *Focus.* Adam kicked off his pants. In only his boxers, he stepped onto the edge of the boat and dived into the icy water, barely causing a ripple.

He stayed under for what seemed like an eternity. Rationally, I knew there was no reason to be worried, but still, I leaned over the edge and anxiously scanned the water.

His head finally broke the surface just below me. When he spotted me, he grinned. "You fancy joining me?"

I stood back from the edge. "Not a chance."

He hauled himself up the ladder, dried off, and got dressed. He rubbed his hair absentmindedly with the towel as he walked over to me and sat down.

"Aren't you frozen?" I asked him, concerned, as I pulled my legs up to my chest and pulled my jacket tighter around me. I put my hand on his arm but his skin was warm to the touch.

"Powers have their advantages. I can regulate the temperature of the water," he explained with a grin.

We settled down to eat, but I could only nibble at my sandwich. I couldn't stop thinking about my powers and my evoking or lack of evoking. I was still amazed by how much I'd felt my power intensify over the past week. I couldn't believe I had used it without even knowing that day with Caitlin. And that wasn't the only time. At home the other night, I'd been staring at one of my schoolbooks and suddenly I realized it was hovering in midair. It seemed so simple, like breathing. It was all about manipulation of the air around me; there was so much I could do that I hadn't initially realized.

I hadn't pushed my power to the limit by any means, but I felt like I could do anything I put my mind to.

Unfortunately, though, two weeks had passed and the Dublin Order didn't have any updates for us. Fionn was still in the dark as well, though he was spending most of his time buried in translations of the Druid Scribes.

I was so deep in thought I didn't realize Adam was watching me with concerned eyes. "What?" I said, looking at him.

"Don't think about it too much, please. It only makes it harder. We'll make this work."

"I know," I said, and smiled. "So, when can I see your new and improved powers?"

"All in good time. Let me digest first." He stretched out beside me, putting his arms behind his head and closing his eyes. I gently ran my fingers over his face, along his eyelids, down his nose, tracing the line around his lips.

"This is so nice," he murmured after a while. Then he propped himself up on one arm. "Ready for some magic?"

"Absolutely."

He jumped up and pulled me with him. Then he looked out to the sea and slowly closed his eyes. The boat was absolutely still on the water. The ocean around us seemed solid, like glass. About thirty feet out from the yacht, though, waves began to jump and dance. I followed the crests as they created a perfect circle, with us at the very center. I looked up at Adam, but his eyes were closed. All of a sudden, the waves shot up in a vertical wall, surrounding us in a circle of water. It was smooth, almost transparent. It rose at least fifty feet in the air.

I looked at Adam again. He had his hand out in front of him now, palm out, as if holding the wall of water in place. He slowly opened his eyes and looked down at me to gauge my reaction.

His eyes were ebony, with irises that glowed like the water he was now controlling. I was speechless and felt my element jolt in my chest. I spun around with my mouth open, finally turning back to him, drinking in the power that seeped from him, and quivered as I felt his power mix with mine. I sensed my element's hunger for the connection and how it was drawn to his eyes. It scared me—they scared me—but then I saw the green flicker through the black and swirling blue and Adam smiled. I felt a very different pull—it was warm, comforting, and just as strong, but it had nothing to do with elements. I smiled back at him.

"It's so beautiful."

"That's nothing—watch this."

He threw his arms up again. This time the wall rose higher and arched inward, until it finally met above our heads. It was like being underwater, our own private water cave. I could see fish swimming through the liquid ceiling high above us. The sun behind it turned the sea dome a shimmering aquamarine. It glittered and sparkled like nothing I had ever seen before.

"It's so . . . magical."

He smiled. "Pretty cool, isn't it?"

I looked deep into the black eyes, seeing my own reflection. "You are truly a wonder, Mr. DeRís. And for the record, I'm seriously starting to dig the new eyes." I stretched up to kiss him, slowly at first, but then deeply and passionately. He put his arms around my waist in response, squeezing me tight to him. The wall of water held for a moment more before it dropped with a great whoosh and crashed back to the sea surface. The boat rocked, but Adam held me firmly and kissed me back with a burning urgency. We were both left breathless.

"We'd better start heading home." His hot, ragged breath caressed my ear. "It's another two hours back to the marina, and we'd better get in before nightfall."

"You're right." I released my grip on him.

But he didn't let go of me. His mouth stayed at my ear. "Don't let me go," he whispered.

I laughed. "I'll never let you go, Adam. You know that."

"No, I mean literally. Don't let me go." The black and swirling blue eyes faded to green and he looked at his feet.

"What are you talking about?" I said, following his eyes. Then I did a double take. We were hovering about four feet above the boat's deck. "Aghh!" I screamed. We both dropped to the deck and landed in a heap.

"How did you do that?" he asked urgently, pulling me to my feet.

"I don't know. I didn't even realize I was doing it."

Adam frowned. "Has this happened before?"

"Not this floating thing; that's a first. But . . ." I paused, knowing he wasn't going to like what I was about to tell him. "Well, other stuff has been happening. I've tried to stop it. I swear."

Adam's brow furrowed. "You should have told me."

"I didn't want to worry you."

"No matter what happens, we have to work this out. Do you hear me? We have to work this out."

I nodded nervously. "I try to control it; it's just—I feel the power running through my veins. I'm not doing these things; the power is."

The sea around us began to get quite choppy, and dark clouds started rolling in above our heads. "We need to get back," he said, turning away abruptly. He got to work and busied himself the whole way in, leaving me to nurse my insecurity and bruises.

Adam had just seen everything I was fighting to hide. How much longer could I keep it from everyone else? How soon would it be before my eyes started changing color and the element overtook me? We needed time to unlock the code of the Druid Scribes; we had to find the answers.

But my time was running out fast.

Nineteen

FEELINGS

Everything changed after that day at sea. Adam was still loving and attentive, but I felt him pulling away from me. I knew he was freaked out by my sudden growth in power, but every time I broached the subject, he told me not to worry about it. Instead, he buried himself in translations, and spent all his free time researching and becoming more and more obsessed with finding some answer in the writings of the unnamed pair. He'd exhausted every avenue with the translations he had at home, and had decided to go to Dublin for a week to work with the Order on the encryption keys— determined to uncover the secrets of the unnamed pair, believing their story to hold the answers we were look-ing for.

On the Sunday before he left, Adam came over to say good-bye. Dad was out on a date with Petra, and we were lying on my bed together. He had been quiet all evening.

"So what's your excuse this time for missing school?" I asked, smirking.

"Work experience."

"And what about the yacht club? Aren't they going to miss you?"

"There's nothing going on at the club this time of year. They'll survive without me. How has your Mark been?" he asked. "Any more flare-ups?"

"Nothing major." I said, pulling his arm around me. "Do you have to go to Trinity? Couldn't you just bring the Druid Scribes down here?"

"Trust me, the last thing I want to do is leave you and go to Dublin. But the Order won't let the relics leave the crypt." He rubbed his hair in frustration. "I still can't believe I'm pinning my hopes on a fictitious book writ-ten by a bunch of delirious druids."

"You don't believe that. I know you don't. You believe there's wisdom in the Scribes."

He shook his head. "I don't know what I believe any-more. I don't want any of this to be true, but if it is, and there's a solution, I need to find it. I wish the Order would help a bit more, but it seems like they're determined to keep the answers hidden—to keep us apart. They're always harping on about something. If it's not the Druid Scribes, it's the Fifth Prophecy." He gazed into space.

"What is the Fifth Prophecy, anyway?"

"Hmm?" He snapped out of his thoughts. "Oh, don't mind me; I'm just thinking out loud."

"No. They mentioned that when we were in Dublin too. What is it?"

He shrugged a little. "It's a book. Like the Scribes, it was written in an ancient language, but it was transcribed while the Order still held the knowledge of the encryption key. It tells of the coming of a fifth element."

"There's a *fifth*? Why hasn't anyone ever mentioned it to me?"

"No, there's no fifth—at least, not yet. See . . . the fifth isn't a Marked One. The fifth is created, using the four Marked. The fifth combines all four powers with its own to create an all-encompassing power—one that is supposedly too powerful for this world. The Order governs itself based on the Fifth Prophecy; that's why they're always harping on about keeping the bloodlines pure."

"Pure?"

Adam sighed. "Yeah, the fifth is said to come from royal blood. Hence, the carefully selected partners for Carriers of the Mark."

"So they're not just looking for the neutral gene?"

"The neutral gene is just part of the selection process, but knowing that the genetic line is clear of royal blood is more important, and there's no test for that. The Order has no idea who and where the royal bloods are. As they see it, pairing a Carrier with royal blood could bring about the fifth."

"I'm of royal blood. . . ."

He smiled. "Yet another reason why you are an enigma. Carriers were always of direct descent. But you are a Carrier *and* a royal blood."

"Is that a problem?"

Adam shrugged. "It's just not something the Order ever prepared for."

"So I take it the coming of the fifth is not a good thing?"

"The fifth element is spirit. In order to release the element a door to the spirit world must be opened."

"And that's bad?"

Adam nodded.

"There's more . . ." I insisted, watching his eyes. "You're not telling me something."

"I can't believe we're talking about this now." He scratched the back of his head in irritation. "You don't need to know all this; it's totally irrelevant."

"Adam, it's obviously not! You believe in the Fifth Prophecy."

Adam remained silent and turned toward the window,

squinting at the evening sun.

"You can't keep me in the dark. If this affects me, I deserve to know."

He sighed. "The Fifth Prophecy foretells the end of the Marked line."

"The end? What does that mean? That we die?"

Adam's eyes glazed over as he began to recite softly.

> Taken of the four, and born of royal blood, the fifth will die before it can live.
>
> A mother's sacrifice, a father's anguish, an evil descends to consume all.
>
> The air fills with voices of those past.
>
> Elements, darkness, and worlds will collide.
>
> The lion's heart returns to its place, knight turns on knight, and loyalties divide.
>
> The strength lies in the unknown.
>
> All ends here.

He looked back at me and shrugged.

"That's a bit cryptic," I said.

"Well, that's how it translates. It's all we have to go on."

"Am *I* the royal blood?" I asked quietly.

"No! Of course not . . . Oh, I don't know—don't you see; that's the point! We don't quite know what you are." He took my hands and lifted my chin up to make me face him. "There are many components required to bring about the fifth. So far there is no sign of the others. Unless you've seen a lion and some knights strolling around nearby," he said sarcastically.

"Don't make a joke of this; it's serious."

"We can't bet our lives away on something that *might* be. We can cross that bridge *if* we come to it."

"You should have mentioned this to me before."

"Before what, and for what purpose? Nobody knows what the fifth is or how it comes about."

"But how else could an element be born if not from a Carrier of the Mark?"

"But that's my point exactly. We don't even know if it's a person. The prophecy states the fifth is created using the four Marked and combining them to create the fifth—a fifth that must die before it can live. That doesn't sound like a living, breathing being to me. There is nothing linking you to this prophecy other than the fact that you happen to be the first Marked of royal blood. The Order is just looking for reasons to keep us apart."

"I don't know, Adam. Maybe I shouldn't evoke at all," I protested. "If I am a link to the fifth, I could stop it from coming by not performing the evocation ritual. It would be the answer to a lot of problems."

He smiled sadly. "The Order would never allow that. Besides, you're too far gone. You're not going to be able to stop this. That's why I'm going to Dublin." He pulled me up and held me tight. "I'm going to find the answer."

"*If* there's an answer." I burrowed my face into his neck.

He pulled away and dropped his head to mine and gazed into my eyes. "There's an answer. I need you to believe that."

I dropped my eyes. "I'm trying hard to Adam, I am. I . . ."

"Well, I believe enough for the both of us." He sighed. "I'm sorry, but I have to go," he said, giving me one last hug. "I'll be back at the end of the week."

"Sure." I managed a smile for him.

"Trust me, this is all going to work out."

I nodded and waved him off.

The Dublin Order was pushing for some trial evocation rituals, but Adam insisted we wait until he had covered all the options. Fionn was still supporting Adam and me for now, but I knew my hand would be forced soon, and I was a mess at the prospect.

With Adam in Dublin during the week, school had lost its shine. He'd only been back from his previous break a week and now he was gone again. Jennifer and Caitlin were always hanging out with Darren and Killian, and despite their gallant efforts to involve me in everything, I felt like a fifth wheel most of the time.

On the other hand, Áine had become a little clingy and was getting really friendly with Caitlin and Jennifer too. It was actually a little irritating having her shadow my every movement, and I finally confronted her one day after school.

"What's up with the chaperoning?"

"Nothing," she said, avoiding my eye.

"Áine?"

She sighed. "Adam asked me to keep an eye on you."

"Why? Isn't Randel enough?"

Áine looked behind her surreptitiously. "We need to talk."

"We do? What's going on?"

She took my arm and dragged me through a gap in the hedge at the side of the road. We emerged onto a little shingle beach that was deserted except for an upturned boat and some discarded crab pots.

"Listen," she began quietly. "I told Adam to tell you, but he said you had enough on your plate."

"Tell me what? What's wrong?"

"We're not sure, but Randel's been agitated for a few weeks now. I'm not reading him well at the moment."

"Is there something wrong with him?"

"No, I don't think so. I think there might be something wrong with me, though. I'm not seeing with my usual clarity."

"Seeing what?"

"My earth sight—what I see through the animals and

their senses. It's a bit . . . blurry. I'm missing things."

"Are you all right?"

"I'm fine . . . I think. I'm not sure. Adam told us that you've been experiencing some flares in your Mark."

"Yeah, I have. But I thought they were just growth spurts."

"We don't think so, Meg. Flare-ups are usually a sign of some sort of danger. If there's a threat to you, your Mark reacts."

"But . . . if we're in danger, wouldn't your Marks have flared up too?"

"I know. It doesn't make sense. We're trying to figure it out, but in the meantime, we have to stick close to each other. Just in case."

I felt the blood drain from my face. "You really think we're in danger? From who? The Knox?"

"Please don't panic," she pleaded. "Adam made me swear not to tell you, because he was worried you would freak out. Anyway, it's probably nothing. The Knox have never found us here. We're just being cautious." I must have still looked as concerned as I felt, because she immediately started fretting. "Oh, I shouldn't have told you. I'm so sorry. Damn."

"No! You did the right thing. I need to know what's going on."

"Don't tell Adam I told you. Please?"

"I promise. Now come on and walk me home."

When I set off to school the next morning, I was exhausted. I hadn't slept much, between imagining phantom pains in my Mark and keeping my ears on high alert for noises that didn't come. Adam was probably right: Áine shouldn't have told me. Maybe I was better off being blissfully unaware of the potential threat.

Caitlin was waiting for me at the school gates, as always, only this time there was no sign of Killian, which was unusual.

"Hey, Meg."

"Hi, Caitlin. Where's Killian?"

"He's already in school," she said. Suddenly her eyes welled up. I pulled her away from the gates and around the corner.

"What's wrong? What happened?"

Her face crumbled. "Oh, Meg, I don't know where to start." She put her arms around me and started sobbing.

"Caitlin, I'm sure everything will be okay." I rubbed her back and cast a subtle glance at my watch. We were already late for school. If we went in now we'd be in more trouble than if we didn't go in at all. "Come on," I told her, tugging on her arm. "My dad's not home. Let's ditch."

She pulled back and looked at me through reddened eyes. "You'd do that for me?"

"Of course! Now let's go, before someone sees us."

Once we got to my house we went to my room,

armed with sweetened tea and plates of cookies. We had just settled onto the bed when she finally started telling me what happened.

"Killian broke up with me."

"*He* broke up with *you*? But he's so into you!"

"I thought he was, but apparently he snogged a girl a couple of weeks back at some show-jumping event."

"Did he tell you that?"

"No. He was feeling really guilty and told Darren, who told Jennifer, who told me." She picked up the cookies and started shoving them into her mouth in between sobs. "Why would he do that to me?"

"I'm sure he didn't do it on purpose."

"Yeah, he accidently fell openmouthed into another girl's arms. I'm sure he had no option but to slip her the tongue."

I grimaced and patted her back, waiting for her to continue.

"So anyway, I confronted him last night, and do you know what he did? That total prick."

"What?"

"He . . . he said . . . 'sorry.'"

"And that's a bad thing?"

"Of course it's a bad thing! I wanted an argument. I wanted to tell him exactly what I thought of him and where to stick it. But *no* . . . he goes and apologizes and gets all teary eyed on me. He tells me he's a twat.

Then he broke up with me because he thought he wasn't good enough for me!" She shoved another cookie into her mouth.

I was lost for words.

"Actually, now that I hear myself telling the story, it doesn't sound too bad, really. In fact, it sounds like a whole load of crap." She started laughing. "He's right—he is a twat."

"Did he really cry?" I asked, feeling my straight face start to give way.

She nodded and kept laughing, even though there were tears still in her eyes. I laughed along with her. I couldn't believe how good it felt to talk about normal girl stuff again.

"Oh, I'm sorry. I shouldn't let it get to me like that. I suppose at the very least he has given me enough fodder for lots of teen angst to torment my mum with." She pasted a smile on her face, covering up a hurt I knew she felt deeply. "So enough about me. What's the story with you and Adam these days? He's been acting kinda strange. And why does he keep missing school? Is everything okay with you two?"

"He just has a lot on his mind." I looked down at my feet. "He's been in Dublin this week, so I haven't really seen much of him."

"It sounds like you could do with a few of these biscuits too," she said, holding out the plate. "What is he doing up there, anyway?"

"Work experience." I sighed, taking a cookie.

"Wait, work experience? I thought work experience was done in fourth year. . . ."

"Um, yeah, it is, but this is some sailing thing, and the timing wasn't right last year or something. I'm not sure." I couldn't meet her eyes.

She shrugged. "What we need is a girls' night out."

"Yes! That would be amazing."

"And maybe if we leave the boys to fester on their own for a while, they might start to realize just what they're missing." I was glad to see some of the sparkle return to Caitlin's eyes. "So let's hit the cinema Friday after school."

"You're on! I'll ask Áine to see if she can borrow Adam's car, and you let Jennifer know."

"Adam didn't take his car to Dublin with him?"

"No, the, uh, people he's working with are springing for his flights." *And the lies just keep on coming.*

"Nice. If we have the car we might be able to squeeze dinner in too."

With our plans decided, we closed the curtains and turned off our phones so that no one would be able to track us down and catch us ditching. We then proceeded to watch hours of daytime TV. It was the most relaxed I had felt in a long time. We heard knocking at one point and peered out the window to try to see who it was, but no one was there. It looked like we were home free. Finally, at three forty-five, we cleaned up and crept back toward the school so we could look like we were walking home when the last bell rang. We stood hidden in the bushes until we saw the uniformed masses start streaming toward us; then we stepped out and blended in with the crowd.

"Thanks a million for today. It was just what I needed," Caitlin said, giving me a hug.

"Me too. I'll talk to you later."

"Will do." She waved good-bye as she turned off down her road.

I started puffing my way up the steep hill back to my house and turned my phone back on. It rang immediately. Adam. "Why weren't you in school today?" were his first words.

"Well, hello to you too."

"This is serious, Megan. Why weren't you in school?"

"I just ditched with Caitlin. She's having guy trouble."

"Jesus, Megan. You should have let us know. We've all been on high alert looking for you."

"What?"

"You don't show up at school. Your phone is off. Fionn called your house, but there was nobody home. Your dad says you're in school. We've all been at our wits' end."

"Adam, people ditch. I don't like you checking up on me." I couldn't believe my absent boyfriend was berating me. I felt like I was being lectured by my dad. "If you're so worried about me, stop wasting your time in Dublin."

"I'm not wasting my time. I'm doing this for us. Do you really think I want to be up here away from you?" His voice was getting louder. "What more can I do?"

"Well, you could start telling me the truth," I spat in an acid tone. Part of me knew I was being a bitch, but I felt like he was treating me like a child.

"What are you talking about?"

"You know what I'm talking about. Áine told me everything," I blurted out.

"She told you?"

I winced, knowing I had let her down, but I barreled ahead. "Somebody had to."

Adam was silent. I could tell by his heavy breathing that he was livid.

"Look, Adam. You're mad. I'm mad. We should talk about this later when we've both calmed down."

"Fine," he snapped, and the line went dead.

Ugh. What a crappy way to end a good day. I stomped home, feeling terrible about our fight. I tried several times to reach Adam, but his phone went straight to voice mail. Feeling utterly dejected, I opened the front door. Dad wasn't home yet, so I headed to my room. All I could think about was locking myself away for a few hours and having a good cry.

But as I turned the doorknob I got a funny feeling. I

looked down at my arm and watched the goose bumps form slowly, working their way from my wrists up my arms. Then I heard a whisper at my ear, just like in the café with Caitlin.

"Who's there?" I gasped, spinning around. But I was alone.

I pushed the door open slowly, but stayed in the hallway. Nothing looked out of place. I stepped into the room and cautiously looked around. I still didn't see anything out of the ordinary, but something definitely didn't feel right.

I bit my lip. I wasn't going to start calling Fionn or Áine now, especially if they were all pissed at me for disappearing today. I backed out of my room and went downstairs, then sat in the kitchen with the TV volume on high until my dad came home.

I didn't sleep that night. I kept imagining noises, and I was hyperaware of my Mark. I kept expecting Adam to call at some point to clear the air. But the call never came.

Twenty

STRANGER

Aine was so mad the next day, she barely spoke to me.

"You said you wouldn't tell him," she muttered on our way to class.

"I know. I'm sorry. It just came out."

She grabbed me by the sleeve and pulled me into a deserted classroom. "What were you thinking? You have to get used to the idea that you are a Marked One now. You can't just go off on your own and not tell anyone. Have you any idea how vulnerable you are?"

"I guess not."

"Exactly. Adam, Rían, and I have all evoked. We are

strong, and we can protect ourselves. We also live on protected lands that the Knox are blind to. You have only just started using your power, and yet you go swanning off on your own after I tell you there's a potential threat in the area. Exactly what part of the warning didn't you understand?"

I shrugged. "I just didn't think."

"Don't you even care what you are doing to my brother?"

"What do you mean?"

"Adam is tearing himself apart up in Dublin. He's working night and day to find a solution to *your* problems. Let's forget for the moment the fact that he's missing out on loads of school, school that he'll have to make up for when he gets back. And the fact that Fionn has to lie through his teeth to allow that to happen. Christ! Megan, you know that he pines for you when you're apart; you've seen how it affects his power. He's facing the struggle of a lifetime with his element and it's all for you."

I didn't know what to say. I couldn't believe I had never thought of it from Adam's point of view. "I'm so sorry, Áine. When you put it like that . . ."

Áine's glare softened. "Yes, well, I didn't mean to be so harsh. It's just that he's my brother and he's hurting."

"He won't answer my calls," I said, feeling my eyes well up. "How can I apologize if he won't talk to me?"

"Leave him a message. He'll call you back, I promise."

I nodded, swallowing hard.

"Now, come here." She pulled me in for a hug. "Let's get to class. Take good notes. Adam's going to need them when he gets back."

At lunch, I called Adam. As usual the call went to voice mail.

"Adam, it's me. I'm sorry for being so horrible yesterday. I don't know what I was thinking. Please forgive me?"

Ten minutes later my phone rang, and Áine glanced over and gave me an I-told-you-so look.

I jumped up and ran off to answer the phone in private. "Adam, hi."

"Hi, Meg. I'm sorry."

"No, don't be. It was my fault. I never stopped to think. And I was a total bitch."

He laughed. "You weren't a *total* bitch. Anyway, you didn't realize you were doing anything wrong."

"So am I forgiven?"

"Well, am I?"

Relief flooded through me. Everything was going to be okay.

"Oh, Adam, I can't wait for you to get home."

"I should be back Friday night."

"Oh." I winced.

"Is there a problem?"

"No, it's nothing. I was going to go to a movie with Caitlin and the girls, but I'll cancel."

"No, don't cancel. I won't be down until late anyway."

"Are you sure?"

"Of course I'm sure."

"In that case . . . any chance Áine can borrow your car?" I smiled, knowing he'd be more likely to say yes to me than to his sister.

"My car? Oh, I don't know about that. Áine's driving sucks."

"Oh, come on, Adam. Please? We'll take really good care of it. I promise I'll make it worth your while."

"Well, when you put it like that, how can I refuse? Roll on, Friday!"

I hung up the phone and ran back to the gang feeling better than I had in a long time.

"Well? Are we all friends again?" Áine asked sheepishly.

I nodded. "He'll be back on Friday."

"Aw, does that mean our movie night is canceled?" Caitlin whined.

I sat down beside her. "Nope, in fact it just got a little better."

"What's this about?" Áine inquired.

I smiled at her. "Girls' night out on Friday."

"Oh, can I come?" Áine asked, looking a little unsure.

I laughed. "Of course! You're driving." Jennifer and Caitlin exchanged excited glances.

"I am? In what?"

"Adam said you could drive his car."

"Are you serious? He never lets me drive his car. Excellent. This can double as my birthday party."

"It's your birthday on Friday? Adam never mentioned it."

"Oh, Adam doesn't *do* birthdays, but I do. This is great. We'll have so much fun."

That Friday after school, Jennifer, Caitlin, Áine, and I all packed into Adam's car and drove to the movie theater singing along with the festive songs on the radio. By the time we got there we were hoarse from screaming along to Wham!'s "Last Christmas." We fell out of the car laughing and got in line for tickets.

Jennifer and Caitlin were chatting about whether to buy one popcorn or two, but I tuned them out as my happiness faded. My Mark was starting to sting a little. I scanned the foyer. Nothing seemed out of the ordinary. I was just coming back to focus on my friends when my eyes stopped on a man in the next line. There was something about him that felt wrong, weird. When he saw me looking at him, he swiftly turned away.

The whispers were back. This time they swirled around my head, moving from one ear to the other. I shook my head to clear it and shifted closer to Áine, hooking my arm through hers.

"You okay?" she asked, looking around the room automatically.

I shook my head. "Something's wrong. My Mark is stinging."

Áine paid for the tickets on autopilot and turned back to me. "I'm not sensing anything."

"Maybe it's nothing. My Mark has stung before and it's been nothing."

"I have a bad feeling about this, Megan. I think we should go home."

"No, not yet. Let's stay for the movie. If it gets worse we'll go. Please?"

She nodded reluctantly. "Okay. But tell me right away if you feel anything else."

We walked toward the theater and joined Jennifer and Caitlin, who'd walked on ahead. It was a great movie, judging by Caitlin's and Jennifer's cackles all the way through it, but I couldn't focus on the screen. My Mark was stinging nonstop and the whispers kept whirling around my head. I looked around the theater, but I couldn't see anything in the darkness.

Áine glanced at me. "Is it happening again?"

I put my hand over my Mark and nodded. "I keep hearing whispers."

She stared at me, wide-eyed. "What are they saying?"

"I don't know. I can't make them out."

"Oh, Christ. Why didn't you tell me that? I'm going to have a look around." She sat bolt upright, her eyes closed, and stayed like that for the rest of the movie. I wondered what animal's or insect's eyes she was looking through. What would be in here? A fly or a mouse maybe?

When the movie finally ended and the lights came back up, I got up from my seat. Jennifer and Caitlin were looking at Áine strangely, and Caitlin reached over and shook her shoulder. "Áine, hello, it's over. Were you asleep or something?"

Áine's eyes opened slowly. "Oh. I think I dropped off. Sorry, guys. Was the movie good?"

Jennifer laughed. "It was great! I can't believe you fell asleep." She put her hand down to Áine and pulled her up out of the seat. "Come on; let's go get some dinner. I'm starving." Jennifer turned to Caitlin. "What do you fancy?"

I looked nervously at Áine, but she said nothing. We made our way out and were heading in the direction of the restaurant next door when Áine suddenly turned and leaned against a wall.

"Actually, guys, I'm really not feeling well." She had a pained expression on her face. "Would you mind terribly if we just went home?"

Jennifer's face fell. "Oh, what's wrong?"

"I think I'm coming down with something. I feel weak."

Caitlin walked over to her, looking concerned. "Are you okay to drive?"

"Oh, of course, I just need to sit down. Why don't you guys go in and get some dinner to go and then meet me back here. That will give my stomach a chance to settle. Megan will look after me out here."

Caitlin looked torn. "Are you sure? We could just go now. I can wait till we get home."

Áine shook her head. "No, honestly, go on ahead."

"That sucks, Áine," Jennifer said, reaching into her pocket. "We even had a special treat to go with your dessert." She held up a box of pink candles and Áine gave her a weak smile.

Caitlin turned back to me. "You want anything, Meg?"

"No, I'm good." I waved her off and they both headed into the restaurant.

As soon as they were out of earshot, I spun back to Áine. "What is it?"

"There was a man at the back of the theater who stared at you through the entire movie."

My heart started to pound. "I think I know who you're talking about. I saw someone who gave me the creeps right before we went in. Small guy, right? Early forties, slightly bald?"

"You noticed him and you didn't say anything?"

I shrugged, feeling stupid. "I didn't think it was important."

She rolled her eyes. "How long have you been hearing the whispers?"

"A few weeks. I thought I was imagining them at first, but tonight they were louder."

"Shite. I need to ring Fionn."

"What is it? Have you heard the whispers too?"

"I used to hear them all the time. If there's danger close by, the Sidhe warns us to guide us out of harm's way."

"But you haven't been hearing them recently?"

"No. And I don't know why. I stopped hearing them around the time my earth sight got fuzzy. It's like what Randel's been saying."

"What do you mean? What has Randel been saying?" I demanded.

"He's not seeing anything either. None of us are, but Randel has been uncomfortable, anxious. It's like we're being blocked somehow. We have to get home to the boys; they need to know about this."

Áine took out her phone and dialed. "Fionn, it's Áine. Listen, I think someone might be snooping around. Megan noticed a man. Yeah, I know. Fionn, she's been hearing the Sidhe warnings. No, I didn't. I know; we're coming home now. Okay, I'll put her on." She handed the phone to me.

"Megan, are you okay?" Fionn said.

"I'm fine. My Mark was stinging during the movie, though. Áine thinks there's someone watching us."

"You heard the Sidhe warnings? What was he saying?"

"I couldn't make it out. I didn't even realize they were warnings. I'm sorry I didn't mention it sooner."

"Don't worry about that now. Just stay close to Áine and get home as soon as you can. Oh, Adam wants to speak to you."

"Megan, are you all right?" Adam asked breathlessly.

"I'm fine. Don't worry. We're going to leave now and head to your house."

"Rían and I will come; we'll meet you guys halfway. Just watch out for us."

"You don't need to meet us. We'll be fine." But he was gone already. I sighed and looked at Áine as I handed her back the phone. "He's coming to get us. Rían's going to give him a ride."

"To tell you the truth, I'll be glad of his company," Áine said, flicking her eyes around nervously.

Jennifer and Caitlin arrived back with their bags of food. We all went to the car and climbed in.

"Are you feeling any better?" Caitlin asked as Áine got into the driver's seat.

"Not really. Adam is coming to meet us to help drive home." Áine looked around uneasily, quickly scanning the other cars. I did the same, though I was happy that my Mark was no longer stinging.

We had only been driving for ten minutes when I saw Adam and Rían up ahead of us. Rían pulled the bike to the side of the road, and Áine pulled over in front of him. My heart fluttered as Adam handed his helmet to Rían and headed over to us.

Jennifer sighed loudly from the backseat. "It's just not fair that Megan gets to snog *that*. Really, Megan, you should share. Sharing is caring and all."

I smiled back at her.

Áine made a gagging noise. "That's my brother you're talking about. Yuck."

Adam opened the driver's door. "You okay?" he asked Áine. Then his eyes met mine.

We both nodded.

Adam sat in the driver's seat, and Áine got in the backseat with Jennifer and Caitlin. Rían followed us, watching all around him. It felt silly being escorted home, but I had to admit it was nice to feel protected. Adam dropped Jennifer and Caitlin off at Jennifer's house; then we headed back to the DeRíses' place. This time, Rían drove ahead of us. As we pulled off, I noticed Randel flying alongside us.

"Now, tell me exactly what happened," Adam said.

Áine told him the story. Once she was finished, he asked us to describe the man. Unfortunately, there wasn't much we could say. As soon as we reached the house Adam and Áine jumped out of the car and Fionn came running out to meet us. "Is everyone okay?"

"We're fine," I replied, stepping out of the car. "This could all be nothing."

Fionn gave me a stern look. "If you felt there was something wrong, you were more than likely right. You have to learn to trust your Mark."

We filed into the kitchen and sat down at the table, except for Adam, who was too tense to sit. He stood behind me with his hands on my shoulders, and I melted into him, letting myself relax.

Fionn stood at the head of the table. His face was calm, but he was gripping the wood so tightly it looked like the bones in his knuckles would break through the skin.

"We have to stay close to home for a while. If you need to go out, I want you to travel in pairs." He looked toward Áine. "Does Randel have anything for us?"

She shook her head. "Nothing. There's definitely something that's not right, but he's still not sure what." She looked to the window, then back to Fionn. "There's something else, though. I didn't sense the man at the cinema. It was Megan's tension that alerted me to him. Even when I went looking for him, I found it hard to locate him, like I was being blocked. I don't understand."

Fionn's forehead creased. "Well, we have to assume the Knox have someone sniffing about." He looked around the table. "They can't know about Megan; nobody else in the Order has been told. They must have been following the residual energies of Adam's surges. If they were sure they had found us they could have just taken the girls tonight, but they didn't. That makes me think they're unsure."

"Do you really think it's my fault?" Adam asked from behind me.

"It's most likely the case that they followed your residuals, Adam, but it's not your fault. They're following the same pattern as when they located us through Rían's residuals, back in the U.K."

"How do they follow the energy? Does it leave a trail?" I asked.

"They have the amber shard of the Amulet of Accaious. Remember when I told you about that? The amulet, even just a shard of it, is sensitive to the Marked energies. If the energy is strong enough, the Knox can track it. That's why we've also been careful to confine our using the elements only within protected lands." He paused and took a deep breath. "We can't take anything for granted now. Áine, tell Randel to keep an eye on Megan's house for the next few days. I want feedback on anyone who gets within a hundred feet of that house. I'd be a lot happier if she wasn't alone at night either, so, Áine, you can arrange to stay over with her some nights, and I'll keep watch on the nights you're not there. So far, we have no evidence to suggest the Knox have been in Kinsale, so that gives us some breathing space."

I looked around at them. "I think that Knox guy was in my room on Tuesday."

Everyone looked at me in shock.

"When I got home on Tuesday afternoon, I went up to my room and my Mark started stinging and I heard the whispers. I stood at the door, but I felt like I couldn't walk into it, so I just sat downstairs until my dad came home."

Adam took a breath behind me. "How did this happen?" He spoke quietly and slowly. He let go of me and stepped back from the table.

Fionn stood away from the counter. "Calm down, Adam. Now is not the time to lose it."

I turned to him. Adam's eyes were already black, with vivid blue swirling around them.

"Adam, I need you to focus. I don't know how this happened," Fionn said.

"The Order must have blabbed," Adam growled through gritted teeth.

"They wouldn't. They would never do that. This guy might just have been following your residuals to her house. Adam, think about it. It makes sense. Megan hasn't evoked. Her residuals wouldn't be readable yet."

"Someone was in her room, for Christ's sake. In her room!"

"But I don't think he was still there when Megan got home. If he had been, he would have acted right then and there. I'd say her Mark was sensing that he'd been there earlier."

Rían shook his head. "How is he getting around our senses? We've always known when the Knox are close. This is bad."

Adam was pacing back and forth behind me. I reached out to him, catching his hand as he passed, and pulled him close, forcing him to wrap his arms back around me. I hoped it would calm him, and it worked; I could feel his heart slowing and his breathing evening out.

"I have to look into this," Fionn said. "Adam, you keep close to Megan. Stay as long as you can tonight. I will take over when you leave."

I felt Adam nodding behind me. "It's getting late; I'll take her home now."

Rían stood up. "I'll drive ahead of you to make sure everything is clear."

At the front door Adam held me back and let Rían go first. Rían was already on his bike, his eyes scanning the yard, before Adam would let me go to the car. Rían nodded up to Adam and he set off down the driveway with us behind.

I looked up at Adam's frowning face. "What's going to happen? What do we do?"

"We keep calm and you lie low for a while. This will blow over. They've been close before, but what saves us every time is that they don't really know what they're looking for. So we keep our heads low and they move on to the next town. It's been years since we have even seen a tracker in Ireland."

"Is that what the guy in the theater was? A tracker?"

"I think so. We can't be sure at the moment, but he fits the usual profile. There's something different this time, though; he's getting around our defenses. We just don't know how he's doing it."

"But why would he come after me?" I said, still upset. "I haven't even evoked my power. I wouldn't be much use to them, would I?"

He looked at me with a pained expression in his eyes. It was a look I had seen before. He knew something that he wasn't telling me. I put my hand on his. "Please tell me."

"If they do know about you, and I'm not sure they do, you'd most likely be their first choice." He took a deep breath, letting his words sink in. "You're only just learning about your powers, so you can be molded into what they want. And you're also still figuring out how to control your powers, so you're not in a position to fight back or put up much resistance. And, of course, there's the fact that you're a Carrier of the Mark. It's what they've always wanted."

"Adam, I'm scared. I wish I could be stronger. I wish . . ." I didn't know what I wished. I just wanted life to be a little simpler, easier.

"Only over my dead body will they ever get to you. Just trust us and let us take care of you," he said, rubbing my leg. "Look, we're at your house, and your dad's not here. I'll stay with you until he comes, and then Fionn will be on the night shift. He can camp out in the Discovery and keep watch from a distance. You will be perfectly safe." He started to get out of the car, but I grabbed his arm in a panic.

"Don't leave me here."

"I'll be right back. I promise." He got out of the car and walked over to talk to Rían, then came back to me and opened the door.

As I got out, Rían flashed his lights at us and headed down the road.

"Where's Rían going?"

"He's going to do a quick sweep of the area, and he'll check in by phone if there is anything to report." Adam walked me to my front door, watching over his shoulder as I dug out my keys. "Do you sense anything?"

"No. Everything seems fine," I replied, opening the door and stepping in.

"Just let me have a quick look around, all right?" He left me in the hall and ran upstairs. When he came down a few moments later, he was smiling. "It looks like we're all good."

It was a relief to hear that, but it set me off. The tears came and they just kept on coming. I couldn't stop them. It was panic, fear, and confusion all rolled into one. I thought I had finally come to grips with my new life and all the dangers that came with it, but I was wrong.

Adam pulled me to him and sat down on the couch. He said nothing; he just held me, cradling me gently, letting the tears run their course. When they eventually dried up, I clung to him, afraid to let him go, not wanting him to leave.

The ringing of the phone broke the spell. It was my dad, apologizing for being so late and wondering if I would be all right if he went home with Petra and I stayed on my own tonight.

I was secretly relieved. That meant Adam would stay here with me. I told my dad not to worry, and I turned back to Adam to tell him the news.

"I'll stay here with you then; there's no need for Fionn to do a night shift tonight." He opened his phone and dialed. "Hi, it's me. Everything is clear here. Look, Caleb isn't going to come home tonight, so I'm going to stay with Megan. Let me know if you find anything out." There was a pause at the other end while Fionn spoke. "Okay. Talk to you tomorrow. Bye." Adam threw the phone onto the table in front of him and pulled me back into his arms.

"I'm so sorry about before, all the crying. I don't know where that came from," I said, pressing my face into his shirt.

"Don't apologize. I hate to see you hurting like that. Please believe me when I tell you that I will make you safe."

"I do believe you. I just hate being so weak and needy."

He pulled away from me so he could hold my face between his palms. "You are one of the strongest people I have ever known. Look at what has been thrown at you over the past months. And with each thing you rise to the challenge. It leaves me breathless sometimes. *You* leave me breathless."

"I love you," I said as I gazed up into his magical green eyes. I'd felt the words coming. They'd been building for a while, but I was still shocked when I heard them come out of my mouth. I did love him. I loved him beyond any elemental attraction.

"I love you too," he whispered back, his eyes sparkling.

I knew then, at that moment, that I was not going to evoke my element. My love for Adam was real and true, and I could not accept the idea of anything standing in the way of our future.

We sat there all evening. I closed my eyes as he traced patterns on my face, and his touch calmed me with every stroke. I must have fallen asleep, because the next thing I knew he was tucking me into my bed and climbing in next to me.

"It's been a while," he murmured into my hair. "I nearly forgot how good this feels."

"Happy birthday," I whispered.

He smiled. "Thanks."

I fell back into a deep and comfortable sleep in his arms.

The next morning when I woke up Adam was gone. I jumped out of bed and was about to run downstairs when I heard a noise coming from the kitchen. My heart pounded, and I crept down quietly and peeped around the corner.

"Megan? You slept late." My dad was sitting at the kitchen table drinking a cup of coffee.

My brain was struggling to catch up. Where the hell was Adam? I peeked out the window to where his car should be, but it was gone.

"Yeah, I guess I'm, uh, really tired. Did you have a good night?"

"It was great. We had dinner in that new restaurant on the waterfront. What were you up to?"

"The girls and I went to a movie in Douglas, then got some dinner."

"That's nice. Oh, it looks like Adam is here. Another date today?" he casually asked.

"Oh, yeah! I completely forgot. I'm not even dressed yet." I ran to open the front door, suppressing a some-what hysterical giggle. "Hey, Adam."

He winked at me. "Still in pajamas?"

I rolled my eyes at him. "Yeah, I guess I slept in. I'm

going to get dressed. My dad's in the kitchen," I said, my tone heavy with meaning.

I ran upstairs and heard Adam say good morning to my dad. By the time I got back to the kitchen, Adam and Dad were discussing some upcoming event down at the yacht club. I got some breakfast while they chatted. I offered Adam a bowl of cereal, but he shook his head and said he had eaten earlier. This all made no sense.

"Are you ready to go?" Adam asked, as I put my bowl in the sink.

"Sure. See you later, Dad." We moved quickly to the door.

"Bye, guys," Dad called, and we walked out and got into the car. We didn't speak until Adam had reversed out of the driveway.

"Where the hell did you go?" I eventually asked.

"Áine rang and said Randel had seen your dad on his way home, so I parked down the road and out of sight for a while to give your dad time to get in."

"I freaked out when I woke up and you were gone. You could have let me know," I said indignantly.

"Ah, but you're so beautiful when you're asleep, and you seemed to be having a nice dream. I couldn't have woken you." He smiled at me. "I'm starving, by the way. It was torture watching you eat your breakfast there."

"Why didn't you have some?"

"I didn't want to give your dad any room for suspicion."

"That's silly! He'd never have thought you'd stayed here."

"I wasn't risking it, just in case. Come on, let's get back and see if Fionn has any news."

When we got to his house they were all there waiting for us.

"Anything?" Adam asked.

Fionn shrugged. "Nothing. My contacts in the U.K. said they hadn't seen any Knox activity for at least eight months. They were as surprised as we were that the Knox could have come so close without being detected."

"Do you think it might be a false alarm?" Adam asked.

"I don't know. It's worrisome that your senses aren't picking him up, but at least Megan's seem unaffected. We need to trust them for the moment, to be on the safe side. Áine has been scanning the wider area and she's also coming up blank, but I'm not convinced we're in the clear." He shook his head and his thoughts seemed far away. "I won't rest until we are safe."

Twenty-one

THE HACK

After that scare, things calmed down. The strange man didn't appear again, and nobody in the Order had any information on any current Knox activity. As the weeks passed, a sort of strange normality settled in. We tried to put the theater incident behind us, and though we remained cautious, we resumed our old lives. One thing that had changed, though, was that we had discontinued training. That was fine with me. I wanted to put distance between me and my element.

The New Year started with Hugh figuring out a new section of the Scribes. He was sure he was close to cracking the key. With that news, Adam began spending weekends in Dublin, working with the Order. Progress was slow and Adam was very unhappy with the evocation date fast approaching. He began retreating back into his research, spending most of his time either in Dublin or scanning through photocopies of old texts. He marked each passing day on his calendar with a black "X," and with each one his mood sank further. It wasn't just me he was withdrawing from now, but his family too. He let his schoolwork slide and didn't even bother attending most of the time. Fionn was covering for him, but the school was beginning to ask questions, and Fionn was running out of excuses for Sister Basil. But Adam didn't seem to care, and when Fionn pressed him on it, Adam just snapped that he was eighteen and Fionn was no longer his legal guardian.

With Adam so wrapped up in text translations, I had plenty of time to myself. And the more time that went by, the more I realized I could not live without Adam. Since the day on the boat when I'd felt my own love for Adam exist alongside my elemental attraction for him, I knew our love could survive beyond the elements. And I had heard it in Adam's voice the night he told me he loved me. I was going to make myself fail to evoke at the ritual planned for February, and I would continue to fail until it was too late. I hated myself for being so selfish, and I knew that letting go of my element would be like killing a part of me, but it was a sacrifice I had to make.

This meant that I had to learn how to channel the excesses of my power, which kept struggling to exist, into something else. So I focused on control. Since I'd made my decision not to evoke, I saw my power with better clarity and found it easier to manage. Despite the element's best efforts to free itself, it no longer slipped out accidentally. More recently I actually felt like my power had given up the fight. I slowly became confident that I could avoid evocation. Now I just had to work on my acting skills so that it actually *looked* like I was trying to evoke during the ritual.

As I stuck to my plan, Adam grew more and more distressed about the Druid Scribes. I didn't want to tell him that I wasn't going to evoke—I knew he wouldn't agree to it. But I hated watching him suffer. And, of course, if he found a solution, I would be overjoyed to be able to keep my power and keep Adam. In the meantime, even when I didn't hang out with Adam, I knew his moods were just getting worse and worse, because of the storms and floods that ravaged Kinsale throughout December and early January. I suspected that much of the freakishly bad weather was caused by Adam's black mood, and I wished I could press fast-forward to get to the summer.

I was back to spending a lot of time with Caitlin, which was great. We studied together in the evenings, filling the void the boys left in their absence. Caitlin and Killian had tried getting back together, but Caitlin couldn't get the image of Killian cheating on her out of her head, and so she ended it . . . again. Poor Killian was devastated. But something told me that she still had feelings for Killian and that his suffering would be short.

One evening after we finished our homework, we started talking about our plans for the summer. Caitlin informed me that she was stuck working at the bed-and-breakfast from spring right through to the fall, so she wouldn't have a lot of free time.

"We should do something this weekend. In fact, we should do something each weekend up to when the tourist season kicks off." She sighed. "I'll smell like a full Irish breakfast until the end of the summer."

I laughed at her. "It can't be that bad."

"You haven't smelled me during the summer months. I'm telling you, I won't be able to even look at a sausage until Christmas."

"So what do you want to do this weekend? I was actually thinking it would be fun to take a ride at the stables. We haven't been down there since the whole Killian disaster went down."

She looked out the window. "In case you've missed it, we're sort of in the middle of storm season here."

"I'm predicting good weather this weekend."

"Oh, you are, are you? What have you got, some kind of magical barometer?"

I grinned. "Yeah, something like that. Look, I'll take care of the weather. You acquire the horses."

"I'm not sure, Megan. Things are still awkward with Killian. I don't know who has the harder task: you in appeasing the rain gods, or me in coercing Killian into giving me his horses."

"Something tells me it won't be a problem."

"Oh, fine. You're on." She sounded reluctant, but I could tell by the gleam in her eye that she was secretly glad to have an excuse to talk to Killian.

"Great!" I finished my tea and started gathering my stuff. "I'd better get home. I'll see you tomorrow."

She waved me off and I headed home, spying Randel on the tree across the road. I waved discreetly to him. Even though there no longer seemed to be a threat, he still kept a constant watch on me. While the rest of us had moved on, Áine had told me Randel was still unhappy. So he shadowed me, a constant and reassuring presence that I was now well used to.

I was walking for about ten minutes when Adam pulled up and rolled his window down.

"Want to let your inattentive boyfriend give you a lift?"

I looked into his tired eyes and smiled. Despite the fact that he had been hard to talk to lately, I was thrilled to see him.

I leaned over the window and gave him a kiss.

"You're far too forgiving," he murmured, as I climbed into the passenger seat.

"No way. Maybe I should be thanking you," I teased. "Your absence from my life is what's going to get me into Trinity. I'm going to whip your butt in the exams," I joked.

"And what makes you think that?" He tapped the side of his head. "This brain is a lean machine; I'll whip *your* butt, hands down. All I need is a few nights of cramming."

I ran my finger along the purple rings under his eyes. "All you need is a few nights' sleep."

He sighed. "I can't sleep these days. My brain won't shut off. I told you, lean machine." He tried to laugh, but it didn't quite come out.

I cupped my hand under his chin. "What you need is another night with me. I'd make sure your brain shuts off. It's been a long time."

"I know. I'm nearly there, though. It won't be long now, I promise."

"You don't have to do this, Adam," I whispered.

He opened his eyes and sat upright. "Yes, I do. Time's nearly up. Come on; I'll get you home."

I played with the idea of telling him I was giving up the element, that I had it under control now, but I knew he'd freak out. I sighed and leaned back in my seat as he drove the rest of the way to my house. When we pulled up, I saw that my dad was already home.

"I won't come in," Adam told me.

"Will you be in school tomorrow?" I asked hopefully.

"Not tomorrow, but I can see you Saturday."

"Well, we were thinking of going out for a ride on Saturday, Caitlin and me. I haven't asked Áine yet, but I'm sure she'll be up for it too. Do you mind?"

"Of course not. Maybe I'll see you Saturday night then."

"That would be nice." I gave him a good-bye kiss, then stepped out into the rain. "Adam."

"Yes."

"Any chance you could think happy thoughts on Saturday? Riding in the rain isn't much fun."

Adam's lips curled into a little smile. "I'm sorry; I don't even notice I'm doing it." He put out his hand and flicked it to the side. The clouds broke above my head and the first bit of clear sky I'd seen in weeks peeped through the clouds.

"I'll save all my happy thoughts for Saturday," he promised, and he backed out of the driveway and drove away.

"Hey, Meg." Dad walked out to greet me. "Is Adam not coming in?"

"No, he had to go study."

Dad looked at me thoughtfully. "Is everything all right with you two? We don't see much of him around

315

here these days. I haven't seen his name on the duty list in the club either."

"Everything's fine, Dad; he's just studying a lot." I decided to change the subject before he could ask any more questions. "Caitlin, Áine, and I are going to go riding on Saturday."

"That sounds nice. Too bad the weather's been so bad."

"I think the forecast is calling for a break in the rain."

"Really? Well, if that's the case, maybe I'll head down to West Cork with Petra."

"Sounds good. Anyway, I'm going to hit the books," I said, plodding up the stairs. I was so tired. I couldn't help feeling sorry for myself too. I missed the real Adam. I couldn't wait for the time when he and I could just be together, without anything hanging over our heads.

Saturday was indeed beautiful. I wondered what happy thoughts Adam could have come up with to produce such a perfect day. We were all up bright and early and down in the stables before ten a.m. As I had expected, Áine was delighted to hear about the riding trip, and had been talking about it all week. When we got there, Áine and I found Caitlin and Killian talking happily together. When she saw us approaching, she hugged him and ran over to us.

"Well, well, well, what do we have here?" Áine teased.

She blushed. "It's hard to stay away long! I guess I just can't resist a man in jodhpurs."

I laughed. "I knew it was only a matter of time. I bet he'll be much more attentive this time around. No screwups."

The three of us turned and looked at him. He happened to glance at us at exactly the same time, and when he met our eyes, he spun around fast to look busy doing something. Unfortunately for him, he tripped over a wheelbarrow and caught himself just in time to keep from falling on his face. Then he tried to gather his dignity and saunter away looking nonchalant. We all burst out laughing, but tried to smother the sounds so we wouldn't hurt his feelings.

"Come on," Áine said when she managed to get her breath back. "Let's get going."

Killian had tacked up three of the yard's best horses. I stretched my foot up into the stirrup and hauled myself up. As I sat in the saddle my Mark stung for a split second. I spun my head around, but there was no one else nearby, and Áine was still smiling away.

I must have imagined it. My hair was probably caught on my riding hat. I reached back to free it.

Caitlin leaned over. "Here, let me help." She hooked her finger under my hat and pulled out my hair.

"Thanks, that's better. Come on, guys," I shouted, and trotted off down the path.

"Hold up," they called after me, kicking their horses into action, trying to catch up.

It was a gorgeous morning. We trotted all the way out to Sandycove beach, letting the horses go into the water up to their chests to cool them down; we all got a little wet in the process, but it was fun. We had our picnic on the beach, under the soft glow of the winter sun, and then doubled back toward Kinsale. We were making our way to a particular field that Áine said was long enough to ride through at a gallop. When we arrived at the field the horses all got giddy and excited, prancing around the place and shying from imaginary things in their excitement to get going.

Áine put her hand up in the air. "On your mark, get set, go!" she roared, and all the horses took off, half rearing up in their first stride. All that could be heard was the thudding of hooves, and I gloried in the feel of the wind in my face.

Something tugged me back. I didn't see anything; I just fell to the ground, totally winded. I could see Caitlin and Áine galloping out of view with my horse hot on their heels. They hadn't even realized I'd fallen. Then something covered my mouth. I tried to scream but I couldn't. I couldn't even breathe. I was being held down and dragged.

I felt the blackout coming . . . and then I felt nothing.

Twenty-two

FOUND

It was dark and cold. There was no air. I tried to move my hands to push off whatever was on top of me. But my hands wouldn't move. They were bound. I didn't know which way was up or down. I screamed and kicked my legs against anything I could hit, but it did no good.

My eyes finally adjusted to the dark and I could see I was in a small, enclosed space, with a tire wedged against my back. And I was moving. I was in the trunk of a car. I tried to reach the lock, to see if I could activate it from the inside, but I was too tightly bound. I screamed again and tried to use my power, but nothing happened.

Suddenly the car skidded to a halt, slamming me into the trunk wall. My head took the brunt of the blow and a stabbing pain sliced across it. Fear gripped me. What was going to happen? What was this? Logic told me it was the Knox; they'd come for me. How long had I been unconscious? Was it minutes? Hours?

At least I could be sure that Áine would have figured out by now that I was missing. She would have told her family. Adam would know.

Adam. His name stabbed through my heart. He would be frantic. They all would. This was the one thing they feared above all else, and now it had happened. It hurt to imagine how Adam's face must have looked when he heard the news. I knew how it would crumble, how his eyes would narrow and darken. Even here, in my little prison, all I wanted was to somehow get to him and tell him not to worry.

A car door banged close by and I heard footsteps, then a clunk as the trunk was opened. I was blinded by the light that poured in. All I could see was the silhouette of a person with the bright sky behind. Then there was a hand over my nose and mouth again. I struggled, calling on my power in vain, but not for long. My body went limp before my brain shut down.

I was being dragged out of the trunk. My legs hit the ground as the blackness took hold.

320

I felt sick and drowsy. I remembered waking up in the dark trunk of the car after falling from my horse, and being smothered by some choking chemical. I had no idea where I was. It was damp and cold. I could hear lapping water. I looked around me.

Was I on a boat? I must be, but the floor was at a funny angle. I tried to stand up, but my hands and feet were still bound and I fell over. I heard footsteps clumping down the stairs.

"Good morning, sunshine. You awake again?" a voice with an English accent rang out. "Are you going to be a good girl this time or do I have to drug you again?" The words were heavily laced with sarcasm. I shook my head frantically from side to side, trying my best to convey to him that I would play along.

He pulled me roughly off the floor and sat me down on a makeshift bed.

"Now you stay quiet, right, or it will be night-night for you again," he threatened, and removed my gag. My mouth was sore and cracked where the gag had been tied tight. I opened and closed it a few times, trying to ease the pain in my jaw. I tried once more to tap my power, but it was dead.

"No point in tiring yourself out. Your powers won't work on me," he said right into my face. My expression must have revealed my shock, because he laughed and held out a charm that was on a chain around his neck.

"You see, I have the Amulet of Accaious."

"You can't," I croaked out. "That was destroyed years ago."

He chuckled to himself and dragged a crate over beside me to sit on. "I may as well introduce myself, since you'll be seeing quite a bit of me. I'm Lyonis Fleet." He held out his arm as if to shake my hand, then started laughing. "Oh, I guess you're all tied up, aren't you?" He cackled at his own pathetic joke.

"As you can see, the amulet wasn't destroyed," he went on. "It was simply disabled. We had the missing amber shard. All we needed was the remnants of the Amulet." He held out the amulet that dangled on the big gold chain and moved it closer to me. It looked like a bronze sun with pointed sunbeams radiating from it. At the very center there was an unusual amber stone; I could see the cracks where the shard had been fixed back into it. The amber glowed bright.

"This little beauty was a gift to us from a friend of ours in the Order of the Mark. Look at how it glows when it gets close to you." He moved it closer to me to prove his point and the glowing grew more intense. "All we had to do was insert the amber shard and hey, presto, your little earth element Áine couldn't see me coming."

"But *I* sensed you coming."

"A minor flaw. It only blinds evoked elements. But it binds all the elemental powers, evoked or not, so you can't touch me."

I held my breath. The Knox had a weapon that Adam, Áine, and Rían would be powerless against. I had to remember every shred of information that this man told me. I had to keep him talking.

"What about me?" I asked quickly.

"Ah, indeed, what about you? When we learned the fourth had been found and guided by the Sidhe himself, we knew something was stirring."

"I don't know what you're talking about." *Christ! Who told them?*

He leaned in and pulled my hair away from my neck. "An activated Mark from royal blood . . . and a Carrier too. Who could have imagined such a creature? But here you are." He put his hand on my Mark. I cringed away from his touch.

"Don't be frightened; I'm not going to hurt you."

"Does drugging me and dumping me in a car trunk not qualify as hurting me?"

"Ooh, and she's feisty too." He laughed. "What a combination. Listen, girl, you should really play along. The Knox aren't half bad. You might even like us."

"I doubt it," I spat, and turned away from him.

"Well, they're on their way here now to collect you, so you might want to rethink that. Trust me, little girl: The fifth will come. You'll want to be on our side when it does."

"The fifth? This is all about the fifth?"

"Of course it's about the fifth. It's always been about

the fifth. That's what we've been doing all these years. Biding our time. And now that time has come."

"The fifth has nothing to do with me."

"It has *everything* to do with you," he sneered.

"Get away from her!" Adam's voice filled the small cabin as he came down the steps from the deck above.

"Adam." I gasped.

Adam didn't know about the amulet. I had to try to warn him. Suddenly a ball of water from outside the boat shot through the window right at Lyonis. It got about a yard from him and then the water splashed against thin air, like it had hit a glass wall.

"What the . . . ?" Adam looked around the cabin in shock.

"The amulet! Adam! The am—" I was cut off mid-scream as a fist slammed into my face.

"No!" I heard Adam shout as I fell sideways and landed on the floor, dazed and groggy. There was blood in my mouth, and my cheek and jaw pounded. I was using all the energy I had just by focusing on staying conscious.

Lyonis and Adam were fighting, struggling against each other. They lurched to the left, smashing into the side wall, and then they both went right out through the rotting hull. I could hear Rían's voice outside.

"No, Rían, don't attack him! He's got . . . Rían, *no*!" Adam shouted.

Flames engulfed the boat, and my lungs ached as dark,

noxious smoke filled the air. I struggled off the dirty makeshift bed and shuffled across the floor, the cable ties binding my hands and feet making my progress slow.

Suddenly a wall of water smashed through the cabin, dulling the flames.

Seizing my opportunity, I threw myself toward the wooden stairs, where the remains of the fire licked their way upward to freedom. I gritted my teeth and reached over to hook the cable binding my wrists on a jagged piece of scorched metal that I could see through the flames. Turning my face away from the searing heat, I tugged down sharply and felt the tie snap. I screamed as the flames burned my skin, but I didn't have time to worry about the pain. I needed to get out, to warn the others. I had to make sure they were okay.

With my hands free, I released my ankles and scrambled up the still-burning stairs to the deck. I was on a half-sunken old fishing trawler that was listing at an odd angle where it had run aground, in what looked like a boat graveyard. The smoke had curled its way up from the wreckage and was slowly starting to clear. Through the haze I could see a group of people on the shoreline.

Lyonis was standing in front of Rían, Fionn, and Áine, pointing a gun at them. They were motionless, staring at the ground. My eyes followed their horrified gaze to the body lying facedown at the water's edge.

It was Adam. He was lying flat, deathly still, with blood oozing out of him. It soaked through his shirt, pooling on the damp sand.

Horror filled me, along with anger, despair, loss. I could hear the blood whooshing through my veins, pumping through me. Every pulse was so loud in my ears I could hear nothing else. I started moving toward Lyonis. The man who had drugged me, threatened me, beaten me, and now had taken my reason for living away from me. My fear was a distant memory. Not once did I look down to negotiate the dangerous maze of broken boats, water, and debris. I would have vengeance. That was all there was left in the world.

"I'll be with you soon," I promised Adam as I moved closer to my target.

Lyonis was aiming his gun at the others. Áine was sobbing, Fionn looked desolate, and Rían was shaking, a picture of rage.

Lyonis didn't see me coming, but Rían did. His face changed as we locked gazes. What was that I saw in his eyes? It looked like fear, but I didn't care. I was beyond caring. I could feel a surge of strength building in me like a bomb about to explode. I felt like I was floating; there was no longer ground beneath my feet. There was no need for it, no need for substance. I wasn't moving through the air; I *was* the air.

My beautiful Adam. I could see part of his face now

where he lay in a crumpled heap, his eyes hidden by lids that were closed forever.

Lyonis. That animal had taken my precious Adam from me. I screamed in pain, a scream so loud it ripped through the valley. In the same moment I saw Fionn throw himself toward Lyonis. Lyonis pulled the trigger and Fionn fell forward beside Adam. As he went down he snatched at the amulet around Lyonis's neck, ripping it free. Lyonis shrieked in horror as the realization hit him: He was no longer protected.

Then I heard a roaring. It was so loud I could hear nothing else.

Rían and Áine covered their ears and cowered on the ground. They crawled over to the bodies of Adam and Fionn and threw themselves down over them. The roaring continued and I looked around.

I suddenly realized that I was up in the air high above them. I appeared to be radiating a bright light. The air around me swirled until I could no longer see the land. River water started rising up and spinning around me. Next the boats lifted, then some trees, their great roots torn from the earth by the brutal force emanating from me. It was a massive vortex, spreading out farther and farther until the riverbed was visible, the water swirling high above it. The boats and the trees that had been tugged up swirled so fast that their outlines became a blur.

I saw the object of my rage running away. He was making for the woods, but I pushed out the great vortex of moving air and debris so that he stayed constantly in my sight. There was no way he could break through its impenetrable wall.

"*You*," I snarled. My voice was not mine. It was a mixture of howling wind and cracking thunder. "You will pay." I clasped my hand, as if to pick up his little body far below me on the ground, and he rose right into the air until he was at my level.

"I'm sorry! I'm sorry!" he screamed, flailing his legs and trying to shield himself from my glare.

"Too late for that." My voice reverberated around the valley.

I looked at Adam, his lifeless body. Rían and Áine were standing now. I saw them waving up at me, but I was beyond caring what they wanted. The power inside engulfed me, took over my very core, and it needed vengeance. I glanced back to Adam one last time just to look at his physical body before I went to meet him in the next life. I knew I could do it. I wouldn't be dying. I would simply cease to exist. I knew exactly what to do and how to do it. It was instinctual. I just needed to turn the power on myself.

Lyonis was still screaming. It was irritating me, ruining my last few moments with my beloved's body.

Adam's hand moved.

Shocked, I looked again. Now his whole arm moved.

And then I saw that his eyes were open, green, clear, and beautiful.

Adam.

Adam was still alive.

Lyonis's screaming was really getting on my nerves.

"Oh, shut up," I roared at him. I felt my power disperse a little. The glow around me dimmed, and the great whirling vortex of water, trees, and boat debris faltered slightly.

"Megan." I heard Adam's voice clearly, as if all other sound in the universe had stopped for one moment. "Megan, I'm all right. Come back to me," he pleaded.

Come back to him—of course I'd come back to him. I was his. I dropped lower and let Lyonis fall to the ground with a thud. Water started splashing back to earth. Trees, boats, and rocks all came crashing down around us in a big circle.

"Adam," I breathed. My voice returned to the one I recognized. "I thought you were dead."

"Me too, baby, me too," he said weakly.

I threw myself into his arms.

"You are one scary girl. Beautiful, amazing, magical, but damn scary," he whispered into my hair, then groaned. He stretched out and grabbed Fionn's arm. "Are you still with us, Fionn?"

"Just about," Fionn croaked, and rolled over.

Twenty-three

EMPOWERED

ionn looked warily at me. "Well, that's one I have never seen before," he said in a weak voice. "Rían, check on that bastard, will you?"

Rían picked his way through the debris to where Lyonis lay in a heap. "He's alive," he announced. "More's the pity." He gave the unconscious man a good kick and walked back over to where Adam and I were lying on the ground. "Have you disarmed her?" Rían asked Adam jokingly. He gave me an admiring look. "Jesus, girl! Remind me never to get on your bad side."

I snuggled into Adam's arms. The tears were pouring down my face, my human emotions flooding back into my body.

"We'd better get you to a hospital, bro," Rían said. "Looks like Fionn could do with some patching up too." He turned to me. "Now, don't take this the wrong way and get all freaky mad, O very scary one, but you have seen prettier days. Your face is a mess, and those burns on your hands look really painful." He winced.

Wow. I had completely forgotten about the punch I got in the face, and about my burned hands. I glanced down at them. They really did look bad. "Ouch," I said.

"That bastard," Adam said through gritted teeth.

"Come on. Let's get you lot to hospital and call the Gardaí for this asshole," Rían said, walking by Lyonis and kicking him in the ribs again.

"Will you give him one for me?" Adam said.

"It would be my pleasure." Rían kicked him again.

It wasn't long before there were squad cars and ambulances on the little lane that led down toward the boat graveyard. They had to bring the stretchers on foot, since they couldn't get the ambulances down to where we were. Adam and Fionn were taken away first to the hospital.

I was going to ride with Rían and Áine and get seen to in the ER, but we had to speak to the Gardaí first and make statements. Rían recounted the story of my abduction. He claimed Lyonis was some deranged psychopath who claimed to be a member of a weird holy order. He'd kidnapped me, beaten me, and then shot Adam and Fionn when they came to rescue me. It did the trick.

Lyonis was taken to the hospital under a Gardaí escort. I doubted we'd be seeing much more of him.

I was desperate to be with Adam, so as soon as the Gardaí were finished with us, Rían, Áine, and I set off for the hospital. Now that I was sitting still in the back of the car, the pain in my hands really started to take hold. They throbbed all over.

I looked over at Áine. "How did you find me?"

"I sent Caitlin home with the horses and then we looked for you everywhere. I knew something was blocking me, and instead of trying to see past it, I focused on it and looked for it. It led us right to the boat graveyard."

"He had me drugged. I don't even know how long I was gone," I said.

"He must have been waiting for you. He pulled you off with a sheephook. We found it in the field along with a wad of cotton that was doused with chloroform. You were only gone a couple of hours."

"Does my dad know?"

"He thinks we're still out on the horses. Caitlin promised not to say anything as long as I explained to her what was going on. So at the moment he doesn't even realize there is a problem, but your face and hands are going to require some explanations, so best to let him know now, before he hears something through the Kinsale gossips." She handed me her phone with a sympathetic look.

I dialed his number. "Hi, Dad."

"Megan, whose phone are you calling from? Is everything all right?"

"Um, yeah, but there was sort of an incident. I'm all right, but we're on the way to the hospital." I tried to phrase it so he didn't immediately think the worst, but as I thought it through, I realized he was going to absolutely freak out when he heard about our injuries. I'd save that for later.

"It's a very, very long story, Dad, but I'm fine; I just have a few bruises. Look, I'll be at Cork University Hospital. They're taking Adam and Fionn there too."

"Adam and Fionn are going to the hospital too? Christ, Megan, what the hell happened?"

"Dad, I can't tell you over the phone; just come to the hospital and I'll tell you everything."

"Of course I will. Who's with you?"

"Áine and Rían. Honestly, I'm fine. It's Adam and Fionn we should be worried about." Saying it out loud reminded me that Adam had been severely injured. I'd been so overwhelmed at his not being dead that his injuries hadn't registered. The tears came again; I could hardly finish the phone call. Áine took the phone from me.

"Hi, Mr. Rosenberg, it's Áine. Yes, don't worry, we're looking after her. I think she's suffering from shock. Yes, of course we will. See you in twenty minutes. Bye."

I looked at her and she put her arm around me. Her hug made me fall apart completely. Maybe she was right. Maybe I was suffering from shock; the tears just wouldn't stop.

Still holding me with one arm, she flipped open her phone again. "Just one more call to make," she said, smiling down at me.

"Caitlin, hey, it's Áine. Yeah, we have her. Yes, I've told her dad. She's a bit worse for wear; we are taking her to hospital. I know—look, I'll tell you all about it later. No problem. Bye."

"Is she okay?" I asked Áine.

"She's fine, just concerned about you. She knows there's something up with us, though. We're going to have to think about what to tell her. Let's get you fixed up first. We'll sort that out later. She's going to keep quiet for us in the meantime."

When we arrived at the hospital, I wanted to go right up to see Adam, but they told us that he was in surgery and wouldn't be out for a while. They also said I needed to be seen by a doctor before I could do anything. So I let them put me on a bed and tend to my bashed-up face and burned hands. The nurse who was cleaning my face winced as she wiped dry blood from a large cut along my hairline. I'd forgotten about that impact on my head in the trunk. The side of my face had puffed up and my upper lip was bloody and swollen. Once she'd finished applying the paper stitches I finally got to look in a mirror. I hardly recognized myself.

"Don't worry, pet," the nurse reassured me. "That swelling will go down quickly, and the stitches are on your hairline; they won't even leave a mark."

I attempted a smile for her. To be honest, I didn't care; I just wanted to get down to see Adam. They draped my hands in gooey gauze and bound them thickly with bandages.

I saw a nurse approaching with my dad. "Oh, my God," he whimpered.

"Dad, it's not as bad as it looks; I promise. Please calm down."

He rushed over to me. "I heard what happened; the Kinsale Gardaí called me, and Áine spoke to me outside. How could this happen? Why you?"

"Dad, this guy is psychotic. It could have happened to anyone. I was just really lucky that Adam and Fionn caught him in time."

"How are they?" Dad asked, taking my bandaged hands gently in his.

"I don't know. They won't let me out of here, and Adam's still in surgery. Dad, can you talk to the doctors and see if you can get them to release me? Please?"

My dad was deathly pale; he looked like he was the one in shock. "I'll see what I can do." He got up and walked out of the exam room. He was back in a few minutes with the news that Fionn's surgery had gone well, and that while Adam had lost a kidney and a lot of blood, he would also be fine. The feeling of relief was overwhelming.

As soon as I was released, I crept into Adam's room. A nurse who was checking on him turned to me as she adjusted his position. "He will be out for quite a while, love. You should come back in a few hours."

"No, no, I'm staying here."

"Whatever you want, dear, but you look like you need some rest of your own."

"No," I said firmly. "I'm staying." I sat in the chair by his bed.

My dad stood at the door.

"Let me take you home, Meg. Please? You're exhausted."

"No, Dad, I'm not leaving him."

My dad sighed and went out to sit in the waiting room.

I put my head down carefully on the bed beside Adam. Being here with him, even in his unconscious state, made me feel safe and protected, and soon exhaustion overcame me. I fell into a deep sleep.

A comfortable, warm sensation woke me, a hand rubbing my back, another sweeping over my hair.

"You're awake," I whispered.

"How are you?" He gently traced his hand over my face.

"I'm fine."

"And your hands?"

I sat up. "Don't worry about me. How do you feel?"

"I've been better, but it's not too bad." He laughed, then grimaced in pain.

"So . . ." I said slowly, "it would appear that I have fully evoked my element by accident."

"I'll say! That was awesome."

"But where do we go from here? What will we do now?" I asked, searching his eyes.

He gazed back at me for what seemed like forever and then gently traced his finger along my cheek. "Don't worry about that now. No matter what happens we're in this together. Right?"

I reached up, covering his hand with mine, and nodded. "Right."

We were interrupted when Rían popped his head around the door. "Hey, you two. How are you feeling, bro?"

"I'll survive. All things considered, I'm feeling pretty good. How's Fionn?"

"He's good."

"And that jerk Lyonis?"

"He's in hospital too, but in Garda custody. Megan here landed him right on his head, so he has a serious concussion and a fair amount of bruising to his abdomen and ribs." He winked at us. "Megan, you're going to have to go home with your dad today at some stage. The poor man's asleep in the corridor."

Adam looked at me. "Take your dad home. Get some rest."

"Okay." I kissed Adam good-bye and went out to the hallway to get my dad and head home. Suddenly, I had an overwhelming sense of relief—it was finally over. No more running from what I was. I had evoked. Now we just had to deal with the consequences of that, but no matter what, Adam and I would be dealing with them together.

Things quickly went back to normal in the aftermath, with a few notable exceptions: My dad was neurotically overprotective, Caitlin was seriously suspicious of the DeRíses, and Adam and I found ourselves at the center of school gossip . . . again.

There wasn't much I could do with Dad; I'd have to ride that one out. And I knew that the gossip mill would move on to something else soon. But Caitlin's suspicions needed to be dealt with. Luckily, Fionn was on the case. He invited her over to their house for dinner one night, and I listened as he fed her the most amazing story. It was told so well, I nearly believed it myself.

According to Fionn, Adam, Áine, and Rían were in a witness protection program. Their parents had been killed by a gang and all three of the DeRíses knew their identities, so the gang was constantly looking for them in order to dispose of the witnesses to the murders. Fionn claimed that he had been enlisted by the program to protect them and keep them hidden, and that was why they moved to Ireland and lived a very quiet life. What had happened with my abduction was a simple case of mistaken identity. Fionn told her that a member of the gang had located the DeRíses and abducted who he thought was Áine, but was in fact me, and Adam and Fionn got shot trying to rescue me.

Caitlin was mesmerized by the story and on a complete high at being involved and having to keep the DeRíses' identities a secret. I felt bad about deceiving her yet again, but Adam pointed out that a lot of it was so close to the truth that it wasn't even too terrible a lie. And, most important, it was for her own good.

Fionn lured the Order to Cork shortly afterward. They were enraptured by my evocation and talked excitedly of the alignment, but Fionn quickly put a stop to any celebrations, accusing them of treachery. They each vehemently denied being involved with the Knox, but M.J. did admit that he had told the council about me. He felt it was his duty to warn them because of my relationship with Adam and the potential problem with the Fifth Prophecy. So that meant that there were more people who could have betrayed our trust. We just didn't know who to blame—and who we could turn to in the future.

As for Adam and me, we'd each gotten a glimpse of how life would be without the other, and that wasn't going to happen again. Our future was full of obstacles, but we would face them one at a time, together. We'd simply play along with the Order for an easy life.

So as the Dublin Order members fought with Fionn in the study, we sat obediently on the couch and pretended to listen. They had moved on by this point to fighting about the Amulet of Accaious, which Fionn now had. He was adamant that it would stay with him to ensure it would never be used against us, but the Dublin Order couldn't accept that they weren't allowed access to it. We had planned to go to dinner with the three Order members that night, but as their fight with Fionn heated up, that looked less and less likely.

"Come on," Adam said, getting up. "We don't need to listen to them now. Let's take a walk. They won't even notice we're gone."

Adam held my hand. We walked quietly out into the yard and down the field to the copse of trees at the side, our usual haunt when we wanted some alone time. Once we were under the privacy of their canopy, he swung me around and caught me in his arms.

"Have I told you today how amazing you are?" he breathed.

"Let me see now." I did some fake pondering. "You

know what? I don't think you have."

"Well, let me show you how amazing you are, then."
He bent his head down to mine and kissed me softly.
The leaves in the trees began to stir and rustle as a gentle
breeze blew around us, warm and soothing.

"Wow," he whispered. "I'll never get used to that."

Shortly after I'd evoked my full power, we had
discovered that when we were together now, the
atmosphere around us changed. It seemed to absorb
some of our power and become part of us. And when
we kissed each other, the air around us would caress
and kiss us in the most sensual and earthmoving way.
I thought I'd had the most fantastic relationship with
Adam before I evoked, but neither of us realized the
depth and intensity that it would attain after. It was
now truly magical.

I leaned back against the trunk of a tree and caught
my breath. I raised my face up toward the branches
above my head, watching the last of the residual energy
that we had created work its way through the leaves
until it faded away. Adam moved in closer to me, put
his lips to my neck, and started working his way up
toward my ear. My breath quickened again, and I felt
the energy emitting from me mixing with his and
swirling around us, leaving us once again breathless.
I let myself slide onto the ground. He followed me
down and hovered over me on his hands and knees.

The power was all-encompassing. We just stared at each other and then he lowered his lips to mine and kissed me passionately and deeply. The air whipped up around us, shaking the grass we were lying in and scattering leaves down on us from the trees above. He rolled over onto his back and followed my gaze up into the trees, watching the magic disperse.

"Do you think we should mention this to anyone?" I asked breathlessly.

"Let's keep this our little secret. Anyway, it might not always be like this. Let's just wait and see."

We heard voices coming out of the house in the distance.

"I guess that's our cue," he murmured, catching my eye and smiling.

"I love you so much," I whispered. "I will be with you always, no matter what."

"I love you too. Forever," he said, reaching out and taking my hand. He held it to his chest. We stayed like that until we heard car doors opening. Adam stood up slowly, then bent down and took both my hands and pulled me up to him.

"Ready?" I smoothed his hair back into place.

"As we'll ever be." He smiled and started walking backward toward the house, pulling me with him.

ACKNOWLEDGMENTS

Thank you to everyone who made this book possible. Special thanks to the gang at HarperTeen, including my amazingly talented editor, Erica Sussman, TJ, Becki, Christina, Elyse, and Kristina. You guys eased my way into the publishing world with lots of laughs and fun, and for that, I'll always be grateful. To my fabulous agent, Tina Wexler, who makes the magic happen behind the scenes. A HUGE thanks to the people of www.inkpop.com, without whom I wouldn't be here. Hugs to all the wonderful Inkies who supported me and my book from day one, especially Morgan Shamy, my advocate and friend.

A big shout-out to my proofreaders-slash-babysitters, Jennifer Galvin, Paula Conroy, and Betty Bowe, who were unfortunate enough to holiday with me in the middle of writing this book; I'm sure it wasn't pretty, but they never once complained. Thanks to Lorna Grehan and Valarie Feehan for their editing skills, and to my dad, Liam Conroy, whose idea it was to write this book in the first place.

Most importantly, thank you to my family; in particular, my long-suffering, gorgeous husband, Michael, and my wonderful children, Chloe, Megan, Fionn, and Rían. You guys endured desertion, crankiness, takeout food, and self-absorption during the months I was writing and editing *Carrier of the Mark*—thank you for being so patient. I love you guys all the way to the moon . . . and back.

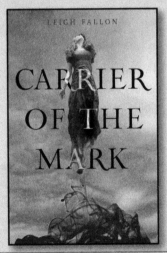

JOIN

THE COMMUNITY AT

Epic Reads
Your World. Your Books.

FIND
the latest
books

DISCUSS
what's on
your reading
wish list

CREATE
your own book
news and
activities to share
with friends

ACCESS
exclusive
contests and
videos

Don't miss out on any upcoming
EPIC READS!

**Visit the site and browse the
categories to find out more.**

www.epicreads.com

HARPER TEEN
An Imprint of HarperCollinsPublishers